Into the Prairie

THE PIONEERS

**Center Point
Large Print**

Into the Prairie

THE PIONEERS

Rosanne Bittner

CENTER POINT PUBLISHING
THORNDIKE, MAINE

This Center Point Large Print edition
is published in the year 2007 by arrangement with
St. Martin's Press.

The text of this Large Print edition is unabridged. In other
aspects, this book may vary from the original edition. Printed in
Thailand. Set in 16-point Times New Roman type.

ISBN-10: 1-58547-933-0
ISBN-13: 978-1-58547-933-7

Library of Congress Cataloging-in-Publication Data

Bittner, Rosanne, 1945-
    Into the prairie : the pioneers / Rosanne Bittner.--Center Point large print ed.
      p. cm.
    ISBN-13: 978-1-58547-933-7 (lib. bdg. : alk. paper)
    1. Frontier and pioneer life--Fiction. 2. Tecumseh, Shawnee Chief, 1768-1813--Fiction.
3. Indians of North America--Fiction. 4. Indian captivities--Fiction. 5. Mothers and
sons--Fiction. 6. Women pioneers--Fiction. 7. Indiana--Fiction. 8. Large type books. I. Title.

PS3552.I77396I54 2007
813'.54--dc22

2006030728

I would like to dedicate this book to my uncle, Harold Swope, born in Greentown, Indiana. His grandparents walked to Indiana from Kentucky and built a little log cabin there that later became a six-hundred-acre farm, land upon which Uncle Harold still lived when he died in 2003 at the age of ninety-seven. He served on the Kokomo police force, where he was considered a sharpshooter and an expert in fingerprinting; he was a lieutenant for the Indiana National Guard; and after retirement from the police force he became an editor/photographer for the *Kokomo Tribune*. He accomplished all of this without a high school education.

Uncle Harold represented the best of the descendants of early prairie settlers.

FROM THE AUTHOR

The prairie land of America once covered more than 640 million open, treeless acres, from Indiana in the east to the eastern border of Nebraska. Over seventy-two species of grasses thrived there, often growing over six feet high, as well as hundreds of varieties of flowers. Only the invention of the breaking plow made cultivation of the prairie possible, and Indians likened the ripping sound that it made to a cry of pain from Mother Earth.

But there were other cries of pain that came with settling America's prairies, the cries of humans who suffered indescribable loneliness, hardship, and loss. The characters in this story are fictitious, but their experiences are based on real history and real experiences of countless prairie settlers during the first half of the 1800s.

It should be noted here that the history used in this story concerning the great Shawnee leader, Tecumseh, and his brother Tenskwatawa (also known as the Prophet) is all true. The Shawnee settlement of Tippecanoe was also referred to by some as Prophetstown. The Potawatomi Indian character in this book, Windigo, is fictitious.

The New Madrid earthquake of December 9, 1811, really did occur. It was the most cataclysmic earthquake ever seen in the United States. If the same earthquake took place today, as well it could, it would very likely destroy every building in Illinois, Missouri, Arkansas, Tennessee, and Kentucky and more in surrounding states. Tecumseh predicted the New Madrid earthquake months before it happened.

Historical dates and facts for this story were primarily taken from *A Sorrow in Our Heart—The Life of Tecumseh* by Allan W. Eckert (Bantam Books, 1992). For anyone wanting to learn about America's early history, Allan Eckert's books are necessary reading for a vivid, factual account of this country's exciting past.

I also used *Tecumseh—A Life* by John Sugden (Henry Holt, 1997); and *Shawnee!* by James H. Howard (Ohio University Press, 1981). Both of these men are also inspiring authors who can bring America's past alive.

I have written this book to honor the incredible bravery and fortitude of America's first prairie settlers, and to continue the stories of the descendants of the (fictitious) Wilde family that began with *Into the Wilderness*.

1

April 20, 1810

"You're crazy."

Jonah Wilde rolled his eyes at his older brother's remark. "No crazier than our grandfather Noah. He never stayed long in one place either."

"And he ended up dying too young, just like our uncle Jeremiah did. Ma named me after him because the poor man didn't live long enough to leave any heirs."

"Grandpa was killed fighting in a war, and so was Uncle Jeremiah. This is different. All I'm doing is heading west. We've both heard plenty about the prairie land out there, wide-open land that can be farmed. I can claim all the land I want."

"You can't be serious, Jonah. Last I knew, most of it was promised to the Shawnee and Delaware, and that Shawnee leader they call Tecumseh is doing a damn good job of forming a confederacy of all the tribes against any American settlement west of the Ohio. And it looks like we're going to end up at war with the British again. You know how they will use Indians against Americans. You couldn't be heading west at a more dangerous time, Jonah, and with a wife and a son!"

Sadie Wilde glanced nervously at her husband. She

knew Jonah was truly worried about her and little Paul, but he also had a dream, and he came from a long line of dreamers who'd risked their lives for what they believed in. "Surely a little farm out in the wilderness won't draw much attention," she spoke up in Jonah's defense.

"Yeah, Jeremiah, leave him alone." The words came from Jeremiah and Jonah's fifteen-year-old brother, Matthew.

"No one asked for your opinion," Jeremiah snapped.

Matthew made a face at Jeremiah, his soft blue eyes glittering with the desire to tease. "Who says you're always right?" he taunted.

Sadie considered the contrast between the fair-haired young man and Jeremiah, whose straight black hair and deep brown eyes betrayed the Indian blood he carried from his grandfather and great-grandfather, men who had greatly sacrificed in the building of their young country. Jonah was a grand mixture of white and Indian, with the same dark hair, only with more curl in it, and very blue eyes. His handsome looks still stirred womanly desires in her that had not changed with three years of marriage and a two-year-old son.

"All of you stop this." Jeremiah's wife, Regina, set an apple pie on the table. "I am tired of hearing you argue," she continued. "Maybe it's best that Jonah *does* leave. We certainly will have more peace and quiet around here." She glanced over at Sadie. "I'm sorry, Sadie, but this subject has been discussed to death."

"I agree," Sadie answered, glancing at her brother-in-law. "Jeremiah, if I am perfectly fine with this move and it makes Jonah happy, you might as well let us go with your blessings."

Jeremiah sat down beside the cooking fireplace in the main room of the Wilde family home, a fine wood and stone structure built by their father, Luke, who now lay buried beside his wife, Annie, who died when Matthew was born. Sadie knew the story about how the home had been burned by Indians and Loyalists during the Revolutionary War . . . how Luke and his brother Jeremiah had gone off to fight in that war, Jeremiah losing his life . . . how Luke came back here to the Ohio Valley to rebuild. He'd died, leaving this beautiful farm to Luke and Jeremiah, but now both men had families, and since Matthew also lived with them, the family was outgrowing the farm.

Jonah leaned back in the chair where he sat at the kitchen table. "You heard Sadie," he told Jeremiah.

Jeremiah scowled. "I need you to help with the farm."

"You have Matthew, and three kids of your own," Jonah answered. "Heck, young Mark is eleven years old, plenty big enough to handle a lot of chores. Ruth is eight and a wonderful help to her mother already, and little Luke begs you to give him things to do. This farm isn't big enough to feed all of us and still make a profit. We all know that. I have a wife and a son and with God's grace I'll have more children. The family has grown, Jeremiah, and this farm has always seemed more yours than mine. You were the firstborn. I want something that really feels like my own. And with Ohio already getting more and more settled and being a state now and under rules and taxes and—"

"Indiana is on its way to becoming a state, too," Jeremiah reminded him.

"That's a long way off," Jonah retorted. "By the time that happens, I intend to be one of its biggest landowners."

"The Shawnee might have something to say about that," Jeremiah reminded him, rubbing his eyes.

"We're going, Jeremiah. You can't stop this."

Jeremiah sounded a disgruntled chuckle. "No more than anyone could stop our grandfather Noah from getting mixed up in the French and Indian War, or our uncle Jeremiah from running headstrong into the Revolutionary War and nearly getting our father killed for it, let alone losing his own life."

He turned to look at Jonah, grinning in resignation. "No, I can't stop you, although if I had any sense I'd get you in a choke hold and drag you to a tree and tie you there." He turned away again. "We've heard how our grandmother Jess suffered after Grandpa died," he added. "And we know how our mother and father used to mourn Uncle Jeremiah. Now I suppose Regina and Matthew and I will end up mourning *your* death, maybe yours and Sadie's both."

"You are too focused on the dark side of things, big brother," Jonah tried to joke.

"Yeah, well, with the struggle it's been to live here

fighting Indians and the elements to hang on to this farm, that's pretty easy to do."

Jonah stood up, running a hand through the dark waves of hair that grew so fast it seemed Sadie was always cutting it. Her husband walked over to stand behind Jeremiah, reaching out and squeezing his brother's shoulders. "We'll be okay, Jeremiah. Lord knows I've fought off Indians before. The whole family has, even Sadie. The Wilde clan is good at those things. Besides, Grandpa and our uncle Jeremiah were both killed by *white* men, remember, both of them killed in different wars but both by British soldiers. I'm not worried about the Shawnee. In fact, that Tecumseh is all for peace, they say."

Jeremiah reached around and grasped one of Jonah's hands. "Maybe so; but don't forget things look bad between the United States and Britain again over this damn mess with France and Napoleon. God knows you could all die at the hands of the British instead of Indians."

"I could go to help protect Jonah and Sadie and little Paul," Matthew offered.

Jeremiah rose and walked toward the front door. "Kid, Jonah and I have raised you from the day our mother died giving birth to you. You're more like a son than a brother to me. I couldn't bear to watch you leave, too. Besides, I need at least one of you left here to help with the farm. And regardless of what Jonah said, this place is as much yours and his as it is mine. Pa would have wanted it that way." He glanced back at Jonah. "And it will be here when you give up and come back," he told the young man.

Jonah chuckled. "You know better."

Jeremiah watched him with sadness in his eyes. "This valley is home, Jonah."

"It is your home. And Indiana will be *my* home—mine and Sadie's. She's as much for going as I am."

"Sadie is crazy in love with you. She'd follow you into hell and you know it."

"She understands the potential," Jonah replied. "Think about it, Jeremiah! You know good and well that settlers are going to keep heading west. There was a time when this valley was inhabited only by Indians, and now it's full of settlers and farms and towns. This country can't help but keep growing westward, and people will need a place to stop and buy supplies. I intend to be one of the first out there and be the supplier. I'll be a rich man someday, you mark my word, and little Paul will be even richer. This is as much for him as for me."

Sadie thought what a wonderful father Jonah was, and she prayed he was making the right decision. Openly she fully supported him, but deep inside she had her moments of doubt, mostly at the thought of how lonely she would be away from the family. Leaving this farm, and her friends in nearby Willow Creek, would be the hardest thing she would probably ever do.

Jeremiah slowly nodded. "Your mind is made up. So be it. When will you go?"

"Soon as spring planting is done. I don't want to leave you high and dry for that. And that will give me time to stock up on what we'll need."

Jeremiah glanced at Sadie, who gave him a smile and a nod. "We'll be fine, Jeremiah," she told him, wanting to show as much confidence as possible.

Jeremiah turned to Matthew, giving him a commanding look. "There are chores to be finished, kid. Let's go."

He walked out and Matthew grumped. "Kid!" He stood up, looking at Jonah. "When will he see that I'm grown up?"

Jonah chuckled. "Well, I'm twenty-nine years old, and he still thinks he has to take care of me, if that tells you anything."

Matthew left, and Regina turned to Jonah. "Your mother told Jeremiah to always watch out for the both of you," she told Jonah. "She knew that you especially had the wandering blood of your uncle Jeremiah and your grandfather Noah."

"Well, Ma always was good at figuring people," Jonah told her. "And I guess she was right about me. I've put this off too long already, Regina. Now with Tecumseh opting for peace, I don't see why this isn't a good time to try for Indiana and all that rich prairie land. Besides, you know I'm right about this farm getting too small for all of us."

Regina glanced at Sadie, who noticed that in spite of only being thirty years old, her sister-in-law was showing gray hairs. That's what farm life could do to a woman, let alone living with a man whose last name was Wilde. She was only twenty-one herself, but she wondered if she, too, might gray prematurely.

"We'll all miss you so," Regina told her with sudden tears in her eyes. "Especially little Paul, although he'll look at this as quite an adventure, I'm sure."

"Adventure is probably putting it mildly," Sadie answered.

Jonah looked at her lovingly. "And you're the bravest, finest woman a man could ask for," he told her.

Sadie gave him a smile, walking to where he stood to lean up and kiss his cheek. So brave and determined he was, and such a good man, a caring, gentle husband. "Jeremiah was right," she told him. "I'd follow you anywhere. Maybe I'm not brave at all. Maybe I'm just crazy. I guess we'll find out, won't we?"

Jonah drew her close, hugging her tightly. "I'll take good care of you, Sadie. You know that."

There was such comfort and sureness in his arms that in that moment, all of her fears were gone. "I know."

2

Jeremiah will make sure we have plenty of provisions to help us get by the first year." Sadie listened to her husband's reassurances with doubts she refused to voice. She loved Jonah Wilde beyond her own fears and wants. She'd known him for years, since they were little and often saw each other at social gatherings in Willow Creek. His father and mother were practically famous amid the community for what they'd suffered and sacrificed in the War of Independence.

Any woman would be proud to be married to a man who bore the name Wilde, even though she knew that meant the possibility of being married to a man who was brave enough to forge his own way on the frontier or risk his life in war. Jonah chose to brave the frontier, and so she would have to do the same.

"Thank goodness we'll start out with everything we need," she answered her husband. They lay together on the feather mattress of their bed, in their own cabin near the main house. Young Matthew would make this cabin his home once they left, and Sadie had no doubt he, too, would marry in the next two or three years and start raising his own brood of Wilde descendants.

She turned to Jonah, snuggling against him. "I'll miss Regina and the children. That's the only thing that hurts, Jonah, our little Paul growing up without his cousins to play with."

"More settlers will follow, Sadie, you'll see. We won't be alone out there for long. And we'll have more children of our own."

But how long before I have other women to talk to? she wondered silently. *And what if Paul takes sick, or I have problems birthing a baby?*

Those were not questions she felt she had any right putting upon her husband and his dreams. And what more able man could she be traveling with than Jonah, who was an accomplished hunter and farmer, a man who'd always provided for her and his own, who had not a fearful bone in his body?

Jonah moved an arm around her and kissed her hair. "Have I told you lately how beautiful you are?" he asked.

Sadie smiled. "That's because the lantern is so dim."

Jonah chuckled. "You know better. You'll match the prairie with your yellow hair and green eyes; and Lord knows you're far stronger than this skinny frame of yours would lead one to believe." He moved a hand over her ribs.

"Well, since you're my husband, I'm glad you think me beautiful," she told him, still taking great pleasure in his touch. She moved a hand over his muscled chest and arms. Her husband's dark skin and hair revealed the bit of Indian he'd inherited from his grandfather and great-grandfather, but his eyes were as blue as a September sky, a gift from his father. "I might not stay so beautiful once we're settled on the prairie," she added. "They say there are no trees there—no shade from the sun. I'll be a wrinkled-up old lady before you know it."

"We'll *plant* trees," Jonah answered. "And I'll build you a sod house as fast as I can so you'll have a place to get out of the sun whenever you need to. They say sod houses can actually be quite cool in summer. If we can find the right location, I'm told it's even safer and cooler to dig a house right out of a hillside. Nothing can get to you in a house like that—no animal, not the elements, not even Indians. There are no windows for them to climb through and they can't burn it."

No windows for light, Sadie thought. *We'll live underground like the moles and the prairie dogs, where we won't hear the wind or see the sun.*

She couldn't entertain such thoughts. It wasn't fair to Jonah. She had to stop feeling sorry for herself. Would it be any better to let him go off alone to do this, never knowing whether he'd made it? Whether he was all right? Never knowing when he would return? Would it be better to sleep alone at night, wondering if perhaps she was a widow and didn't know it?

No. She would go with him. It didn't matter what they might face, as long as she could lie in Jonah Wilde's arms like this at night. She'd married him for better or for worse, and it was her duty to follow her husband wherever he went and do it without complaint. And little Paul needed his daddy. That, too, was important. Their beautiful son slept nearby, excited about going on a "big trip" in a wagon.

"We should take plenty of whiskey," Jonah was saying.

"Oh? Do you plan to get drunk a lot?"

He chuckled. "For medicinal purposes, and you know it." This time he kissed her eyes. "I know you don't exactly look forward to this, Sadie, but I just know this is the right time to do this. Treaties or no treaties, people are going to keep heading west. There is just too much free land there to ignore, and the first ones to settle it will end up literally building their own settlements and reaping all the benefits."

He moved on top of her. "I promise to take good care of you, to protect you and Paul above all else and make sure you have a decent house there someday. The first summer and winter will be hard, but things will get better after that. I'll make sure of it."

She moved her arms around his neck. "I know you will. I love you, Jonah, and I'm not afraid."

He leaned down to meet her mouth with his own, at the same time reaching down to push her flannel gown up to her hips. "The next few weeks will find us worn and tired and working hard, Sadie. There won't be much chance for this on the journey."

She closed her eyes and opened herself to him, never even considering turning this man away in the night. He was her husband, and he should be allowed his pleasure, especially when she took so much pleasure of her own in return. He moved inside of her with all the glory that was Jonah Wilde, the only man who'd ever invaded her most private self with such power and yet such gentle intimacy. She arched toward him in return, gasping at the way he had of making her feel wanton and wild and exploding with love and desire.

Her groans of pleasure mingled with his own as she gladly served his needs and answered his hot kisses and allowed his lips to trail down to where he'd opened her gown to reach inside and cup her breast. He pulled at her nipple like a babe, an act she found intriguingly delightful, for a strong, brave, grown man to seek out that which he knew as an infant and to still take such delight in it.

He surged into her until she felt his life spill from him. More heated kisses were followed with a deep sigh as he moved to lie beside her again. "We'd better get some sleep," he said, squeezing her hand.

Yes. They were leaving tomorrow. And he was right. There would be little time for enjoying their sweet love physically once they headed into the prairie.

3

May 19, 1810

"Oh, my, we'll miss you so! And worry so!"

"Reggie, we'll be all right. Just keep us in your prayers," Jonah told his sister-in-law. "And surely others will pass through wherever we land. I'm sure we can find someone to bring you a letter."

As they and the rest of the family mingled and hugged, Sadie fought hard to keep her smile of confidence. Inside, her stomach churned at the thought of leaving this family she'd grown to love. What if she never saw any of them again? There was a very good chance of that.

Oh, how her heart ached! Jeremiah, the oldest brother, dependable and steadfast, had kept this farm going, with his faithful Regina by his side. Little Paul would so miss his cousins, whom she now hugged one by one with relish . . . Mark, who at eleven hated hugs; Ruth, who hugged her almost too tightly, and six-year-old Luke, who seemed to think this was all just fun and games. She hugged Matthew, thinking how someday he would fall in love and marry, and she and Jonah would miss all of that. They would miss seeing Jeremiah's and Matthew's children grow up.

Next came Regina, and Sadie clung to her lingeringly. How long would it be before she again enjoyed the company of another woman, especially one who knew and understood her so well? She'd lost her mother so long ago, her father even longer, and her only sister had moved back east with her soldier husband. Regina was the only person in whom Sadie could confide the way only women understood.

Jonah was doing his own hugging, the kind of quick, almost embarrassed hugs men give each other. He picked up each of his nephews and his niece and embraced them. Everything was happening too fast . . . too fast. It felt strange to experience so much joy and so much sorrow at literally the same time.

Everything was packed, farm tools and implements, plenty of flour, sugar, salt, pork fat with smoked ham packed into it to preserve it, jerky, spices, soaps, dried fruits and vegetables, coffee, tea, whiskey . . . plenty of whiskey. They'd also packed planting seeds, a few fruit trees as well as hardwoods, their roots packed with dirt and wrapped in damp cloth. Sadie's wagon also carried tableware and even a bit of her china, packed in straw; a mantel clock; a rocking chair; cloth for clothing and curtains; sewing supplies; a couple of rag rugs; a butter churn; cooking pans; coffeepot; their clothing; blankets and pillows; towels, washtubs, and washboard; candle wax and candles; lanterns and oil; some of Paul's stuffed toys and a toy wooden horse Matthew had carved for him for his second birthday, plus a toy wagon Jeremiah had made for him. Then, of course, they'd taken apart and packed the brass bed Jonah had ordered all the way from New York City before their marriage.

They were taking so many supplies that each of them would drive his and her own wagon, and hitched to Jonah's wagon was a smaller open-bed wagon filled with firewood, enough to get them through a few days once they reached open, treeless country, something Sadie had trouble picturing.

They would try to settle someplace not too far from the edge of where the woods ended. Jonah would have to travel to cut wood from then on. Jonah had even carefully packed four square-framed windows so her future sod house could have light. The windows could be reused in a real wood house someday, and Jonah would make shutters to cover them against bad weather . . . or Indian attack. For the time being it was the only way she could handle the thought of a sod house.

It was time! Jonah walked her to her wagon, placing a switch in her hand.

"Remember the commands I taught you," he told her, kissing her cheek. She'd driven horse-drawn wagons plenty of times, but she'd never guided oxen before. They were driven by commands and a switch, not by reins; and the guide walked alongside them rather than sitting in the wagon and using reins. They would walk to the prairie.

"I can do it," she assured Jonah. She took a deep breath and adjusted her slat bonnet against the sun. Six oxen were hitched to Jonah's wagon, since he was pulling the extra wagon filled with wood. Sadie's wagon would be pulled with four oxen, the huge beasts rather intimidating but gentle and easier to command than she'd thought before learning how to guide them.

Jonah placed Paul on his shoulders and walked to his wagon. Oh, how Sadie prayed her baby wouldn't get sick on the way with no doctors available to help. She told herself to trust in God. She always had, but never before had faith been so important.

At least the day was beautiful, sunny, cool, dry. For the first several days they would pass other settlements before being completely alone. That was good. It would give her time to adjust to first leaving the family, then gradually leaving other people and civilization behind. Last night so many friends from Willow Creek had come to visit for the last time that she'd gone to bed later than she preferred. She was already tired, but so be it. She was determined to make this first day without complaint. A letter was on its way to her sister in Philadelphia . . . a loving sister she would likely never see again.

She breathed deeply against the pain in her heart. More good-byes. Jonah got his oxen moving. Sadie did the same. A milk cow and two calves were tied to the back of her wagon, and she looked back to see their ropes yanked tight at first until the animals started walking to keep up. Jeremiah had given them the cow and calves, and so many other things with which to get started.

They started down the pathway that led to the main road. After a few days there would be no roads, no bridges. They would have to forge their own way through undergrowth, forest, tall grasses, over rivers.

"God help us," Sadie whispered as they reached the end of the driveway. Her throat swelled with a need to cry. *Don't look back.* Regina would understand. Sadie told her last night that she would not . . . could not look back once they got under way. A last look at the family home, their own small home next door, the barn the whole town had helped raise years ago, faces of loved ones. How could she turn and see all of that and not drop her switch and run back?

Jonah did look back. He smiled and waved . . . so self-confident, so sure all would be well and that they would even be able to come back and visit one day. When men dreamed they saw only the good of it, the excitement, the potential. Jonah was a proud man who wanted to forge his own way, and he didn't know the meaning of fear.

He glanced at her then. "You okay?"

She smiled and nodded. She couldn't answer verbally. If she opened her mouth she would start crying. She would not do that to him. He looked so happy, and he needed to think that she was happy, too. He might have stayed if she'd insisted, but she would never see the same joy in her husband's eyes as she saw there now.

The voices that still shouted good-byes began to fade. The oxen turned at the end of the driveway and lumbered down the road, headed west. Sadie's eyes were so brimmed with tears that she could barely see.

Be strong, Sadie. You can do this.

4

May 22, 1810

"Why should we be so patient?" Windigo rose from the council fire to face the heralded Shawnee leader, Tecumseh. "I am Potawatomi," he told Tecumseh. "The things the white men have done to us are unspeakable. I for one am not so sure I and my people can sit around while you preach to us to hold back from what is in our hearts, which is to show the whites that the Fort Wayne Treaty means nothing to us!"

He faced Tecumseh squarely and with enough youthful warrior's pride to match Tecumseh's pride in being a respected warrior and leader of the Shawnee.

"Listen to me, Windigo," Tecumseh answered in the deep, commanding voice that had won so many tribes to his side. "I am not saying we will never war against the Americans. I am only saying we must wait until even more of your people, and more Miamis and Wyandots and Delawares and Ottawas and others, join us here at Prophetstown. You know yourself that the numbers of *shemanese* who live east of *Spraylaywith-eepi* are as great as the stars in the heavens. We will never defeat them without building our own numbers and fighting them *together!*"

Spraylaywitheepi. The Ohio River. Windigo knew the Shawnee tongue as well as his own. He used Tecumseh's language when speaking to him. Windigo's own father had been Shawnee . . . until white men killed him! Yes, he, too, remembered a time when the Indian Nations thrived east of the Ohio, where now white settlements flourished and were swarming like ants to the other side and into western lands.

"I understand what you say, Tecumseh," he answered. "I greatly respect your plans. I even agree with them. I am only telling you that since the death of my Shawnee father and the horrible rape of my Potawatomi mother by six white men, my heart burns with a desire for revenge! The Potawatomi also are eager to destroy these new white settlements. I brought many of them here with me, all desirous of hearing what you have to say, and most of them in agreement. But the deprivations against us make waiting nearly impossible! And when I think of how Governor Harrison tricked many of our leaders into signing that treaty, and how he claimed it was valid when in fact hardly any of those who truly represent us signed it, I dream of sinking my knife into the white leader and running it up his belly to his throat and then taking his scalp!"

Others who were gathered in the Shawnee *msikah-miqui,* or council house, raised fists and voiced their agreement with Windigo. His name meant "Man Eater" in the white men's tongue, and he'd proven that the name fit. Once he, Windigo, then only nineteen, had torn the heart from an American captive and eaten of it, showing other white captives how sorry they should be for setting their log houses on Indian land, and in sweet revenge for his father's death and his mother's abuse. He still enjoyed the memory of the horror and terror in the captives' eyes at his act. He enjoyed frightening whites. He most enjoyed killing them.

"I, too, have given much thought to killing Harrison," Tecumseh told the circle of various tribal leaders, turning to make eye contact with each and every one of them.

Windigo sat down as the great Shawnee orator continued. Although he disagreed with waiting too long for war, he fully respected Tecumseh's ability to unite so many. It was not an easy task, given the fact that many of these tribes had at different times warred against one another. Old hatreds and bad feelings ran deep among some of them. Tecumseh faced a formidable task in trying to get all of them to band together against the white man. Windigo had to admire the deep-voiced, handsome specimen of man who continued to travel extensively in his efforts to bring all tribes into unison for one cause.

"It is true that William Henry Harrison, who the American settlers made leader of this land they call Indiana, *our* land, has betrayed us with the Fort Wayne Treaty. He once called us friend, and I called *him* friend! What he has done should not be forgiven, and it only shows us again how deceitful the Long Knives can be. I only implore all of you to reason with me and wait for revenge. It is always wise to first do all that is possible to avoid war, for we know what war does to our women and children. And to make war before we are truly united and ready would only bring disaster. First we must talk to Harrison one more time and explain that the proper leaders did not sign nor do they agree to the treaty. I propose a council meeting with Governor Harrison."

"He will just lie to us again," Windigo grumbled. "No matter what he tells us, it will not be the truth."

"And while we wait, Tecumseh, more Americans will come into this land they think is theirs by treaty." The words came from the Wyandot spokesman, Stiahta, who had spurred the execution of Leatherlips, a Wyandot man who'd signed the much-reviled treaty. The ritualistic execution consisted of four tomahawk blows to Letherlips's head, his punishment for going along with a treaty that gave away three million acres of prime Shawnee and Wyandot hunting grounds, land also used by other tribes for survival. "The only ones I believe we can trust now are the redcoats, who hate the Americans and are nearly ready to make war with them again."

"I will try to arrange a council with Harrison as soon as possible to avoid too much American settlement taking place before we can talk," Tecumseh answered. "I will send my personal aide, Sauganash, to Vincennes to set a time for this meeting."

In spite of his own desire to make war right now against new settlers, Windigo took some solace in the very presence of Tecumseh, who seemed to draw crowds wherever he went. He was an eloquent, sincere speaker, a man who could be trusted and believed. If anyone could reason with William Harrison, it would be Tecumseh, even though hard feelings had developed between the two men.

Windigo became lost in thought as other leaders voiced their opinions, some understanding each other, others using interpreters, for many here spoke other tongues. Windigo glanced at Tecumseh's brother, Tenskwatawa, the Prophet. It was mostly Tenskwatawa's fault that rumblings of war had begun. To Tecumseh's surprise, the brother with whom he'd once been close had gone against Tecumseh's wishes and literally betrayed him. While Tecumseh was in the south trying to gather support from southern tribes, Tenskwatawa had jealously proclaimed himself the wiser, stronger leader and had advised all tribes already gathered at Tippecanoe to make war on the Americans and, in particular, to attack and destroy the Indiana capital at Vincennes. Rumors of such an attack had driven a deep wedge into the intercourse between Governor Harrison and Tecumseh, who was being blamed for instigating the rumors. Tenskwatawa, who'd always proclaimed he was able to see the future, had begun painting his face as a warrior and a leader, though he could never handle either job in the outstanding way of Tecumseh.

Now Tenskwatawa sat silent and meditating, his face no longer painted, his sightless right eye drooping as the man appeared lost in thoughts of his own. Tenskwatawa no longer wore the fancy Shawnee regalia he'd been inclined to wear during Tecumseh's absence, for when Tecumseh returned and learned of the damage the Prophet had done to his relationship with Governor Harrison, Tecumseh had sharply reprimanded his brother, demanding that he stop trying to start a war and cease his outrageous behavior that had cost so much in Tecumseh's quest for peace.

There was none other like Tecumseh. The greatest of leaders of other tribes knew this and respected it. The man had been a renowned warrior by the age of twelve. His leadership and oratory abilities were unprecedented. His very build and voice, wisdom and intelligence, demanded leadership. The man's unique abilities in these areas were the reason so many representatives from other tribes, including Windigo, had come here to Prophetstown to consider joining an amalgamation of all tribes to put up a united front against Harrison, the great father in Washington, and indeed, all whites.

But the waiting was sometimes more than Windigo could handle. If not for the cruel way his own father had been tortured by white men, and his mother's multiple rapes, Tecumseh's plan would be easier to accommodate. But the death of his father and the shame brought upon his beloved mother had set a fire in his heart that burned constantly, fueled by a need for revenge.

5

May 24, 1810

Sadie took heart in the lovely weather and beautiful hills of Ohio as she and Jonah drove the oxen ever westward. Soon they would cross the border into Indiana, and still the country was hilly and covered with hardwood trees. Perhaps, Sadie thought, the land ahead was not so wide-open and treeless as they'd been led to believe. After all, people always tended to exaggerate when telling their tales of adventure. And how could there possibly be a place where trees did not grow?

The few days they'd traveled helped still the initial agony in her heart over leaving the family. Still, she could not help picturing what they might be doing now, Jeremiah and Mark hoeing the fields, Regina hanging a wash, Ruth gathering eggs, Matthew feeding the stock, little Luke cleaning the horse stalls. She knew every day's routine and missed it, but a taste of the adventure of travel far beyond any place she'd ever been soothed the sting of being apart.

Jonah seemed so happy. This new venture might not be so bad after all. Little Paul brimmed with excitement, but whenever he rode in one of the wagons Sadie worried that he might fall. So far the boy had been mindful of obeying his father's order to stay in the back of the first wagon where Sadie could watch him. There he played with a straw horse and could see his mommy and wave to her, and he often fell asleep in one of the stacks of quilts.

They still followed a decent roadway that led west and southwest, encountering a cabin here and there where settlers let the oxen drink from their water troughs and kindly offered food. Always the women seemed eager to visit with another female, and Sadie welcomed their company in return. The one threat to Sadie's positive outlook was the same warning from everyone they met . . . "Be on the lookout for Indians. Most will be friendly, but some won't." . . . "Stay to the southern end of Indiana. Tecumseh is gathering tribes in the north at Tippecanoe."

Sadie breathed deeply every time she gave thought to the prospect of running into Indians, especially Shawnee. No one who'd lived in the Ohio Valley was unfamiliar with the horrible damage and suffering angry warriors could cause. And Sadie could barely stand to ponder some of the stories of torture she'd heard exchanged by men discussing such things. She could only pray it was true that the one called Tecumseh was a man of peace.

"Looks like a settlement up ahead," Jonah called out. "We'll camp there the night."

Sadie took relief in the words. Her feet screamed to be left alone and her back and hips agreed. Maybe she could talk Jonah into staying here more than a night. She and the oxen needed a good rest, and she didn't doubt Jonah did, too. He'd be too proud to admit it. She'd have to use herself as an excuse to stay over.

"Thank God," she called out. "Could we please stay more than one night this time, Jonah? Surely one extra day won't make any difference."

He turned to look back at her, flashing the handsome smile she so loved. "I was already considering it. It wouldn't hurt to rest the oxen, and Paul deserves a day of running and playing."

Sadie smiled. "Oh, thank you!"

Both of them switched the oxen into a slightly faster pace, and Sadie had to grin with curiosity, wondering if oxen ever ran. She'd never seen one move fast, which was why it was easy to keep up with them on foot. She supposed that if she were as big and lumbering as one of these beasts, she wouldn't be able to move very fast either.

Thunder rumbled in the west just as they approached the small settlement that consisted of a few log dwellings, a trade store, a tavern, a black-smith's barn, and a livery where several horses were penned. The few people in the street stared and nodded, most grinning and welcoming them.

"Headed west?" a man in front of the livery asked.

"Sure am," Jonah answered. "Free land."

The man nodded. "Sounds good, long as you can keep your scalp while you're there. I've known some that's done fine out there on the prairie, and some that never made it . . . even some that come back with stories that would curl your hair." He looked at Sadie. "Sorry, ma'am. Don't mean to scare ya."

It's a little late for that, Sadie wanted to reply. "It's all right," she answered aloud.

"Say, is there a barnyard around where we could turn the oxen loose for a night or two . . . maybe sleep in a barn on hay instead of in the wagons?" Jonah asked.

The man scratched at his beard. Sadie guessed him to be perhaps in his forties. His face was tanned and deeply wrinkled, and a few teeth were missing; but she could see he'd once been a nice-looking man. Hard living destroyed that quickly, although he still looked strong and healthy, a rather short man but stocky and solid.

She wondered what years of toiling in a new land would do to her handsome husband. And Lord knew what it would do to her. Still, she could never stop loving Jonah Wilde no matter what age and the elements did to him, and she knew he felt the same way about her. The kind of love they shared went beyond outside appearances.

"Me and the missus live right back yonder." The livery owner pointed to a cabin and barn they'd passed coming through the settlement. "My son Jack, he's sixteen—keeps the barn right clean—one of his chores. You're welcome to put up there. Got a well where you can bring up whatever water you need in a bucket. Got a right sturdy outhouse, too."

"We're obliged," Jonah replied with a nod. He removed his floppy leather hat to wipe sweat from his brow. The weather had turned warmer than any they'd experienced since leaving Willow Creek.

"Say, my name's Marvin Stockton," the livery owner told them before they could leave. "Wife's name is Louise. I gotta tell ya, we've been thinkin' on goin' into the prairie ourselves. Might be a real boon to Jack's future if we got settled there and he got in on one of the first Indiana farm settlements, you know? With so many people wantin' to go there because of the new treaty, it's bound to grow."

"That's the whole idea," Jonah answered. "I don't intend to let Indian worries stop me. Seems to me like Governor Harrison is in pretty good control of things."

Marvin nodded. "Still a worry, though. Only reason I brought it up . . . well, there's been others come through here. Where they ended up I'm not sure, but . . . well, I'm thinkin' maybe you and the missus would like company." He grinned at Paul, who stuck

36

his head out of the back of the wagon and grinned the chubby, dimpled smile that would win anyone's heart.

"Hi, mistuh," he said, waving to Marvin.

Marvin waved back. "The missus would love bein' around a little one again. All we have is Jack—never could have more after that." He rubbed the back of his neck as though in thought.

"You saying you want to go with us?" Jonah asked.

Marvin shrugged. "Well, it's kinda sudden to you, I know; but it's somethin' we've been thinkin' on for over a year now, and you two look awful young. Most likely you'll need some help, what with your woman havin' to look after the boy and all. You comin' along like this just kind of hit me that maybe it's time for me and the wife to take our son to settle on his own on free land. He's been itchin' to go, you know? We're worried he'll take off on his own, and that would break my wife's heart. This way we wouldn't have to worry so much about him 'cause we'd be with him."

Marvin shook his head then, laughing in a funny, contagious way that made Sadie smile.

"Listen to me," the man continued, "rattlin' on to complete strangers. I don't know why I got this good feelin' about you two. It just come over me of a sudden, you know? You must think I'm crazy."

Jonah chuckled in return. "Well, there are plenty of folks back in Willow Creek who thought I was crazy to head into the prairie, so I understand. The wife and I will go get settled and we can talk more about it. Fact is, it would probably be of some relief to my wife to have another woman along."

So, he understood better than she thought. Sadie wanted to run over and hug her husband. Things were looking brighter after all. She felt happier and more confident than she ever had since leaving Willow Creek.

6

May 27, 1810

The "orchestra" consisted of one fiddler who knew only four slow tunes, but that didn't matter to the thirty-five settlers in Stockton. Sadie was glad that after Marvin and Louise Stockton left the tiny establishment, they would forever be remembered by its name, as they were the first ones to come here. Now, after ten years of toiling away to make their little settlement livable, they would go on to Indiana and do it all over again.

She smiled at Jonah as he gently whirled her around on the dirt floor of Marvin's barn, where a clearing had been made for the good-bye celebration. They'd stayed here six days while the Stocktons prepared for their own journey. The respite had been a welcome break and a boon to Sadie's spirits.

"Maybe wherever we settle in Indiana, we'll build our own town that will be named after you," she told Jonah.

38

Jonah frowned. "Hmmmm. Wilde Town. Doesn't sound too tame, does it?"

Sadie laughed. "Well, maybe we can call it Jonahville."

He chuckled, flashing the smile she loved. "Not too bad, I guess. How about something like Paulston, after our son?"

Her eyebrows arched in approval. "Not bad." She glanced over to where little Paul was holding hands with a girl of about ten. He was jumping up and down in his own form of "dance." "He looks so much like his daddy," she commented. "And that's a very good thing."

Jonah pulled her a little closer. "Well, if he looked like you, that wouldn't be a *bad* thing, you know."

She watched him lovingly. "If he was a girl I'd agree. Maybe the next one will look like me in every way."

He leaned down and kissed her forehead. "You'd like a little girl, wouldn't you?"

"You know I would, but I can wait. A new baby is certainly the last thing we need right now—or even a pregnancy! We'll both have too much work to do." She saw the disappointment in his blue eyes.

"This won't be easy, Sadie."

She knew he was talking about more than the work involved in building from scratch. They had agreed that they must abstain from making love until they had a decent house to live in and had cleared a little land. He would need her to help with some of the physical

39

work, and that might endanger a pregnancy.

"Then we'll just enjoy each other more over the long, cold winter," she answered.

He rolled his eyes. "Don't even talk about it. You have no idea how enticing you are even when you're covered with dirt and sweat, Mrs. Wilde."

"Well, it's the same with you, so we'll *both* have to suffer through it."

He chuckled. "Luckily we'll be too dang tired most of the time to care." He whirled her again. "It's just . . . times like this . . . when we're relaxed and happy—"

"I know." The music stopped. "Maybe we shouldn't even dance anymore," she suggested.

Jonah ran a hand through his hair. "Maybe you're right." He put an arm to her waist and led her to a table covered with pies and cakes. Someone had removed a large coffeepot from a fire outside and brought it in, along with coffee cups donated by each family to use for the celebration. Most of them were tin, and Sadie felt a tug at her heart at realizing it would be a long time before she could set a decent table and use her china.

People began lining up to eat, and the friendly women at the table wished them good luck and said they would include their family as well as Marvin's in their prayers.

"You're so brave," one woman named Hilda told Sadie.

"It's my *husband* who's brave," she answered. "I'm not so sure about myself."

They both smiled, but Sadie knew by Hilda's eyes that she understood what she was going through as a woman with a small child going into a new land. Only another woman could understand.

"At least Louise Stockton will also be going," she added. "It will be so good to have another woman along."

Hilda nodded. "And you couldn't ask for someone more understanding or more adept," she answered. "And their son is a strong young man who will be a big help."

Sadie agreed. She took her pie and some coffee and walked over to sit down beside Louise, to whom she'd warmed immediately upon meeting. God was surely smiling upon her and Jonah, to have led them to these wonderful people who would travel and settle with them.

"Mommy, me some pie!" Paul said, running over to her. Sadie smiled and fed him a bite of berry pie.

"He's such a sweetheart," Louise told her. "And Lord knows I'll enjoy having him to dote on."

Sadie looked at her, studying the stout woman's kind brown eyes surrounded by the heavy lines of hard living. Her brown hair was heavily splashed with gray, and beneath all that Sadie could tell that like her husband Marvin, Louise had once been fine-looking. She'd learned the woman was only thirty-eight, but she looked much older. "I'm so glad you'll be along so we can take turns watching him while the other helps with the work."

"Yes, this is going to work out fine, all right," Louise answered in a rather scratchy voice.

Sadie caught the hint of sadness in her eyes. "It will be hard leaving all your friends here, won't it?"

Louise reached over to pat her hand. "Not as bad as you having to leave family," she answered. "I reckon we'll both be havin' some soulful memories."

"More, Mommy!"

"Say please, Paul."

"Pleeeze." The boy flashed his dimpled smile.

Sadie gave him another bite of pie. "Yes, we will," she answered Louise's comment. "I'm sure that's why God led us to each other, Louise, to help us bear the parting by forming a new friendship."

"Well, I reckon you're right there." Louise smiled and shook her head. "It's the price of marryin', I guess. Men get an itch, and their women have to scratch it."

Sadie laughed. Louise was prone to surprising, amusing comments, which would certainly relieve the boredom once they settled in . . . if they had time to get bored. "I suppose you're right!" She'd kept shoveling bites of pie into Paul's mouth during the conversation, and already it was nearly gone. "Paul! You ate all of Mommy's pie!"

Paul grinned, his teeth and lips red from the berries. He ran off to hop around to another tune from the fiddler, and Sadie shook her head. "I'm glad we brought a good stock of food," she told Louise, "or that boy will eat us into starvation before winter is over!"

"Just wait till he's Jack's age!"

"Well, at least Jack is old enough to help plant and harvest the food he'll be eating!" Sadie glanced over to where Jack stood talking to Marvin and Jonah. He was as tall as Jonah and had to look down on his father. Yes, the strong young man would be a wonderful help. Sadie could hardly get over their stroke of luck in finding these people to travel and settle with. The Stocktons had come here from Pennsylvania, Marvin having the same "itch"—as Louise had put it—to go to new places and have something of his own. The price of living had gone too high in Pennsylvania, and he'd lost his livery business to competition from a much wealthier man who could afford all the most updated tools, a bigger building, and hired help. Also wanting land to farm, Marvin left in 1800 and had come as far west as he dared at the time because of Indian problems. Now with a new treaty between the Shawnee and other tribes and Governor Harrison, they felt relatively safe in going even farther west.

"Marvin says that it will actually be easier getting started in prairie land because we won't have any trees to clear," Louise told her.

"My goodness, I never thought of that, Louise." Sadie leaned back to watch Paul. "I guess that's because I can't picture a land with no trees in it. Do you really think it's like that? Surely there are *some* trees."

Louise shook her head. "I reckon we'll find out, honey."

Sadie nodded. "I guess we will." She thought back on the big autumn barn dances they used to have back at Willow Creek, with at least five times the number of people here, and in a much bigger barn . . . Jonah and Jeremiah's barn on the Wilde homestead. She'd gone to one at sixteen, and that was when she'd ended up falling in love with Jonah Wilde, womanly desires blossoming where once she'd seen him only as a friend. They had danced . . . and danced.

7

May 29, 1810

"What do you think he'll do, Marvin?"

"Tecumseh?" Marvin puffed on a pipe and watched the flickering flames of their campfire. "Hard to say. He's incredibly popular among all the various tribes, I'm told—even with some whites. At the same time he has a reputation for being a fearless warrior. Some say he had that reputation by the time he was fourteen or fifteen years old. A man like that could go either way. All this fuss over the Fort Wayne Treaty and Harrison and Tecumseh and all them Indians getting together— with somebody like Tecumseh at the head of it all, it might be good for us . . . might not."

Jonah rolled his eyes. "You aren't helping me, friend."

Marvin chuckled. "I gave up long ago tryin' to pre-

44

dict what Indians might do."

Sadie and Louise listened to the conversation with keen interest. Their safety could depend on the decisions of an Indian leader whose name was apparently known as far away as Washington. Before leaving Stockton a courier who made his living by daringly carrying news all over southern Michigan, Ohio, and Indiana had brought a newspaper from Detroit to the little settlement. He was handsomely paid by people hungry for news. Even though the paper was several months old, it was read aloud to a town gathering by William Stringer, a former schoolteacher from eastern Ohio.

Everyone had listened intently to an article about the great and rising leader of the Shawnee named Tecumseh, who was being called a great orator, a magnificent and fearless warrior, a natural-born leader who was influential with all Indian tribes as well as many white leaders, including Governor William Henry Harrison of Indiana. However, according to the article, the Fort Wayne Treaty of 1809 was being declared illegal by Tecumseh, and because hundreds of Indians from many different tribes from far-reaching areas were gathering at Tippecanoe, Tecumseh's primary home, Governor Harrison feared a planned uprising. This was not good news for people like themselves who were planning to settle in Indiana on land now deemed to belong to Americans.

Jonah rubbed his eyes and sighed. For the next several seconds the only sound was that of crickets and the crackling of the fire. They still had not left hilly, forested country, and a soft wind rustled the fresh green leaves of trees that had fully opened up only a month ago. Little Paul slept soundly in his wagon, and all seemed so serene.

"Surely if we stay more to the south like others advise, we won't have to worry," Louise spoke up. "We have to go there anyway to file our claims. Surely they will have suggestions for us."

Jonah nodded. "True, but I don't want any Indian leader dictating where I choose to settle. With any luck, the safest available land will be what we're all looking for."

"I ain't afraid of no Indians," Jack told them confidently. He poked at the fire with a stick, creating little spurts of embers that sparked upward, some of them floating off with wisps of soft wind. "I expect that Governor Harrison has a good militia set up and can handle anything that there Tecumseh wants to throw at him, especially since he's the one who handled the treaty in the first place. According to that article, Harrison has apparently been dealin' with Tecumseh for a lot of years. He probably has him figured pretty good and knows what to watch out for. If the governor of Indiana wants that land opened up, he'll make sure it's safe for new settlers, I'll bet. You just watch."

"Ever the optimist, are you?" Jonah asked with a sudden grin.

The smile did not fool Sadie. She knew her husband was concerned for her and Paul. Still, she also knew he wouldn't let the Shawnee stop him from his dream. It was such a relief having Marvin and Jack with them now . . . extra help in case of a run-in with unwanted visitors . . . the two-legged kind.

"Why, heck yes," Jack answered. Then he frowned. "What's an optimist?"

Jonah chuckled, and Sadie had to smile, too. Jack was reckless and handsome and fearless . . . a lot like a young Jonah. He'd not had much schooling, and there was a bright innocence about him that one could not help but like him. His energy and good nature were good for Paul, too, who already loved the young man. The feelings were mutual, and having Jack's help to entertain and often carry Paul on his shoulders was a wonderful relief to the burden of Sadie and Jonah having to watch the little boy constantly.

"An optimist is someone who always looks on the bright side of things," Sadie answered for Jonah. "You certainly are that."

Jack laughed. "Only way to be, I say. No sense frettin' your life away over things that *might* happen. If they ain't happened yet, why worry about them?"

"Well, now, there's a philosophy I like," Jonah said, he and others all laughing together now.

"Leave it to Jack to brighten things up," Marvin told them, shaking his head.

Louise stood up and smoothed her apron. "We'd all best get some rest," she suggested. "Plenty of travelin' to do yet."

"I expect you're right," Marvin answered, also

47

rising. He stretched his arms, then arched his back. "I didn't realize how old and settled I was gettin' till I started out on this trip. I ain't walked this much in a long time."

"Heck, you're plenty strong yet, Pa," Jack told him. "You're built like an oak tree."

"Well, this old oak just might have some dry rot on the inside," Marvin answered, provoking another round of laughter.

"Come on, old man. Get yourself some sleep. I've got the bed all made up in the wagon for ya," Louise told him.

Jack walked closer to Jonah. "How long do you think it will be before we see some real prairie land?" he asked.

Jonah took another drag on his pipe, an old pipe that had belonged to his father Luke. He treasured it. "Well, my guess is within about four days," he answered. "After that it's probably a good week to Vincennes. We'll head southwest, follow the Ohio most of the way, kind of skirt our way between prairie and forest till we can head up to Vincennes and figure out where we'll settle. That way we should stay away from trouble and be close to water and wood for as long as possible till we actually settle farther north."

"Sounds good to me." Jack shook his head, grinning. "This sure is excitin', I got to say. I was gettin' bored to death back in Stockton. I've been wantin' to do this but hated leavin' my folks, you know? I sure am glad they suddenly decided to come along. I guess they just got a good feelin' about you two and finally made up their minds."

"Well, they settled Stockton all by themselves, Jack. It had to be hard for them to leave all their friends there."

"I reckon." Jack rubbed the back of his neck. "They're good people, you know."

"Sure they are. We could see that right off. That's why we didn't mind them coming along." Jonah put a hand on his shoulder. "I come from good people, too. My grandfather Jeremiah was a wandering man who fought in the French and Indian War. My father Luke fought in the Revolutionary War and then built the farm he left to me and my brothers back in the Ohio Valley. We left a lot of family back there, Jack, so you're lucky you can bring yours with you."

Jack nodded. "I know." He glanced at Sadie. "Good night, ma'am." The young man walked off to sleep in his bedroll under his parents' wagon.

Jonah walked over to Sadie, smiling down at her. He placed his hands on her shoulders. "We'll make this work, Sadie. It's like Jack said. Harrison surely has plans for backing up this treaty. If we get all the way to Vincennes without a problem, I think we'll be okay."

Sadie grasped his forearms, taking comfort in their solid strength. "I *know* we'll be okay. I feel much better about everything than when we first left Willow Creek."

A sadness came into his blue eyes, lit by the flicker

of the campfire. "I know how hard that was for you, and I'll make it up to you. I promise."

Sadie smiled. "You've never broken one promise you ever made," she answered. She leaned up for a light kiss.

"I love you, Sadie Wilde," he told her.

"And I love you."

Their gaze lingered until finally Jonah walked off to sleep in the second wagon. Sadie reached down and used a corner of her apron to take hold of the blue porcelain-clad coffeepot and remove it from the fire so it would not sit and boil into something undrinkable by morning. It could be warmed up again later. She walked to the first wagon, where Paul slept soundly. Peering inside, she just watched her son for a while, breathing deeply, his perfectly round little face alight by the moon . . . so sweet and innocent.

"Dear Lord, no matter what happens to the rest of us," she prayed, "please never let anything happen to my little Paul."

She walked around and climbed into the wagon through the front so as not to disturb him and settled into some quilts. The hot day had turned into a cool night after a late rain. She fell asleep to the sound of the singing crickets.

8

May 30, 1810

"I for one cannot wait!"

"I know how you feel, Wapmimi, but Tecumseh says we *must* wait," Windigo argued with his good friend. The two young warriors were camped along a creek fed by the Tippecanoe River. "You have heard him speak. I have come to believe he is right. Only with the strength of many tribes can we make war against the Americans and ban them from this land forever."

Wapmimi smoked a white man's pipe in thought. "I had a dream, Windigo."

Windigo shook back his long black hair, which he wore threaded through hundreds of tiny bone and copper tubes that caused a tinkling sound when he shook his hair or the wind blew it. He studied his friend Wapmimi, whose face was distorted because of a deep scar that ran across the right side over his nose. His right cheek was sunk in, the right corner of his lips grown together, and his nose looked crooked, all from a battle to defend his mother and sister from being killed by American trappers who'd attacked their small fishing camp. Wapmimi was only thirteen then, but he'd never forgotten, and his rage against the white man had never waned.

Dreams and visions were highly significant. Wap-

51

mimi's words alarmed Windigo. The fact that he'd mentioned it, something a warrior seldom did, meant it must be very important. "What was the dream?" he asked Wapmimi.

Wapmimi held his gaze with dark, blazing eyes, and Windigo thought how handsome his friend might have been without the scar.

"You know I would not share it with you, my best friend, if I did not think it was highly important," Wapmimi told him.

Windigo nodded. "I understand, Wapmimi, and I will feel honored if you tell me the dream. But I cannot say that I will be able to explain its meaning."

Wapmimi sighed, taking one more puff on the pipe, for which he'd exchanged furs to a British trader. "This was not a vision like we would have from fasting and praying to Wiske," he told Windigo. "This was a very clear dream, a visit from Wiske to me in the night. The Master of Life spoke to me."

Windigo was all ears. This was extremely important. "What did Wiske tell you?" He scratched at a mosquito bite. He wore only fringed deerskin pants and his moccasins because of the heat. He'd applied bear fat to his body to ward off mosquitoes, but apparently he'd missed a spot.

Wapmimi seemed apprehensive. "He told me . . . that your children would be . . . Kitchimokoman."

"American!" Windigo stiffened. "How can that be? I have not even thought of marriage. If I did, it would be to a Potawatomi or Shawnee woman, not an American! Surely you misunderstood the dream!"

Wapmimi slowly shook his head. "No. The dream was very clear. There was a bright light that made me fall to my knees. Out of the light you rode toward me on a white horse, its mane the color of straw. You said, *Find her for me.* Then you rode away, but the bright light was still there. A voice spoke to me then, the voice of Wiske. *I am the Master of Life,* he said. *Find the white woman upon which Windigo rode. She is to be his bride. Her children will belong to the Bear Clan of Windigo. They will unite the Bear Clan with the Americans so there will be peace.* I swear to you, Windigo, this was my dream. I must fulfill it. I must make war on American settlements until I find the woman of whom Wiske spoke. I must bring her to you. It is my duty. And it is your duty to take her for a wife when I find her."

Windigo frowned, very distraught by the dream. "Why would Wiske bring the dream to you and not to me? I have had no dreams or visions of marrying a white woman."

Wapmimi shrugged. "I only know what I dreamed. I am your best friend. I would not lie to you, Windigo. You know that."

Windigo nodded. "Then I must go away alone to fast and pray about this. I will ask Wiske to speak to me also."

"My dream makes me know I must continue making war, Windigo. I cannot sit around and wait for Tecumseh to decide when is the right time. I am to

53

find this woman, and I can only do that by going to American settlements. It will be dangerous. I will risk my life for you in order to fulfill the dream. At the same time I will be known as a great Potawatomi warrior."

Windigo looked across the fire at him. "I will go with you. That way I can protect this woman once you find her. And together we will be known as fearsome warriors to the Americans and will be respected among our own clans, the Bear Clan and the Deer Clan."

"No, Windigo. This is something I must do without you. You are becoming important as an aide to Tecumseh. Our people need a spokesman, and you're becoming the chosen one. This is a great honor."

Windigo grinned with pride. Wapmimi's scar made him look frightening to those who did not know him, most certainly to those against whom he made war. But for those who knew him well, it meant nothing, especially not to Windigo. They had been friends since they played together as little boys.

Windigo was proud of his own good looks. He did not, of course, show it or boast of it; that would be wrong. But he saw how other young girls looked at him, and his mother often bragged about his muscular build and fine features, saying that he could have his pick of young Potawatomi women, and many tried to get his attention. His mother would not be pleased to learn he must marry a white woman.

The thought wiped away his smile. For now he

could not look at the young women of his own kind. Wiske had told Wapmimi in a dream that he was to take a white woman for a wife . . . an *American* woman. He, too, did not like the thought of it, but a dream was a dream, and it must be followed.

9

June 3, 1810

"I wonder how it got this way." Sadie spoke softly, as though she was in church, for that was how she felt. Ahead of them lay what she supposed was a roadway made by someone at some time, nothing more than crushed grasses that were now springing back up but still lower than the surrounding spring growth. That growth was incredibly thick, a mass of grasses decorated with millions of daisies . . . surely millions . . . and millions.

"Who knows?" Jonah answered, also speaking softly. "One thing is sure, no tree seed of any kind could make it down inside those grasses to take root. They're too dang thick." He knelt down, spreading some of the grasses apart. "My God. I won't be able to till this stuff with the plow I have. This would take a pick and an ax to get through." He looked up at Marvin. "Can you just imagine the kind of topsoil that's underneath all of this?"

Marvin shook his head, amazement in his eyes. "It's

sure to be the best farmland a man could ask for." He, too, spoke softly.

"I ain't never seen nothin' like it," Jack put in, kneeling down beside Jonah.

Louise just sat staring from the wagon seat of one of the family's three wagons. She said nothing. From where she'd climbed into her own wagon Sadie looked across a literal sea of grass. The wind was fairly strong today, with the smell of rain in it. As it moved across the prairie grass, some of it higher than Jonah stood tall, the grass would bend and ripple in a cascade of waves that looked very much like wind on water. She'd seen only one small lake once in her lifetime, when her father took her on a hunting trip when she was little. It was a very windy day, and she remembered the way the water rippled. Surely watching the prairie was more like a much larger lake or even the ocean would look when the wind tore across it.

"Lord, have mercy," Louise finally spoke up.

"Mommy! Look at all the flowers!" Paul squealed. "Can I pick some? Can I?"

Sadie pulled him onto her lap. "No, Paul. There could be snakes down under that grass. Wait till we find a place to make camp and can make sure everything is all right."

Jonah looked up at her. "This is incredible."

Sadie looked back at the distant forest from which they'd come. Ahead lay nothing but open land for as far as the eye could see. "It certainly is."

Jonah rose. "Well, like I said, we'll stick more to the river till we get to the other side of Indiana and can go up to Vincennes, so we'll be okay for wood and water. One thing for sure is we need to settle someplace near water. We'll get a good idea of the best place once we reach Vincennes. God knows we won't have to worry about cutting our way through trees getting there."

Sadie wondered if he was thinking what she was thinking—that this incredibly tall grass was easier to hide in than it was to hide behind trees. If a man was walking in this grass, he wouldn't be able to see what was two feet in front of him. At the same time, someone else could be lurking there without their knowledge . . . someone who knew this prairie better than they and knew how to paint himself to match the prairie colors.

"We'll have to try to drive the oxen from the wagon seats just to see where we're going," Jonah said, as though to read her thoughts after all.

"I reckon," Marvin answered.

It would be so easy to get lost in this grass once a person lost sight of the trees, Sadie thought. How was a person supposed to get around in a place like this, with literally no landmarks to use to find his or her way? She'd have to keep a close eye on Paul. She told herself that surely there were some kind of roadways here and there. They just hadn't found them yet. And surely Jonah would choose to settle near one so a person would have some idea which direction to go in case of trouble or need. And what about fire? Surely

57

grass like this would burn fast and furious.

"How you reckon we'll plow this stuff?" Marvin asked Jonah.

Jonah just shook his head. "A lot of oxen and a lot of plain old gut strength," he answered. "It will take more than one go-through. We'll never be able to plant anything this first year, other than to do our best to dig some holes for the trees I brought. I'm glad we've been able to keep the roots wrapped and wet. Lord knows if any of them will really survive once we get them in the ground. There must be one heck of a root system under here. Grass like this can choke a tree to death."

Marvin nodded. "I'm thinkin' we'll need to do nothin' but till all summer, over and over, then again in the spring when it all tries to come up again. That's the only way we'll kill it off and make the ground useful for plantin'."

Jonah nodded. "Maybe not all of it is this thick. Maybe some places are a little better."

"Maybe," Marvin answered, not sounding very sure of it.

"Heck, we can handle it," Jack said with his usual optimism.

"What if it catches fire?" Louise asked, as though to read Sadie's mind. "How would a person get away from it?"

Jonah and Marvin just looked at each other.

"Well, it won't matter if we live underground instead of in sod houses. I've heard some just dig under the ground and make their houses that way," Jack offered. "Just think how cool a house like that would be, and it would be a shelter from fire and even a good place to hide from Indians." He spoke the words with a confident smile, as though that was all there was to it.

"Under the ground?" Sadie asked. "Like moles?"

"Just for a while, don't you see?" the young man answered. "And it would be a lot warmer in winter, too. No worry about hard winds seepin' through the cracks. The more I think about it, the better it sounds."

Under the ground? Sadie said again to herself. No human being should have to live under the ground. Jonah promised a sod house, not a hole in the ground! She'd lose her sanity living under the ground for a whole winter. She didn't like closed places where she couldn't see the sky or go out a different door. What about windows? What about the fine home Jonah promised to build her within a year? How long would they end up living under the ground if he couldn't even till and plant this first year?

"Jack, you're upsettin' the women," Marvin scolded his son. "I can see it in their eyes. Ain't no woman wants to live under the ground. We'll build fine sod houses at first. They deserve that much."

"Well, let's not jump to conclusions," Jonah said, glancing at Sadie, then back to Marvin. "Let's take one thing at a time. First we have to get to Vincennes. Maybe we'll get some news there about the situation with the Indians and get whatever other supplies we need—get an idea of where to go next. We were told what prairie land is like. We just couldn't really imagine it because we've never seen anything like it before. We'll find a way to manage." He looked at Sadie again. "We always do." He gave her a wink and a smile, but Sadie saw right through it. He was just as amazed and unsure as the rest of them, but he was Jonah Wilde, and Jonah Wilde would never admit to defeat of any kind, certainly not before even putting up a fight.

And that was what conquering land like this would be . . . a fight to the last. It would be the strength of the land against the strength of Jonah Wilde, and who could say who would win?

She adjusted her slat bonnet against the sun, bringing to light another concern she tried to put to the back of her mind. If the trees Jonah had brought with them managed to survive, it would be years before they were big enough to cast a shadow from the sun. In the meantime, what on earth would they do for shade?

"Lord, help us," Louise muttered.

It was evening. Back home Jeremiah and Regina and Matthew and the children would be sitting in rockers on the wide veranda of their wonderful, cool, stone farm home, enjoying the added shade of the huge oak tree that sprawled its branches across the front of the house like a mighty servant ordered to fan its master. Already she missed that mighty oak, and all the other grand hardwoods back home.

10

June 12, 1810

The streets of Vincennes were dirt, but well laid out, with several frame and log homes lining them . . . the kind of homes Sadie could only hope to have sometime soon, homes with front porches and hardwood floors and lawns and flowers.

As they guided the oxen and wagons through the town, Sadie began to feel better about settling out here. Maybe they wouldn't be all that far from Vincennes, where there were dry-good stores, tailor shops, a blacksmith, a clothing store, two churches, one of them obviously a Catholic church, with a statue of the Mother Mary standing in front of it. Sadie knew little about the Catholic faith, but out here in the middle of nowhere, she thought how refreshing it would be to be able to attend *any* kind of real church.

They passed several more businesses, including an attorney's office and the land office. Mixed among everything were a few saloons, and on a slightly higher level at the end of town was a home that stood out among all others, a much grander home than Sadie had ever seen, even nicer than the large brick farm home where Jonah's brothers lived. According to a man from Vincennes, whom they'd met outside of town, the home belonged to none other than Governor William Henry Harrison.

Sadie felt a little nervous. Jonah actually intended to go directly to Governor Harrison's home, as they'd learned the man was in town today. Jonah wanted to talk to him about the Indian situation. Sadie wondered if the man would even agree to see them, as he must be quite important. It was Harrison himself who'd devised and executed the sale of Indian land that had opened up so much more of Indiana to settlers. The man supposedly knew the fearsome Shawnee leader, Tecumseh, personally, and had dealt with the Shawnee tribe many times.

"Now there's one fine home," Marvin commented from behind Sadie's wagon.

"We'll all have one just like it someday, Pa," the ever-confident Jack shouted.

"I'm counting the days," Louise answered with obvious sarcasm. "Right now I'd settle for *anything* that doesn't move and bounce."

They all chuckled as they approached the Harrison mansion.

Harrison owns three hundred acres with the house, the gentleman they'd met on their way in had told them. *Goes right down to the Wabash River. Quite a house, too. He's got his own well in the basement, and if there's Indian trouble, that man will let half the town into his house for protection. He's always looking out for us.*

Indian trouble. Their acquaintance mentioned they'd

experienced problems lately, *but Harrison is taking care of it.*

Sadie spotted a man sitting on the porch of the mansion as they drew closer. From where she stood when they halted their wagons, he appeared simply average in size, shorter and smaller than Jonah, but then Jonah was taller and more muscular than most men she'd ever seen.

Jonah walked to the back of his wagon and hoisted Paul down to let him run and play. He came back for Sadie, putting an arm to her waist as Louise, Marvin, and Jack joined them, all walking around the wagons to hail the man on the porch, who rose and came down the steps to greet them. His nose was prominent and thin, his eyebrows dark and bushy. He wore simple farmer's clothes, making Sadie wonder if he might just be a servant or farmhand.

"Hello!" he greeted. "Might I be of some help?"

Jonah walked closer and put out his hand. "Jonah Wilde. We're looking for William Harrison."

The man shook Jonah's hand. "Well, you're shaking hands with him, sir."

Jonah grinned. "It's good to meet you, Governor Harrison." He turned to Sadie. "This is my wife, Sadie, and the little boy running around chasing the chickens over there is our son, Paul." He continued introductions as Marvin and Louise approached, finishing with Jack.

A friendly Governor Harrison folded his arms in front of him. He wore his dark brown hair combed to one side, part of it over his forehead, and because of his build and thin lips, Sadie was surprised that he did not fit the description of the powerful man he'd become in this new territory.

"It's obvious you have all come to Indiana to settle, perhaps under our new treaty with the Shawnee?"

Jonah nodded. "That's right."

Just from his deep voice and his large brown eyes that had a way of commanding attention, Sadie began to see a hint of an engaging man who could indeed be a leader in spite of his less-than-impressionable build and looks.

"We are wondering about the best place to settle, and if there are problems with the Shawnee that we should know about," Marvin spoke up.

Harrison's smile faded to a more austere pose. He put a hand to his chin. "I'll be honest. There have been problems of late, but as governor of Indiana Territory, I can assure you I have everything under control."

"Everything?" Jonah shifted with indecision. "Does that include Tecumseh?"

Harrison sobered even more. "Tecumseh and I go back a long way, Mr. Wilde." He motioned toward his house. "Would all of you like some lemonade? I can have my wife get some for you. You've been traveling with no amenities for a long time. Surely you intend to stay here in Vincennes to rest up before you head out onto the prairie?"

Sadie felt the man was deliberately evading the question about Tecumseh.

"That would be wonderful!" Louise answered.

"We don't want to put you out," Sadie spoke up, feeling suddenly self-conscious about her unwashed hair wrapped into a bun and her plain gray dress. Her fingernails were dirty in places she couldn't get clean no matter how hard she tried, and she wore absolutely no color on her face and no jewelry but for her plain wedding band. It was impossible to stay properly groomed when walking beside oxen and wagon wheels that raised dust for hundreds of miles in the heat. She'd found it incredible that in spite of the thick growth of prairie grass and flowers they'd traveled through, somehow dust still seemed to make its way into the air.

"Nonsense," Harrison answered. "I am always glad to welcome newcomers to my state! The more the better! It will mean Tecumseh and his followers will be less excited about trying to stop the settlement; and it also means Indiana will grow into a state in no time at all! I always go out of my way, if necessary, for anyone who chooses Indiana as their place to settle!" He headed for his porch, indicating that they should follow. "We have some of the best farmland in the nation! My advice would be to settle perhaps fifty miles or so north of here, along the Wabash." He kept talking as he mounted the steps. "Good water, good farmland, what more could a man ask for? There are even a few trees along the river, but you'll want to settle away from them so you don't have to deal with their roots. Believe me, plowing up prairie land is enough of a problem. Some of the roots of prairie grass run six feet or more into the ground!"

His animation about the land he loved was infectious. Sadie breathed a little easier. His excitement made it seem as though the Indian problem was not something a man needed to be worried about. They all followed him onto the shaded veranda, the women sitting down in two wooden rockers while Harrison went inside to ask his wife to make lemonade. Sadie heard him announce they had visitors, and moments later children ranging from a girl who looked in her teens to one who appeared about four years old came bounding out to greet them, all of the children neatly dressed.

"The lemonade will be here shortly," Harrison told them. "These are six of my seven children. The seventh, a daughter named Mary, is inside napping. She is just a year old. My wife is expecting our eighth. Three girls and four sons currently," he said proudly as some of the younger ones ran out to play with Paul.

Now Sadie felt even better! This man had settled and was raising seven children here in spite of Indian troubles. Surely things weren't all that bad, or he wouldn't have his family here. There came more introductions, and his oldest daughter, called Betsy, a teenager, went back inside to help her mother with the lemonade. Jonah and Marvin leaned against porch posts, and Jonah asked permission to light his pipe. Jack sat down on the steps.

"Seven children in fifteen years of marriage!" Harrison boasted. "A man couldn't ask for more than that."

"I agree," Jonah answered, puffing on his pipe long enough to get the tobacco burning. He gave Sadie a wink. Sadie looked away, blushing.

"My wife, Anna, is also from Ohio, you know. Me, I'm from Virginia. Spent most of my life in the army, so I know about fighting Indians. I was at Fallen Timbers, you know. I was a lieutenant then. I was even present at the Treaty of Greenville that ended that war, so yes, I'm accustomed to dealing with the Shawnee, as well as the Ottawa, the Chippewa, and the Potawatomi tribes." He sobered then. "Actually I suspect it's the British we may be fighting again soon, what with them attacking any of our ships that try to deliver goods to or accept goods from France. It's their war, not ours, but they are certainly doing a good job of getting us involved."

The more the man spoke, the more confident Sadie felt. He certainly seemed to know what he was talking about, and he didn't seem to be the type of man who would mislead them.

"I helped with the Treaty of Fort Wayne just last year. And look how Vincennes has grown! We're the capital of the territory, and now we're building a library."

The rest of them had hardly had a chance to get a word in, and as the governor finished, Betsy came back out with a tray full of glasses of lemonade. She was followed by an older woman, very distinguished.

Sadie had no doubt a man like Harrison would marry only a woman of good breeding and education. If such a woman had come here to settle and raise her children, she could certainly do the same.

Jonah set his pipe on the porch railing and took his lemonade as Harrison reintroduced everyone to his wife, who graciously passed around more of the lemonade. Sadie took a sip of the cool drink with great pleasure.

"The water for this lemonade came from our own well in the basement. The water is always cold, very refreshing in this hot weather," Harrison went on, "don't you think?"

Jonah nodded. "Yes. Now, about the Indians . . ."

Harrison waved him off. "Tecumseh makes a lot of noise, but he's a man of peace, Mr. Wilde. He seems to have a great deal of influence over his people, as well as those of several other tribes. The last thing he wants is war. This latest treaty freed up millions of acres, both here and in Illinois. And as I said, the quicker they are settled, the less likely Tecumseh will try to do anything about it. It would be fruitless, since the government has bought up millions more acres through the Louisiana Purchase. Besides, we have a strong, well-trained militia here in Indiana. And the Shawnee don't usually bother with one little farm where a couple of people live. If they do anything, it will be something much bigger. There have been rumors of attacking Vincennes, but those came from Tecumseh's brother, Tenskwatawa. Some call him the

Prophet. At any rate, Tecumseh told me himself that he's put his brother in his place and ordered him to pull back and stop such plans. He doesn't like this latest treaty and professes it to be illegal, but I assure you it *is* legal, and we plan to uphold it in every way, including going after the Shawnee if they make trouble."

"So, you think we'll be safe settling away from Vincennes?" Marvin asked.

Harrison nodded. "Indiana welcomes you and your family with open arms, Mr. Stockton, and you, Mr. Wilde. I am sure that you will find anything you might need right here in Vincennes during your stay, and I will gladly accompany you to the land office to see about picking out a parcel of land for yourselves, if you like. I know the best places to settle."

Jonah brightened as he thirstily consumed the last half of his glass of lemonade. "Governor Harrison, your generosity is more than we bargained for."

"I am always glad to help out newcomers," the man answered.

The way Harrison rambled on about "his" Indians, Sadie supposed he must be quite the public speaker, certainly a great champion of Indiana, even though it wasn't even his homeland. His enthusiasm won all their confidence. By the time they left with the man to visit the land office, Sadie was feeling quite happy and excited about Jonah's decision to come here. Perhaps before they left she could buy some material for curtains.

11

June 13, 1810

Sadie watched Jonah, Jack, and Marvin practice cutting more sod, following the directions of Otto Krause, a stout old German man whose father had been one of the original fur traders at Vincennes when it was just a trading post.

"First you dig an outline for za house," Otto explained. "All around, maybe six, eight inches deep, you see?" He drove a spade into the root-tough soil near his log home outside of town. "Ve lived on za prairie ourself for a while. My mama get sick and ve come back to Vincennes."

The man shoveled while all watched, Sadie still dreading living in a home made of dirt.

"Vonce you dig outline down, it leaf floor up higher zan ze walls around it, you see? When you lay za sod bricks down in za outline to start, it help keep out snakes, mice, and such, you see? Walls deeper than floor, and two, three bricks thick. Keep out unwanted guests." Otto laughed, and the other men chuckled. Sadie only smiled for the sake of being friendly. Louise remained sober.

"Vonce you get outline dug, you cut down za grass unt za veeds over what vill be za floor of za house. You can even put boards down, you know? Zen you bilt za valls. Dig za sod in sizes of brick, maybe six inch deep, von foot long, unt von foot vide. Stack zem two, three bricks across for goot, strong valls—keep out za varmints and za wind and za cold and snow, and even za Indians. And is cool in summer!"

The man grinned and nodded, actually excited about his sod-building lesson. "Stagger za bricks, just like real vons, you know? I tell you, sod makes vonderful house! You vill see, ladies. You can even go to a creek or river unt collect vood unt split it to make door frames, vindow frames. Some sod houses even haf real vindows unt doors! At first you can cover vin-dows wit potato sacks unt doors vit blankets."

"What about the roof?" Jonah asked, watching Otto carve out one brick. It looked to Sadie like hard, hard work. Surely it would take many days of intense labor to build a decent-sized soddy, as people called them.

Otto grunted as he chopped out his first brick. He picked it up and held it out to Jonah. "Der, you see? Goot, solid brick. It last long, long time. You vill see!"

Jonah took the piece of sod, his eyebrows raising in surprise at its weight. He handed it to Marvin. "I can see why this makes a strong house," he commented.

Marvin cradled the brick. "I guess so!" He handed it to Jack.

"Za roof—you go to find vood. You cut two strong young trees unt use one at each end of soddy vit a fork cut into za ends. Put zem in za ground at each end of soddy and cut another strong young tree to lay across za center of soddy, lengthwise, and put each end into

71

za forked posts. Zen you lay many young trees and branches all along za roofline, side by side, close together, you see?" He was drawing in the dirt and motioning with his arms. "Zen you lay more sod on top of za branches, zen more branches, zen more sod. Goot, strong roof, you see? If you do it right, rain not even come through. Just make hole for heating stove." He nodded and smiled. "Sometimes in spring, roof beautiful! Grass grows on it, sometimes even flowers!" He turned to Sadie and Louise. "You should buy some sheets or lots of cloth. You drape it inside, under za roof—keeps bugs and dirt from falling into za soup!"

He laughed hardily, slapping his knee. Sadie struggled to smile.

"It be fine. You vill see. You got strong, smart husband. He vill bilt you fine sod home." He turned again to Jonah. "If you hilt into a hill, you need not vorry about a roof. Za land is your roof, you see? And you be even safer from za Indians, you know? They can't get in but von vay!" He shook his head then. "But it is not easy to find hill sometimes."

Jonah nodded. "I've already figured that one out." He put out his hand. "Thank you, Otto. We'll pick up some stove pipe and some cloth to sheet the ceiling."

"Vare you going to settle?"

"We've filed with the claims office for land northeast of here. There is supposedly a river nearby, so at least we'll have water."

"Goot choice! Und if you go northeast, you be out

of pathway of Indians if za Shawnee decide to come to attack Vincennes. Zey are directly north, so zey would not come through your place to get here."

Jonah nodded. "That's what I'm hoping, although I hope they don't come at all. Governor Harrison seems to think there is little to worry about."

Otto rubbed his chin. "Vell, I hope he is right. Dat Tecumseh, he's got lot of influence, you know? He is unpredictable. I haf fought Indians in my lifetime, but thank God I haf no terrible tales to tell."

"Well, I don't either, but Indians once destroyed my father's farm and did some pretty terrible things to him and my mother. She was even a captive for a while, as was my grandma Jess. I never knew her, but I wish I had. Both were damn strong women."

"Ya, zat is vat it takes out here."

Strong women. Jonah thinks I am strong like that, Sadie thought. Was she? She could only hope to hold a candle to Jess Wilde and Annie Wilde. She didn't even carry their blood. Jonah did. He was the strong one.

12

June 20, 1810

Still on a quest to bring even more tribes under his control before going against the whites, Tecumseh traveled east with his personal aide, the half-breed

73

Sauganash, to visit one Shawnee chief who vehemently refused to join in the amalgamation.

Windigo and Wapmimi accompanied him, Wapmimi not totally happy at being asked. He'd planned on conducting raids this summer in search of a wife for Windigo.

"Do you think that this time Tecumseh can convince old Catahecassa to join him?" Wapmimi asked his friend.

Windigo's horse shuddered and snorted, and Windigo had to give the animal's rope bridle a yank to keep the roan gelding from straying. He barked a command that kept the horse on a straight path. "Who can say?" he answered. "Old Catahecassa is very set in his ways, and old men like things to be peaceful. He thinks if he is friendly with the Long Knives, he can finish out his years in comfort, living off the gifts they give him and his people. I think he is too old to understand that he is giving away the future of his grandchildren to poverty and death."

"Hmmmmm. I agree," Wapmimi answered.

Windigo enjoyed the hot weather they'd had lately. He and Wapmimi wore only leggings and no shirts, both of them proudly decorated with beaded bracelets, and hoops in their pierced ears. As always, Windigo's hair hung in numerous tiny braids, thanks to his mother. Pieces of tin and beads in his hair tinkled with the rhythm of his horse's gait.

Wapmimi wore a colorful turban, and each side of his face was painted with parallel lines in several colors, indicating he belonged to the Thunder Clan. Windigo had painted stick figures of humans in white on his horse's rump, as he belonged to the Human Clan.

"I should be back home seeking your white woman," Wapmimi complained.

Windigo grinned. "Perhaps Wiske means for you to wait one more winter."

Wapmimi scowled but said no more as they entered Catahecassa's village. Windigo enjoyed the way those present looked at Tecumseh with awe, stepping back and nodding to him. Dogs barked, and children ran alongside them. Some of the younger warriors there shouted to Tecumseh that they were ready to follow him, but others gathered in small bunches, talking low among themselves as they followed Tecumseh to where their old chief stood waiting, having been told who was entering their village.

Windigo noticed several young women watching him and Wapmimi, obviously impressed that they rode with the increasingly powerful and popular Tecumseh. There were six altogether in their entourage, the other two being two older trusted Shawnee men who supported Tecumseh, Chaubenee, and a Wyandot leader Stiahta.

Old Catahecassa raised his bony hand in greeting, and Windigo noticed the aged warrior wore a blanket wrapped around him even though it was hot. He pondered the fact that it seemed old people were, for some reason, never warm enough.

They all dismounted, and most of the people in Catahecassa's village gathered around. Windigo stood proudly erect, enjoying the attention and the importance he felt at being one of those accompanying Tecumseh.

Tecumseh approached old Catahecassa, whose name meant Black Hoof. The old man faced him squarely, and Windigo had no doubt he knew the reason for Tecumseh's visit. Catahecassa still believed the wise thing was to befriend Governor Harrison and the Long Knives rather than take the chance at the destruction Harrison's militia could cause if they made trouble. Tecumseh was not at all worried about anything Harrison might do, and neither was Windigo.

Black Hoof took a piece of paper from a man standing next to him, and he handed it out to Tecumseh. "I know why you come here," he told Tecumseh. He shook the paper open and indicated that Tecumseh should read it. Tecumseh promptly took the letter and scanned it, then held it up, turning so that all could see it. Windigo and the others in their party backed away so that Tecumseh could have some space and speak his words to everyone there.

"This letter is from the white traitor, Governor Harrison!" he shouted in his rich, captivating voice. "Harrison is a devil, and by being friendly and accepting toward him, Catahecassa has *dealt* with the devil!"

With one hand Tecumseh crumpled the letter and dramatically tossed it into a nearby campfire, where it instantly curled and disintegrated. An undercurrent of murmurs moved through the surrounding crowd.

"If Harrison were here," Tecumseh continued, "I would treat him the same way!" His spellbinding gaze moved across the gathering, sometimes lingering on one man or another. "You are *Shawnee!* You are my brothers! Do not trust the whites! They give you little now, and one day they will give you *nothing!* Every word from their mouths is a lie, and anyone who deals with them and gives Shawnee land to them is lower than *a skunk!* They should be greatly ashamed! If I had been present when Harrison came to take our land, it never would have happened; and any man who signed away that land with the print of his thumb should have his thumb cut *off!*"

The crowd stood silent as Tecumseh abruptly mounted his horse and rode away. Windigo and Wapmimi and the others followed suit, leaving behind a stunned audience. Windigo felt satisfied that in those few short words, using only his own particularly powerful presence, Tecumseh had likely won over Catahecassa's people, and probably Catahecassa himself.

"Where do we go now, Tecumseh?" Sauganash asked.

"We go to see Blue Jacket. I am told he is at last ready to join us. Our numbers grow, Sauganash."

"As well they should." Sauganash grinned. "You have scored some great victories, Tecumseh, using only the words you speak. There are few left who will not listen."

"There will always be those who refuse to listen. It

is the nature of man. But most are easily led if a man is wise in his words. I pray every day for such wisdom."

"Then the Master of Life is being good to you and answering your prayers."

Tecumseh nodded. He reined his horse to a halt for a moment and looked at Sauganash. "Hear my words. The day is coming when there will be a great trembling of the earth. I feel it in my bones, and I see it in my dreams. It will be such a great trembling that those who do not yet believe will change their minds. They will know the power of Tecumseh, and they will follow."

He started riding again, and Windigo looked at Wapmimi. "A trembling of the earth?" he said softly.

Wapmimi shrugged. "So he says."

"What would make the whole earth tremble?"

Wapmimi thought a moment. "Perhaps the anger of Wiske."

Windigo nodded. "Perhaps." He started forward again, shivering slightly at Tecumseh's prediction. How could he know such a thing, unless he had a personal connection with the powers of Wiske? Surely Tecumseh was not just a great speaker and leader, but also a holy man.

13

July 1, 1810

A tree. Sadie thought how she would give anything for a tree, just one tree to sit under for a little while. Why did it seem that the shade of a tree was so much cooler than the shade from anything else? Sitting under the lean-to Jonah had built with poles and blankets just was not the same. Sweat poured off little Paul as he slept restlessly there, and she felt no relief from the stifling air even though she was out of the sun.

Several yards away poor Louise lay under one of the wagons for shade, suffering from a sick headache. All morning Sadie had been helping the men stack sod bricks, feeling she should make up for Louise being unable to do her part. Thank God little Paul was satisfied playing with his blocks most of the morning and had not been difficult to watch.

By this midafternoon the heat had become so unbearable that even the men stopped their work. Everyone lay resting in the shade, and Sadie used the time to make an entry in a diary she'd started when they first left Willow Creek back in Ohio . . . Willow Creek, named for the many huge, old willow trees that abounded in the area. What she would give to be lying under one of them right now!

We've settled approximately forty miles northeast of

Vincennes, she wrote, *along the White River. The land office said this area is around thirty miles southeast of Fort Harrison, and close to two hundred miles southeast of Tippecanoe, which the renowned Indian leader Tecumseh calls home. Governor Harrison himself told us that here we should have little worry about Indians as they tend to stay to the north and across nearly to Detroit, and otherwise deal in the area of Fort Harrison and south into Vincennes. The governor seems to think he can handle the man called Tecumseh and that Indiana has the situation under control. We can only pray he is right.*

The heat today is worse than any I ever knew in the Ohio Valley, made even more unbearable by a humidity that hangs so thick in the air that one can literally see steam rising off the rivers and out of the ground.

She paused, thinking how it surely did seem that way, with a vague haze in the air. Sometimes the droning sound of millions of singing insects rang so loudly she wanted to cover her ears. She would welcome the sound of a singing bird instead, but that was a very rare sound out here. Where there were no trees, there were few birds. In this area, there were not even any trees along the rivers and creeks.

She opened the bodice of her dress a few buttons down from the top. In this kind of heat one tended to cast off any sense of modesty. Jonah, Jake, and Marvin wore their shirts completely open, and no one found it embarrassing. It simply did not matter. Thank

God the river was not so far away that they could not go there and fall into it to cool off and fill their water barrels, but there was so much work to be done that they dared not allow themselves the luxury too often. They could not risk winter coming on and they not being ready for it. They'd been told that winter could be as cold and intimidating as summer was hot and daunting. In summer there was nothing to cool them, and in winter, with no shrubs and trees to help hold in the warmth or block the wind, the cold could be more harsh than back in Ohio.

This land promises incredibly rich soil. When we dig up the sod, which is very difficult because of the thick root system, we see dark, moist earth that is surely thriving with nutrients. The three draft horses for which Jonah traded our oxen are extremely strong, but even they have trouble pulling a plow through the relentless roots. We've chopped away enough grass to lay out our humble sod home, and we have planted the trees Jonah brought from Ohio. We can only pray they will survive after our long journey, and with their roots having to compete with the thick undergrowth for water and nutrients.

"What are you writing there?" Jonah stretched out beside Sadie.

"Just where we've settled and that we've planted the trees. Someday we'll be living in a fine home, perhaps in the middle of our town, and I want to keep track of how it all began." Sadie faced him with a smile that she hoped would keep his confidence up. "When we

81

end up one of the richest couples in Indiana, I never want to forget our humble beginnings."

Jonah smiled with a bit of sarcasm. "Humble isn't the word for it." He moved his hands behind his head to cradle it as he lay in the grass they'd pressed down to make a soft resting place. "I can't begin to tell you how determined I am to make sure you have a proper home as soon as possible, Sadie. We might spend this one winter in a soddy, but I'm going to do my best to make sure the next winter is spent in a frame home."

"It doesn't matter, Jonah." She remained sitting, her back against two flour sacks. She reached over and touched his arm. "The important thing is to get the farm going, and Lord knows that will be enough work in itself. It's already too late to plant anything this year. Just getting the ground ready will take all the energy and time we have. If we have to spend next year doing more plowing and doing all the planting and harvesting and keeping the land cleared, then that's what we'll have to do. In the meantime, any kind of home will suffice, as long as we can be together and warm."

He sighed. "Well, right now warmth is certainly not a problem. The sooner we get the soddy finished the better. I keep hearing how cool they can be in summer, so we'll at least get you and Paul out of the sun." He closed his eyes. "And we sure don't have to worry about the animals having something to graze on, do we?"

Sadie leaned her head back and closed her eyes, too. "No, thank goodness."

They both lay there quietly for several minutes, and Sadie finally realized that Jonah had fallen asleep. Good. He definitely needed the rest. She heard a cry from Louise, and her heart ached for the woman, who for years had occasionally suffered headaches so painful that her eyes would swell and she would vomit. This heat could only be making her condition worse, and she prayed that God would take away Louise's pain soon.

She set her diary aside and rose, too hot to rest. She walked closer to where Louise lay, but Marvin and Jack were both watching over her. She made her way through thick grasses and an array of wildflowers she could not name, then stared out across the open spaces that lay unchanging for as far as the eye could see.

She thought how a person could no more count the various kinds of flowers than one could count the stars. She tried to figure how a person could fall in love with land like this. Perhaps if she'd been born and raised here, she wouldn't think so badly of it. The Indians certainly felt it worth fighting for.

"Mommy!"

Sadie turned at her son's shout. He'd awakened and was running toward her, holding something. "Preetee! Preetee!" he told her. As he came closer, she could see he was holding a large butterfly. Sadie smiled.

"Yes, it is pretty!" she told him, wanting to share his excitement at having caught the orange monarch. She could tell Paul was proud he'd been able to catch it. Her son had no conception of hardship and loneliness out here. It was simply an adventure for him, and she was determined it would be nothing more than that, determined he would not suffer in any way, no matter how difficult it might become. "Let him loose, Paul," she told him.

The boy let go of the butterfly, and it gracefully fluttered off, landing on a yellow flower not far away. Paul stretched his neck, trying to see. "Where'd he go, Mommy?"

Sadie picked him up and pointed. "Over there, see? He's sitting on a flower."

Paul nodded, still smiling the dimpled, bright smile that made him so precious. "Bowers!" he said, giving a sweep of his hand. Then he clapped.

"Yes, flowers! Millions and millions of flowers!" Perhaps there was something about this land she could love after all. Perhaps all she needed to do was see it through a child's eyes.

14

July 14, 1810

"What is *he* doing here?" The scar on Wapmimi's face always looked uglier when he scowled. Windigo and Wapmimi watched curiously as other warriors surrounded a white man who disembarked from a flatboat he'd landed on the nearby riverbank. He announced himself as Joseph Barron, sent here by

Governor Harrison to speak to Tecumseh. With obvious nervous fear in his eyes, Barron walked with the guarded warriors who led him to a lodge belonging to Tecumseh's brother, Tenskwatawa. The Prophet sat in a large chair outside his lodge, his wife, Gimewane, sitting on the ground to his right.

Windigo and Wapmimi both gathered close to hear what would be said. Barron was the third visitor in roughly two weeks to come here from Vincennes, always with messages from Governor Harrison. Since the Shawnee had refused a shipment of salt from Vincennes in June, Governor Harrison seemed adamant that they should take the supplies, and was obviously growing more irritated that they'd turned down the annuities. The reason was simple to the Shawnee . . . to accept any kind of annuities was to admit they agreed with the sale of their land under the Fort Wayne Treaty. Tecumseh was determined to point out, in every way, that he would not abide by any treaty he'd not sign himself.

Windigo enjoyed watching Joseph Barron sweat profusely, more than necessary for the hot weather. It was obvious the sweat stemmed from pure terror. Since refusing the salt, two other emissaries had been sent to Tippecanoe by Harrison, looking for explanations and trying to keep the peace. Both times, those messengers were lucky to escape with their lives and had been told that if one more person came here spying for Harrison and the Americans, he would die. The Prophet scowled darkly at Barron, who the warriors left standing alone before the one-eyed man. Tenskwatawa rose to speak. "You are yet the third spy Harrison has sent to us!" he declared in English. "Look down, and see your own grave!" he added angrily.

Barron literally shook in his shoes. "It's Tecumseh I must speak with," he told the Prophet. "Not his brother."

Tenskwatawa sucked in his breath at the insult, rage glowing in his one good eye. Just then Tecumseh himself emerged from Tenskwatawa's lodge, ordering his brother to say no more and facing Barron sternly.

"At the moment you need not fear for your life," he warned Barron, also in English, "but be careful with your insults! Tell me quickly why yet another American dares come here, before my impatience tells me to send just your head back to Harrison!"

Barron swallowed before speaking, apparently trying to find his voice. "I . . . did not mean an insult, but I was instructed to speak only with you, Tecumseh. I brought you a letter . . . written by Governor Harrison," he answered. "He asks that I read it to you."

Tecumseh rolled his eyes in exasperation. "There is nothing more that traitor can say to change our minds about his deceit! Hand me the letter!"

Barron obeyed, reaching inside his waistcoat and handing out an envelope. Tecumseh slit it open with a large hunting knife that made Barron back away slightly. He scanned the letter, and after reading it, he folded it and put it back in the envelope, giving Barron an odd smile.

"So, the most important white man in the west wishes to council with Tecumseh." He scanned the others with pride in his eyes. "The white traitor Harrison says we should not think to make war against the Long Knives. He says the bluecoats far outnumber us, like the leaves that fall from the trees. He says we cannot rely on the redcoats and that they cannot even take care of themselves."

Tecumseh laughed, and the hundreds of other Indians who'd gradually gathered while he read the letter laughed with him.

"Harrison says it is folly for us to gather here," Tecumseh continued in his rich voice, and using the commanding way he had of capturing every ear, "and that his government has never violated any treaties made with us."

That remark brought outcries and raised fists.

"They have violated *every* treaty!" Windigo shouted.

"Harrison tries to make fools of us!" Wapmimi added.

Tecumseh raised his hands to quiet the crowd. "The white father at Vincennes says that if we prove that the cowards who dared sign away the land in this last treaty had no right to do so, the land will be restored to us!"

"Yes! Yes!" everyone shouted, some raising rifles, some tomahawks.

"He even says he will take me to see the great father they call president, who lives in the east . . ." He paused, sobering. "Land that *also* used to belong to *us!*"

Wapmimi and Windigo joined in shouts and war whoops of support for the remark, and Windigo took great pleasure in seeing sweat begin to trickle down Barron's face. Their shouts frightened the man, as well they should!

Tecumseh walked closer to Barron, his dark eyes commanding the man's frightened attention. "You tell the white leader Harrison this. Tell him that the Shawnee leader, Tecumseh, will go to Vincennes. Tell him Tecumseh will indeed prove to him that this last treaty is illegal, that all the three million acres it involves still belong to the *Shawnee!* Tell him Tecumseh has many warriors behind him who also believe this, but who all want continued peace with the Seventeen Fires! That peace can only take place when all the land stolen from us is returned! The old chiefs who signed that treaty are *cowards!* But Tecumseh and every man here are brave men who are willing to risk their lives for that land, as they will *do* if necessary. But peace is as important to us as it is to Governor Harrison. If he *wants* that peace, he will give back our land!" He gave a sweep of his arm. "Now, go!"

Barron gladly obliged, turning and running back toward the river where the flatboat that had brought him to Tippecanoe waited. Shouting, hooting warriors accompanied him the whole way, making sure he wasted no time leaving. Windigo and Wapmimi stayed near Tecumseh, who stood and watched Barron until he was out of sight. He then turned his attention to those who still stood around him.

"I will take warriors with me to Vincennes, my *best* warriors! And I wish that they wear their most intimidating war paint. They must look as splendid as possible! In two days I will call a council and I will point out those who will go with me to see the white man who apparently thinks my word is so important! We will leave in one moon."

The leader walked away then, ducking into his *wigawa.* Windigo turned to Wapmimi. "I want to go to Vincennes!" he told his friend. "What say you?"

"You know I, too, want to go, Windigo, but there is still enough of summer left for me to go and find your white woman."

"Tecumseh knows we are greatly honored as warriors among the Potawatomi, and he will want men from every tribe represented at Vincennes," Windigo reminded him. "He will want to take both of us. Besides, you should wait, Wapmimi. This is not a good time to be attacking the Americans. Harrison will use such raiding against us, and it will spoil Tecumseh's efforts to get back our land."

Wapmimi sighed in resignation. "Then I will wait, but by next spring I *must* search for the white woman! Wiske demands I do so."

Windigo nodded. "I understand." He smiled. "I have

never been to Vincennes. I would like to see this place where the powerful white man lives . . . the man who has cheated all of us from what is rightfully ours!" He signaled Wapmimi to follow him. "Come with me!"

"Where are we going?"

"We will go hunting and bring some fine, fresh venison to Tecumseh and tell him of our desire to be among those chosen to go to Vincennes."

"Maybe we will steal some horses along the way," Wapmimi told him. "Did you see the fine horses Etonah brought back yesterday? He said he'd been all the way south almost in sight of Vincennes and stole the horses by daylight! The whites are getting lazy and unconcerned. If we end up fighting them, they will find us a much fiercer foe than they think!"

15

August 1, 1810

Sadie hung a dress, two shirts, a pair of pants, some long underwear, a few of Paul's clothes, and the white cloths she used for diapers on a line of rope stretched from the top of the wagon across to a corner of the family's sod house. She'd spent the whole morning hauling water, scrubbing and wringing out clothes, and hanging them. Blankets were draped over the wagon top, and it seemed that everything took forever to dry because of the high humidity.

She'd grown accustomed to the constant drone of insects, most of which were hidden somewhere deep within the endless prairie grasses. She'd taught herself to shut out the sound, because it would drive her crazy if she let it. She longed to hear the rustle of leaves from a cool breeze down from the hills in Ohio. She ached to hear bird songs. She dreamed of socials and picnics and church and visiting at the quilting club back in Willow Creek. She thought how pleasant it would be to take a buggy to town and shop . . . but such luxuries would be a long time coming.

Paul played inside, where it was indeed cooler, though far from the coolness of sitting on a veranda under shade trees. The sod house was more like living in a damp cellar. Poor Paul was riddled with red bumps from mosquito bites that sometimes kept him awake at night, and she'd begun to leave him dirty, as it seemed the bugs bit even worse when one was scrubbed clean.

She looked at her own hands. Usually filthy from helping dig sod, today they were clean from doing laundry, although rubbed raw in some places from scrubbing. Next would come the socks and aprons, the hardest part of the laundry. She'd already decided none of their socks would ever be truly clean, but she did her best, wearing a wide-brimmed hat against the relentless sun.

It had rained only twice since they landed here, and that was at night; so there had been no true relief from the sun. She would welcome a cloudy day.

She finished hanging another pair of Jonah's cotton pants, then stepped away from the house to see Jonah and Jack out in a field they had managed to chop into rows for planting. It was back-breaking work, and already Jonah and Marvin were working on plans to design their own plow, hoping to find a blacksmith back in Vincennes next spring who might be willing to try to build such an instrument. None of the plows they had brought with them could stand up to the thick roots of the prairie land.

She wiped at sweat on her brow with her apron. Sweat was constantly running into her eyes until they stung, and often she would splash some of the wash water onto her face. Her heart ached for Jonah and Jack working in the relentless heat. She walked back to a clean barrel of water and dipped a small bucket into it, filling it with enough water to take out to the field and let the two men drink and splash some on their faces.

As she approached, she saw Marvin coming toward her from the direction where he and Louise had built their own sod house. It was visible, but several hundred yards distant.

Poor Louise was having another sick headache, something that seemed to happen more often out here than it ever had at home, so Marvin told them. He'd left Jack and Jonah to go tend to her and was now returning. He cut across the field so that he and Sadie reached Jonah and Jack at about the same time.

Jonah gladly grabbed the bucket of water and

swilled down several swallows, then handed it to Jack.

"How is Louise?" Sadie asked Marvin.

The man shook his head, looking ready to cry. "I tell you, I don't know what to do for her. She says it's the humidity out here, says it makes them worse. I feel so bad, bringin' her here, you know? I just feel like this is my fault."

Sadie glanced at Jonah, and she knew he was wondering the same thing she was.

"You thinking of going back?" Jonah asked him, voicing Sadie's own question.

Marvin sighed and turned away, rubbing at the back of his neck. "It's the last thing I'm wanting to do," he said resignedly.

"Not me! I'm not going back, Pa," Jack spoke up. "I mean, I feel sorry for Ma and all, but I'm growed now and I want to stay here and have a place of my own."

Marvin faced him. "I know, son. I wasn't sayin' you'd need to go back, and I'm not sayin' that I will either. It's just somethin' to think about, that's all. Your ma swears we shouldn't go back on account of her, but I can't stand the pain she's in when these things hit her. And she's frettin' over the work that needs to be done and how she can't help and all. Thank God she got her own wash done a couple days ago before she took sick again."

"Well, you bring over anything else that needs washing, Marvin," Sadie told him. "I'll do what I can."

He shook his head. "God knows you have enough of

93

your own work to do, what with little Paul and all."

"Well, I can at least bake some extra bread later tonight. The wind should die down and I can make a campfire and bake it in my Dutch oven. I'm sure not about to fire up a cookstove inside when it's this hot."

Marvin smiled sadly. "The heat is somethin', ain't it?"

"It's not like anything we ever had back in the Ohio Valley," Jack answered for Sadie. He put down the spade he'd been using, and Sadie noticed one corner was bent. "Come on, Pa. Let's you and me go tend to Ma." The young man put a hand around his father's shoulders and the two men walked off together. "Everything will work out, Pa," Sadie heard him telling Marvin. She looked at Jonah. "Will it?" she asked.

Jonah's face was deeply tanned from working so much outside. "Sure it will." He put his hands on her shoulders. "This is the hardest part, Sadie. Every year things will get better." He kissed her hair. "And I appreciate your offer to help Louise. I know how hard you're working. Come fall we'll take a trip to Vincennes or Fort Harrison and stock up on things for winter. Then we'll all get a good rest when the snow shuts us in."

At the moment snow sounded wonderful. "You'd better take a break yourself," she told Jonah. "Do you think we could go down to the river? I know it's close to a half hour's trip, but it still stays light late, and Paul does so love the water. I feel so sorry for him always having to play alone."

94

Jonah smiled. "All right. We *all* need a break. Go get Paul and some blankets and towels. I'll go tell Jack we're quitting for the day and I'll hitch a wagon to one of the horses."

Sadie's spirits brightened. She went to prepare the necessary items, packing some bread and pork for sandwiches. She saw her own eagerness reflected in Jonah's eyes when he picked her up with the wagon, and after a bumpy ride to the river, Paul pointed, shouting, "Wawa! Wawa!"

Sadie and Jonah laughed at the boy's excitement and had to warn him to wait for them as they undressed, Sadie to her bloomers and camisole, Jonah to his knee-length underwear. Stripping Paul naked, they headed into an area of the river where a sandbar made it easier for Paul to enjoy the cool refreshment.

"Mommy! Mommy!" Paul laughed and splashed his mother as Sadie held him around the waist and dunked him several times over. The wind suddenly picked up into a stronger breeze that, to all their relief, kept the mosquitoes away and helped cool them even better from the rush of air hitting their wet bodies.

Sadie thought how if not for being able to come to the river like this, she wasn't sure she could continue bearing the heat and loneliness here. When they came here they could forget the heat and the hard work for a little while. Tomorrow they would begin digging more sod to build a shed for the animals, so they would have protection from the wind when winter came. Lord knew there was plenty of grass to cut and store so the horses, and the milk cow and her twin calves, wouldn't starve when the snow came. Jonah hoped to find someone closer to Vincennes who had a bull so he could breed the milk cow when she began drying up, hoping to keep her milk flowing through another birth. He also hoped to eventually build a whole herd.

Jonah dived into deeper water and swam for a while, then came up to Sadie and Paul, grabbing the boy and throwing him into the air and catching him again. Paul screamed and laughed, and while they played Sadie laid back in the water to let it run through her undone hair.

For a good hour they played and laughed and splashed, then finally wrapped Paul in a towel and carried him to the grassy bank, laying him on a blanket just as the sun began to set. Enjoying being totally wet, Jonah and Sadie lay down on either side of their son and let the breeze cool them to shivers.

"I never thought I'd enjoy feeling cold," Sadie told her husband. "There is actually a sudden chill in the air. It's wonderful!"

Jonah chuckled. "I agree. It's still pretty humid, though, and I suppose once we're totally dry we'll realize it's not as cool as we think."

Sadie turned to Paul. "Are you warm enough, sweetie?"

"Yes, Mommy." The boy half muttered the words, already getting sleepy. Sadie thought how well he was beginning to talk at two and a half. "He's growing so fast," she told Jonah, running her fingers through

Paul's curly blond hair. She leaned over to kiss his forehead. "I think he's already falling asleep. I hope the wagon ride back won't wake him up."

"Paul?" Jonah leaned up on one elbow to look down at his son. "Heck, once this kid is asleep, a cannon couldn't wake him up. You know that." He reached over for another blanket and put it over the boy. "At least tonight we don't have to worry about mosquitoes eating him alive. We can leave him clean instead of putting mud on him to keep the bugs off."

Sadie laughed lightly, meeting her husband's gaze in the darkening sunset. "Little boys *love* mud."

Jonah leaned across the boy and kissed her. "That's true. I am glad, though, that we're far enough from the river that we don't have to worry about Paul thinking he can jump in whenever he feels like it."

Sadie kissed Paul's closed eyes. "All that cavorting wore him out, and it probably feels good to him to be able to rest without swatting at mosquitoes." She lay back down, and Jonah then crawled over his son and positioned himself over Sadie.

He nuzzled her neck. "This is the most comfortable we've been since we got here, and with being cool and not worrying about bug bites . . ." He moved down to kiss the whites of her breasts.

"Jonah Wilde, Paul is right beside us!"

"He's asleep. We won't wake him." He moved to kiss her heatedly. "It's been so long, Sadie," he said gruffly as he began unlacing her camisole. "My God, we haven't made love in so long."

97

Sadie could not deny that she missed the feel of this man inside her. When they married he'd awakened the woman in her she never knew existed, bringing out a wicked desire that he still could stir deep inside. "You know I can't say no to you, Jonah Wilde." She closed her eyes as he opened her camisole to smother her breasts with kisses. He moved downward, pulling off her drawers and kissing secret places she once never dreamed she could allow of any man. But this was Jonah, a man she'd loved since just a child, a man she'd devoted her life to and now had given up so much to be with him.

His kisses caressed her belly, her breasts again, then consumed her mouth as he moved inside of her almost wildly, bringing forth her own near-painful satisfaction. She loved bringing him pleasure, and took her own pleasure in return as he surged to her depths, bringing forth a quick climax from having denied this need for so long. She arched up to him in wicked delight, running her hands over his muscled chest and arms, glad to be a part of a man of such strength and conviction and devotion. With Jonah Wilde beside her she feared nothing.

His own climax came sooner than would normally happen. It had simply been too long since they'd enjoyed such pleasure. "I'm sorry," he whispered, relaxing.

"It's all right. I'm surprised you even had the energy, as hard as you've been working. I worry about you out there in the hot sun all day."

He kissed her again. "I love you so much, Sadie." He got up and pulled her up with him. "Let's go wash off in the river."

Sadie laughed lightly as he stripped off the rest of her clothes, then picked her up in his arms and ran naked with her to the water, throwing her in. They swam and splashed and laughed, then came back to the bank to dry off.

"When will we go to Vincennes again?" Sadie asked.

"Not till the shed is built and we've got plenty of ground turned up and the weather cools. I want a good head start on next spring."

They laid down again, both falling asleep for a while. Sadie could think of no more enjoyable time since they attended socials back home.

It was pitch-dark when Jonah awakened her and said they should head back to the house. Reluctantly, they both dressed and loaded everything into the wagon, including little Paul, who still slept soundly. Jonah slapped the reins, urging the draft horse into a slow walk. Their eyes now adjusted to the moonlight, they steered the horse along a trail now worn through the prairie grass from the soddy to the river.

"I feel so sorry for Louise," Sadie told Jonah. "And in case you're wondering, I'll be all right if Marvin and Louise decide to go back. Surely more people will come out here. We'll have neighbors sooner than we think, and if I can go to Vincennes once or twice a year, or to Fort Harrison, I can handle the long weeks without a woman's company."

Jonah put the reins in one hand and used his other to take Sadie's hand, squeezing it. "I know it's hard for you. I can't promise everything will be wonderful by next spring, but every year *will* be better. Maybe next year we can buy some lumber and start a real house for you so you don't have to worry about dirt falling on you in the middle of the night."

Sadie smiled. "Just knowing you want that as much as I do is all I need. If it takes two years, it takes two years. The important thing is coming up with a plow that can get through the prairie roots. I've never seen land like this."

He chuckled. "I wonder what Jeremiah would think of the prairie. He'd never believe this. We'll have to write him a letter and take it to Vincennes this fall . . . find somebody who's headed east to take it to him. Or if Marvin and Louise do go back, I'm sure they'd be glad to see that he gets a letter."

Sadie sighed deeply. "I miss home so much."

"I miss it, too; but we have to start thinking of Indiana as home now."

Sadie thought what a pleasant evening this had been. Yes, she had to think of this as home. The more time that passed, the more she would feel that way. She moved an arm around Jonah's waist, and he put an arm around her shoulders. Sadie thought how there had been not an Indian in sight since they settled here. Maybe Harrison was right that they wouldn't likely cause any trouble.

16

August 15, 1810

Windigo's heart swelled. He took great pride in being chosen to sit in on Tecumseh's council with Governor Harrison. Just three days ago he and Wapmimi arrived at Vincennes by canoe with eighty painted warriors, all of whom now waited roughly seven hundred yards distant in the trees beyond Grouseland Estate, as Harrison's land was called.

Windigo and ten others walked along a curving road past manicured gardens to a place where they saw benches and chairs set up under a roofed area the white men called a portico. Under his blanket, Windigo carried two knives, a tomahawk, and a war club, as did the others who accompanied Tecumseh, none of them trusting the Long Knives. The rest of the warriors in the distance had orders to watch closely for any sign of trouble, all of them ready to attack the Americans and defend their leader if necessary.

When they drew closer, an interpreter explained that those with Harrison were judges of the Territorial Supreme Court, military aides, a platoon of seventeen U.S. Army soldiers, a Lieutenant Jennings, General Gibson, Major McCormick, and Captains William Whitlock and George Floyd. It was obvious by their fancy uniforms that many of those men were quite important in the white man's world.

Besides the soldiers who were present, many Vincennes citizens also stood not far away to watch the proceedings, but before anything could begin, Tecumseh refused to meet under the roofed area where benches and chairs had been placed. He told the interpreter, none other than his own nephew, Spemica Lawba, who'd come to accept the influx of whites to Shawnee land. That, of course, did not set well with Tecumseh, but he did trust his nephew to properly interpret anything he said.

Although he could speak English, Tecumseh chose to deliver his words in his own tongue in order to be better able to express himself, and so that his own people could understand him. His first words were to tell Harrison that he would meet only out in the open, on the grass of his mother, the earth. It took several minutes for Harrison's aides to move all the chairs out of the roofed area and in front of where Tecumseh stood while his followers all sat in a semicircle behind him. Windigo noted that Harrison's chair was quite large and had arms, apparently indicating his importance.

Once everyone was in place, Harrison formally greeted Tecumseh and his followers, inviting Tecumseh to speak first, which the Shawnee leader did with relish and conviction. He did not have to raise his voice to make his point, as just its normal resonance demanded attention, let alone the way Tecumseh had of using his eyes and certain gestures.

There was not a single thing about him that appeared nervous or apprehensive or unsure.

From the movement of the sun Windigo could tell Tecumseh's speech lasted a good two hours, during which he berated Harrison and the Long Knives for constantly broken treaties, for stealing Indian lands or cheating the Indians out of those lands, for the cold-blooded murder of a Shawnee chief called Cornstalk when the man visited Fort Randolph on a mission of peace, for the butchery of other, defenseless Moravian Indians at Gnadenhutten, for the bloody massacre of Chief Moluntha, tomahawked to death after peace-fully surrendering himself to Americans.

"You have killed Shawnees, Delawares, Miamis, and other Indians, *after* making peace with them! You have illegally taken lands from us. You push the Shawnee into making war so that you can accuse us of being the bad ones! The treaty you claim legally gives you three million acres of Shawnee land was signed by only a few old men who had no right to speak for all! The great majority of Shawnee were unaware of this corrupt land sale. You took that land through lies and cheating! Nothing you say now or ever can be trusted!"

Tecumseh's words were harsh but true. He spoke with great conviction, unflinching, berating not only Governor Harrison and other whites in power, but also the few Indians there who'd signed the Treaty of Fort Wayne, one of them Winnemac, a Potawatomi chief. Winnemac averted his eyes when the accusations came, and Windigo felt shame that one of his own leaders had agreed to the treaty.

Tecumseh promised that in the future, any chiefs who proposed to sell Indian land would be properly punished by their own people, and he declared that if Harrison continued to purchase such lands, it could only lead to war, with grave consequences for the whites.

Tecumseh glared boldly at Harrison, his dark eyes flashing with determination at his next words. "I remind you, Brother, that you yourself told me that if I could prove that land was sold by people who had no right to sell it, you would restore the land to the Shawnee!" He then pointed at Winnemac. "Those who signed the treaty did *not* own the land, and they had no right to sell it!"

Now he raised his voice. "Those here with me, and the thousands more who wait at Tippecanoe, do *not* agree with the Treaty of Fort Wayne, and if that land is not restored to us, this will be settled in a way that will bring bad things to the Americans!"

He paused long enough that others thought he might be through. "*Hear me!*" he barked then, so crisply that several of those present actually jumped at the words. His penetrating glare toward Winnemac as he spoke seemed as deliberate as a knife in the heart. "You will see what will be done to those chiefs who sold that land to you! They will be *punished!*"

Tecumseh turned, stretching out his arms to indicate all those here with him, then turned back to Harrison.

"I am the leader of *all* the tribes, and *none* of them agree with the sale of our land! Soon we will have a meeting of all the warriors of all the tribes, and we will decide what to do with those who sold the land. If you, Governor Harrison, do not return this land to us, their blood will be on your hands!"

It was then that Tecumseh shouted a tirade of accusations at Winnemac in the Potawatomi tongue, so swift and vicious that the interpreter could not keep up. Windigo could tell by Winnemac's eyes and countenance that he was very much afraid now. His breathing quickened, and he refused to look at Tecumseh. His fate was obviously sealed, and Windigo was glad he'd not been a part of signing the treaty.

Tecumseh went on to tell Harrison he had not come to accept gifts from the Americans, for to accept them would be a sign that they agreed with the sale of their land. He told him a council would be held at which those involved in the land sale would suffer for what they'd done.

"I speak nothing but the truth, Brother," he continued to Harrison. "But you, Brother, are a liar! How can the Shawnee have any confidence in white men like yourself? I tell you now, we only wish peace, just as you do, but that peace will only come when our land is returned to us, as it rightfully should be."

Tecumseh then stepped back and sat down. It was Harrison's turn, and Windigo listened intently to the interpreter, even though he could understand English. He wanted to be sure that Spemica Lawba properly interpreted Harrison's words for those Shawnee present who did not understand the white man's tongue.

Harrison declared that the land they purchased belonged to the Miamis and had been fairly purchased through prompt payment to those Indians by the government. He declared that Tecumseh could not claim to be the leader of all Indians, that the Indians were not all one people as Tecumseh claimed. The Great Spirit had made them all different, given them different tongues, placed them in different parts of the land.

"The Shawnee, and those Indians at Tippecanoe who came here from distant lands, have no right to speak for the Miami or this particular land sale," Harrison declared. He himself had a commanding presence, even though he was not a large or tall man. "The land does *not* belong to you and will *not* be returned to you!"

Now Tecumseh lost his patience, again calling Harrison a liar and a cheat, this time severely raising his voice, so much so that the veins on his neck stood out.

Windigo could see Harrison struggling to remain resonant and confident, even though Spemica Lawba had not even interpreted Tecumseh's words. Tecumseh's rage was enough to alarm the man, and he said something quietly to one of his officers. When the soldier hurried away, Windigo and four other Indians appointed as Tecumseh's lieutenants sprang to their feet, tomahawks drawn.

To Windigo's surprise, Harrison himself, also a soldier, drew his sword. One of the other soldiers also pulled out his sword, and the Potawatomi chief, Winnemac, drew a pistol and clicked back the hammer. Some of the white citizens picked up sticks and rocks, and a man wearing a black suit ran to the governor's house and took up a rifle propped against the front door.

Tecumseh let out a piercing war whoop, and the rest of the Shawnee and other tribes who'd come along made their appearance from the surrounding woods, weapons in hand. At the sight, most of the citizens ran off in fright.

Windigo's heart beat faster at the thick tension in the air. Harrison said something to Spemica Lawba, calling him by the English name he'd taken—Johnny. Spemica Lawba repeated Tecumseh's screamed accusation, wherein he'd again called Harrison a liar and a cheat, saying that nothing he said, before now, or here at this council, could be trusted, that the Shawnee and all other Indians had been cheated by the Seventeen Fires, as were called the seventeen states that made up the United States.

Harrison's face reddened with repressed anger. He glared at Tecumseh and called him a bad man for causing such a ruckus at a peace conference. He told Tecumseh he would not talk with him any further, but promised he and his people could leave in safety as long as they left immediately.

Tecumseh signaled his warriors to hold back, and after a last look at Harrison, he turned and left. Windigo hurriedly followed the man's swift footsteps until they reached their own camp, where Tecumseh addressed his brother-in-law, Wasegoboah. He told him to go back and get Spemica Lawba. He wished to speak with his nephew.

Wasegoboah left, and Tecumseh turned to Windigo and the others. "Listen to me," he told them. "I should not have lost my temper. My actions could cause the Long Knives to decide to make war on us, but it is too soon. I have other tribes yet to visit over the winter and bring into our fold. We are not yet quite strong enough to face all the Long Knives, and we have much planning to do. I will therefore ask Governor Harrison to reconvene the council tomorrow and make amends." A sly smile came over his face. "I will make the lying white man believe that I truly regret my actions and that all I want is peace. But soon he will know otherwise!"

Windigo and the others raised fists and tomahawks in shouted support. War would indeed come as soon as Tecumseh said the time was right! Windigo could hardly wait! And, of course, neither could Wapmimi!

17

October 3, 1810

Life was so much better now. The hot summer was over, and Sadie had actually grown attached to her little sod home. Jonah and Marvin had insulated the house with more sod built up around the outside to make the walls thicker, which would mean a much warmer house when winter came . . . and it would come soon.

She walked with Louise along the wooden side-walks of Vincennes, relishing the autumn visit to town that Jonah had promised. She loved him so! He'd installed a real window for her, and today she would buy material to make curtains. Jonah and Marvin were at a sawmill buying flat board lumber for the floors of their soddies. They would no longer need to walk on dirt! Little Paul wouldn't have constantly black feet.

A real wood floor. She could put down her rag rugs and with curtains up, and a fire in the cookstove, they would all be cozy and warm this winter. Best of all, they would truly have time to rest.

Today they shopped in Vincennes and would stay the night in a real hotel. "Louise, look at this material!" Sadie turned to the woman who'd become her close friend, so relieved that Louise had not suffered from a severe headache for a whole month now, ever since the weather cooled and the humidity dropped.

Louise brightened, reaching out and fingering the deep green velvet.

"Can't you just imagine the beautiful dress this would make for the holidays?" Sadie asked.

Louise smiled and shook her head. "And where would you wear such a dress, most likely trapped in deep snows in the middle of nowhere?"

Sadie touched it to her cheek. "I'd just wear it for Christmas Day, even though no one would see it but our two families. It would just feel good to dress up and put my hair up. You should make a special dress for yourself, too."

"Oh, I have one pretty nice dress I brought along, although once we settled I figured I'd never be able to wear it. Maybe I'll get it out Christmas Day. Either way, no fancy dress could do much for this old lady. However, you, dear, look beautiful in simple home-spun."

Sadie laughed lightly. "That's very sweet of you, but Jonah would have a fit if I bought some of this. It's too expensive!"

Louise touched her shoulder. "Jonah approves of *anything* you do, Sadie Wilde. I've never known a man so eager to please his wife."

They both snickered, and Sadie hugged the material close. "I feel so much better about everything, Louise, don't you? Both our homes will have wood floors and rugs. We both have fireplaces now, and the sheds for the animals are finished. And one good thing about high prairie grass is that the animals can graze all winter. They won't have to scrape very far through the snow to find food. All we have to do is stock up good on flour and beans and potatoes and canned goods, and we'll get through the winter just fine."

Louise turned to look at some checkered material. "Personally I'm just glad for winter because Indians usually don't venture out to hunt and raid when the snows are deep."

"Oh, Louise, we haven't had one problem with Indians." Sadie asked the store clerk to measure out three yards of the green velvet, then walked over to a display of lace trimming. "What do you think of this?" She held up some white lace.

Louise walked over and studied it, then took it from Sadie's hands and pulled some ivory lace from the cylinder it was wrapped around. "Ivory. It would look better against the dark green." She grasped Sadie's hands as Sadie took hold of the lace.

"Sadie, you heard the talk around town. Things aren't good between Governor Harrison and that Indian leader called Tecumseh. The Shawnee are insisting we've no right to settle where we are. People say he brought a lot of armed warriors to Vincennes this past summer for his talk with Harrison, and Tecumseh left angry."

Sadie's smile faded. "I refuse to think about that." She studied the lace more closely. "Governor Harrison insists he has thousands of men ready at his beck and call to quell any Indian problems. And even if the

111

Shawnee did decide to begin raiding, it would most likely be along the Wabash and the western side of Indiana and into Illinois. That's where they say nearly all the raiding has taken place in the past. It's very unlikely they would come into our area. Besides, what could they gain from two little sod houses and just a couple of horses? They couldn't get enough from us to boast about. Jonah says Indians like to raid in places where they know the news will spread easily, so they can more quickly put fear into the hearts of the settlers." She set the lace aside, masking her own inner doubts as she continued. "For heaven's sake, Louise, the Shawnee could slaughter all of us, and no one would know a thing about it for months! What good would that do them?"

Louise sighed. "I hope you're right. It does make sense, but I went through too many Indian attacks back in Ohio in the early days. Even back there things aren't totally safe yet. With all this talk about possible war with England and how the Indians would likely side with the British against Americans, it makes for difficult sleeping at night."

"Well, Jonah and Marvin have both fought Indians, and Jack is certainly handy with a long gun. Even you and I can shoot if we have to." She put her hand on Louise's arm. "Winter is coming, so why fret about it now? The time to be extra cautious is next summer, and maybe by then things will be settled with this Tecumseh. A lot of the tribes are perfectly happy with things the way they are and don't want to start more trouble."

"You want some of that there lace, ma'am?" the storekeeper asked Sadie.

Sadie smiled for him. "Yes! Give me about two yards of it." She brushed Indian worries from her mind, putting her hands to her cheeks. "Goodness, I don't even know what pattern I'll use or how much I'll need of any of this." The door opened as she finished. "I'm behaving like a spoiled rich woman."

"Who's a spoiled rich woman?" came Jonah's voice.

Sadie looked up at her husband, who seemed to completely fill the tiny store with his height and build, even though he'd lost weight over the summer. He held Paul in his arms.

"Mommy!" the boy called, reaching out for her. Sadie walked up and took Paul into her arms, giving him a kiss on the cheek. She led Jonah to where the clerk's assistant was measuring and cutting the green velvet material.

"I said I was *behaving* like a spoiled rich woman," Sadie told Jonah. "I told the clerk to give me three yards of this, Jonah. It's five cents a yard. Is that too much?"

Jonah touched the material, running his thumb over its softness. "Do you have even the slightest idea how pretty you'd look in this color, with that light hair and those green eyes?" He leaned closer. "No, it's not too much. Just be reasonable with your curtain material. We have a lot of other shopping to do yet."

"I will. Thank you, Jonah. Did you find enough lumber?"

113

"I think so. We've got quite a wagon full of things to take back already, and we haven't even stocked up on flour and salt and the like."

"I'll need to make some new clothes for Paul over the winter, too." She gave the boy a hug. "You're going to be big and strong like your daddy, Paul."

"I'm big now!" the boy said, holding his arms out. "This big!"

They all laughed, including the store clerk, who commented what a "cute kid" Paul was. "You folks keep an eye on him," the man added. "Them Shawnee, they're prone to taking young white captives and raising them the Shawnee way."

"No Shawnee will ever touch *my* son," Jonah told the man, taking the boy back from Sadie.

Of course not, Sadie thought. *There isn't a Shawnee man alive who could take little Paul from his father.*

"I'm told most of the raiding has taken place west of here," Jonah added.

"For the most part. Actually, things have been pretty quiet since Tecumseh's visit here. Most think Governor Harrison pretty much convinced that Indian bugger that it's useless to fight this last land sale. I don't expect much trouble over winter, but Harrison will keep an eye out. Even so, you folks better do the same. Don't go out plowing fields without your rifle along."

"Never do," Jonah answered. He gave Sadie a wink. "You finish up here and meet me and Marvin and Jack at the little restaurant two doors down from here. It only seats about ten people at a time. We'll go see if we can get a table." He nodded to Louise and left, and Sadie glanced at Louise, momentarily peeved that the woman had a bit of an "I told you so" look in her eyes.

"Mark my words, Louise Stockton. We will have no Indian trouble where we are. That's part of the reason Jonah chose that particular area."

Louise smiled kindly. "I'm sorry, Sadie. I don't mean to cause you worry, especially over little Paul. I just think we need to do like the clerk says and not fool ourselves into thinking we're too far from all the trouble."

"Here you go, ma'am." The clerk handed Sadie the green velvet material, folded flat and wrapped in brown paper. "That will be fifteen cents for the material, and another five for your lace trim."

Sadie reached into her drawstring bag, again taking great joy in the amenities of a real town. She took out the twenty cents and paid the clerk. Excitedly she took her package, then waited while the clerk wrapped her lace edging. She looked confidently at Louise. "I will not worry about it," she told the woman. "We've had a rough summer, and at last I'm beginning to think of my little soddy as home. I was very depressed when we first settled out there, but now I feel better about it. We're all survivors, Louise, and settling on the prairie won't be any different than when you and Marvin first settled in western Ohio and Jonah's folks and mine stuck it out in the Ohio Valley." She turned and took the lace the clerk handed her. "Now," she said, in more of an order than a suggestion, "let's go eat and put our packages into the wagon. Then we'll come back here and finish shopping for material for curtains and more clothes. Coming here is such a wonderful break from what we've been through, don't you think?"

Louise smiled warmly. "I think you are a woman of great faith and great strength, that's what I think," she answered.

Sadie looked away. "I'm just doing what needs to be done to stay sane," she told Louise. She forced back tears and an urge to give in to her inner fears when Louise walked up and put an arm around her.

"Oh, yes, I know," Louise told her. "I know, child."

18

January 6, 1811

Travel had been easier than usual for winter. The surprisingly mild weather seemed to Windigo and Wapmimi to mean good fortune, and now Wapmimi was sure that the coming summer would be the time to search for the white woman Wiske meant for Windigo. They both accompanied Tecumseh as guards, Windigo serving as an English and Potawatomi interpreter.

In Windigo's mind, nothing but even greater power awaited Tecumseh and those who followed him. It was obvious by their treatment wherever they went among the British towns and even among American fortifications that Tecumseh held great respect and prominence. The British considered him the Supreme Commander of all the Northwestern tribes. It mattered not that there were some members of the various tribes who resented the title given to Tecumseh and refused to follow him. They would regret their jealousies, for one day Tecumseh would be responsible for whittling out a huge area of this land that would be considered a separate nation for all Indian tribes, a place where no American dared settle!

Although Tecumseh and his followers did not fully trust the British, they trusted the Americans even less; and with a possible war coming between those two entities, what better time to befriend the British than now? The redcoats were eager to win Tecumseh and his followers to their side, and Tecumseh considered it a fine idea. With both the British and his own amalgamation of thousands of Indians going against the Americans, maybe they could push them all the way back to the Atlantic! Maybe they could win back much more than just the three million or so acres Governor Harrison had so flagrantly stolen from them!

Now Windigo sat at Tecumseh's left as the leader spoke with the old Indian agent, Matthew Elliott, here at Amherstburg, a British stronghold just east of Detroit. Tecumseh's aide, Sauganash, sat to the leader's right.

"I and my followers turn to you now, Elliott," Tecumseh told the man in English. "If the redcoats wish to go against the Americans and take back much of what was taken when the Americans first warred against you, you will have the help of Tecumseh and his followers. I have many young warriors eager to fight the bluecoats and their volunteers, but we will need supplies."

Elliott's sagging eyes actually sparkled with eagerness. "The king will be glad to know that, Tecumseh. Your needs will be met. You will leave Amherstburg with new weapons, plenty of gunpowder, more blankets, plenty of food, and whatever else you need to both live well during this time of peace, and to fight with when the time is right."

"Those with me, and those who wait at Prophetstown, eagerly await that time," Tecumseh answered. "I have all the Shawnee behind me, as well as hundreds of Kickapoos, Potawatomies, Iowas, Menominees, Sioux, Mandans, and Winnebagos. Even Black Hawk of the Sauk and Foxes has agreed to join my leadership. We are strong, and we are ready!"

The two men and their aides sat around a fire inside a Shawnee *wigawa*, built by some of the twenty or so women who'd accompanied them on Tecumseh's journey. The leader had also allowed several children to come along, always wishing to show that wherever he went, he came in peace. Over one hundred fifty followers accompanied him on this trip, comprised of members of all the different tribes now under Tecumseh's leadership.

Agent Elliott removed a fur-lined, buckskin jacket,

as the mild temperatures outside made it almost too warm inside the *wigawa*. Tecumseh and most of those who sat beside and behind him wore only buckskin pants and lightweight shirts.

"I should warn you, Tecumseh, that scouts inform me that the governor of Michigan Territory, William Hull, has been rallying some of the northern Indians against you," Elliott told them. "He is stirring their anger by telling them you have no right to call yourself the leader of all the Northwestern tribes. He is working on their pride and jealousies to keep them from joining with you."

Tecumseh breathed deeply and pondered the news, then raised his chin proudly. "This only tells me that the Americans are afraid of my strength and power. They are trying to build their own Indian backing, but it will not work. There are too many of us now. Those tribes who have not yet joined us know that. They might claim to be against us, but I know they are really afraid. If it comes to fighting us, they will not do it. Governor Hull's attempts against me do not worry me in the least."

Elliott smiled and nodded. "There is something else you should know. The Potawatomi leader, Main Poche, was here several weeks ago, also looking for supplies. He told me about a meeting he had with Governor Harrison at Vincennes. He told me that Harrison tried to get him drunk, then thought to bribe Main Poche into selling him more land, promised him many gifts. The wise Potawatomi leader refused. He told me that was when Harrison threatened all the Potawatomi with the might of the American army."

Anger filled Windigo's heart at the threat to his own cherished Potawatomi leader. He could feel Tecumseh's anger as well.

"Harrison has become my greatest enemy," Tecumseh told Agent Elliott. "What did Main Poche do?"

Elliott actually laughed lightly. "He became very angry, so he told me, and accused Harrison of trying to divide the tribes to weaken them. He told Harrison that he could not just get an Indian drunk and then steal whatever he wanted. He said that Harrison is always threatening the Indians with the possibility of things that could happen to their women and children if the Americans came against them; but Main Poche told Harrison he should consider the same thing— what will happen to *American* women and children!"

Tecumseh actually chuckled, and Windigo and Wapmimi snickered, along with many others. Tecumseh turned to Windigo and nodded. "Your leader, Main Poche, is a wise man, and a devoted follower."

The remark burned more pride into Windigo's heart.

After several more minutes of talking and directions from Agent Elliott as to when and where to pick up the promised supplies, the meeting broke up. Windigo and Wapmimi returned to their own *wigawa,* which they shared with three other young Potawatomi warriors. They eagerly shared the news of what had taken place at the meeting, and all five of them laughed and raised their fists, letting out war whoops at the thought of a great victory that was surely coming—a victory of Tecumseh and his thousands of followers against Harrison . . . against *all* Americans!

"When we get back to Prophetstown in the spring," Wapmimi told Windigo then, "I will go out and hunt." He leaned closer. "Not for deer or rabbits," he continued quietly, "but for the white woman who will become your wife!"

Windigo smiled almost shyly. "You still believe it must be so?"

"I *know* it must be so! She will have hair like the sun and eyes like the grass. She will belong to an American man, and I, Wapmimi, will steal her from him and *kill* him! If we kill or steal enough white women and children, the Americans will be afraid and will go back to where the sun rises and stay out of our land *forever!* The women and children they leave behind will become Potawatomi, Delaware, Shawnee, Kickapoo. *Our* blood will run in the veins of their children, and thus, through numbers alone, red blood will become even stronger, while white blood grows weaker!"

The two young men pushed at each other and laughed. Life under Tecumseh's leadership was good!

19

March 28, 1811

Sadie patted Jenny's belly, which was growing fatter with a calf that would be born in roughly three more months. "Soon you'll be giving milk for a good long time again, Jenny," she told the cow, which she'd insisted must have a name. She'd become accustomed to talking to the animal as though it could understand her. "All summer and half of next winter, maybe longer. We'll have plenty of butter for a good long time."

She smiled, walking into the sod animal shed, where some of the chickens had chosen to lay eggs in the hay in one corner. How the feathered creatures managed to stay out from under the hooves of the huge plow horses and a cow was beyond her imagination; let alone how it was that the eggs never got stepped on.

She stooped down and gathered the few eggs into her folded apron, thinking how, indeed, she was beginning to love this place as home. The winter weather had been kind to them, and playing games inside most of the time, reading to Paul, having time to talk and pray together . . . it all made life here more bearable. She could only hope this summer would not be as hot as last year's.

Had they really been here nine months already? It

hardly seemed possible. Christmas had been as memorable as she'd hoped. Jonah actually hunted down a wild turkey and plucked and cleaned it for her, and they'd eaten royally of roasted turkey, warm-baked bread, pie made from wild berries growing along the river, mashed potatoes, and beans. Having the Stocktons to share the holiday with made it even more fun, and she'd felt pretty again in her green velvet dress, enjoying the look of appreciation and desire in Jonah's eyes when he saw her in it.

One bad snowstorm with lingering deep snows was all they'd encountered, and Paul loved playing in it. Although there had been some bitterly cold weather at times, for the most part temperatures had been more than bearable, and she thanked God that the wood they'd ordered delivered from Vincennes got them through most of the winter by mixing in tightly bundled prairie grass for more fuel.

And there were the long winter nights she and Jonah enjoyed together after Paul fell asleep. Although she was anxious to give her husband more children, so far she carried no second child, probably a godsend since there was still so much work to do. More children would come soon enough.

In another week they would make their spring trip to Vincennes. The food supply was very low now, but with any luck, by fall they would have a good share of their own food, maybe even some to sell. The two plows Jonah had the blacksmith forge for him last fall seemed to be working as expected, their razor-sharp edges cutting through the thick roots much more easily than Jonah had even hoped. The work caused a loud ripping sound that Sadie could hear even from this distance.

She shaded her eyes against the morning sun to see Jonah and Jack each walking behind a plow horse, leather straps tugging at them as their muscles strained to keep the plows digging deeply while the horses pulled them through the unforgiving prairie. Behind them Louise and Marvin worked with spades, chopping at some of the larger chunks of sod to break them up even more. Sadie was the one chosen to stay closer to the houses today and take care of the regular chores of gathering eggs, feeding the animals, cleaning out the animal shed, and preparing breakfast. She and Louise took turns at such chores and at watching Paul, who played outside the shed this morning.

Sadie watched her son, now three, throw little stones at the chickens, then giggle when the birds squawked and scrambled out of the way.

"Paul, don't throw stones at the poor chickens," Sadie called to him.

The boy turned to her with a grin, then his eyes widened. "Mommy, look!"

Sadie realized he was pointing to something behind her, and when she turned, she gasped in shock and terror, dropping all the eggs she'd gathered. Momentarily frozen in place, she stared into the hideous face of a young, painted, feathered warrior with an ugly scar that ran over his right cheek, his nose and lips, which were grown together at the right corner, making his grin look hideous.

"At last I have found you!" he said in English.

What on earth he meant, there was no time to contemplate. Where had he come from! How had he so easily sneaked right out of the tall prairie grass? Filled with horror, she finally found the fortitude to turn and run, screaming for Jonah.

A hand came over her mouth, a strong arm came around her waist, pinning her arms tightly just as she'd nearly reached Paul. She struggled fiercely, but a second Indian grabbed her legs and the two of them began carrying her.

Terror engulfed her as she saw a third Indian grab up a screaming, kicking Paul. More Indians suddenly charged out of the tall prairie grass on horseback, their war whoops ringing in the crisp morning air. They headed for the fields where Jonah, Jack, Marvin, and Louise worked.

"Do not fight, or your son will die, too!" a voice told her.

Paul! Jonah! What did he mean, *your son will die, too?* Would *Jonah* die today? Young Jack? Poor, sweet Louise? Their good friend Marvin? No! No! This couldn't be happening! Governor Harrison had promised it *couldn't* happen!

She was thrown over the bare back of a horse, and quickly someone tied rope around her wrists, brought it under the horse's belly, and tied it to her ankles, so tightly that it hurt.

"Jonah!" she screamed again.

"Your husband and the others will *die* today!" came the gruff voice.

"Mommy! Mommy!"

"Paul, it's all right," she shouted, hoping to keep the child calm so he would not irritate their captors. "We're going for a ride. Be a good boy, Paul!"

Jonah! Jonah! She could still hear the shouts of the warriors, now mingled with gunshots. It sounded like there were many of them . . . surely too many for the three men to handle.

"Oh, God, Jonah," she moaned. "Jonah!" Tears of terror filled her eyes. It all seemed so unreal. Jonah! Poor Louise! The woman had gone all winter without a headache and was finally beginning to adjust to prairie life. What a horrible way for their dreams to end! And Jack, young Jack, such a happy, good-natured young man, with dreams of building his own empire out here.

Tears spilled hard then, for she heard Louise screaming.

"Oh, God, why," Sadie sobbed. "Why?" She struggled to hold her head up enough to see Paul, but he was not in her line of sight. Now she smelled smoke. Were they setting the prairie on fire? Were they burning the bodies of the dead? Would they kill poor Jenny and the calf in her belly? The chickens? The horses? Would they break her window?

What a silly thought. Why did even her one and only window suddenly seem precious?

She heard Paul crying. "God, please don't let them hurt him," she wept.

The horse carrying her suddenly started running, jolting her to the very marrow of her bones. Where were they going? Why had her captor said he'd "finally found" her?

Jonah!

20

Jonah's first sensation was feeling wet. Something pounded his back, and his head. The feel of it against the back of his head brought fierce pain, unlike anything he'd ever known, not even when he took an arrow in his side from an Indian raid back at Willow Creek. When was that? Was he there now?

Thunder. Yes, that rumbling sound was thunder. Water began to seep into his nose, startling him into alertness when he breathed some in and started coughing. The coughing made the pain in his head almost unbearable. He started to roll over, but he couldn't bear the pressure on the back of his head.

Now he realized the pelting feeling was rain, a torrential downpour of drops so big they actually hurt. He moved a hand under his face to keep the water away from it and lay still, thinking, slowly opening his eyes. In front of him lay soaked sod. He could smell the wet dirt, an odor any farmer appreciated. That first spring planting was invigorating.

Spring planting. Wasn't that what he was doing a few minutes ago? He realized the sun was low and nearly in his eyes. When he was working this morning it had been higher . . . and rising. If it was in his eyes . . . it must be setting. He'd been lying here for hours!

What was going on? Why did he feel this fierce pain? Where was everyone? A loud clap of thunder made him jump slightly. He was soaked to the skin. He watched water run past his face in little rivulets, watched a beetle scurry across the clumps of dirt that remained above the water. As he studied the beetle, he noticed some of the bouncing raindrops turn bigger and bigger and become white.

Hail. He grunted as large hail balls beat against his back . . . and his head. He cried out then, moving a hand to his head to protect it. He felt a sticky warmth, and it hurt to touch his head. The hail soon turned back to rain, and he removed his hand and looked at it.

Blood. It was covered with blood. He struggled to remember how he might have ended up like this. Slowly it came to him. How long ago was it? He was walking behind the plow he'd so proudly invented that did such a good job of slicing through the prairie roots. It had been a pretty morning, although very dark clouds lurked in the west.

Marvin worked with him . . . and . . . and Jack. Yes, Jack and his mother, Louise. That was her name, wasn't it? Why was it such a struggle to remember?

War whoops. He remembered the sound of wild

Indians and thundering horses . . . and a woman . . . screaming. *Jonah! Jonah!* He remembered turning toward the sound. His body physically jerked at the memory of a hideously painted Indian riding down on him. No, not just one. There were several. They appeared like ghosts simply rising out of the ground. No warning. He turned to run for his long gun. He heard a gunshot. A man cried out.

He ran so hard. He almost reached his gun . . . and then came the blow. He could even hear a thud . . . his own skull cracking. That must be what he heard, because at the same time black pain overwhelmed him and he fell. His last thought was that he would soon be dead, and there was nothing he could do about it.

Was he dead? Surely not. If he was dead he would not feel this rain and smell the earth and feel this ungodly pain. Where were Jack and Louise and Marvin? Maybe *they* were dead.

Think! Think! Something was missing. That woman who screamed. He could see her. She whispered his name now. *Jonah. Jonah, help me.* He struggled to his hands and knees as the rain continued to pummel him. A horrible dizziness engulfed him, and he vomited. If he wasn't already dead then he was surely dying. *Daddy!*

"Paul?" Yes! Paul! He had a little boy, and . . . what about his mama? "Sadie!" he groaned.

It all became clearer now. He vomited again, and pain ripped through his head, neck, and shoulders as he forced himself to look around while it was still light. In the distance he saw a soddy . . . his soddy. Between him and the house he saw bodies sprawled . . . two men . . . a woman.

Grief and horror overwhelmed him at the reality that began making its way into his injured brain. "No!" he cried. Unable to get to his feet, he began crawling through the mud. He reached the first body, already beginning to bloat from the warmth of the day.

"Jack!" The young man's chest was split open, his torso riddled with arrows. His eyes were wide-open, frozen in a look of terror. "Oh, God, Jack," Jonah groaned. Such a friendly, good-natured young man. How could God have let this happen? He tried to close his eyes, but the boy had been too long dead. His eyelids would not move.

Jonah fought tears as he managed to crawl closer to the house, and to the next body. It was Louise. A horrid wound to her neck had left her head nearly severed. "Oh, Louise," Jonah wept. "Poor Louise."

He fought sobs as he kept crawling, stopping to vomit again. If Jack and Louise had been so hideously killed, then surely so had Marvin . . . and . . .

"No!" he screamed. Not Sadie! Not his precious little Paul! "God, please! Please don't let me find them!" He crawled faster, making it to the next body.

"Marvin," he gasped. A hatchet remained in the man's face, and his body was riddled with bullet holes. With what little strength he had, Jonah grasped the hatchet, and weeping violently, he managed to yank it out of Marvin's face.

"Bastards!" he screamed through tears. "Bastards! Murdering savages! God damn all of you! God damn you!"

Why had he alone been spared? It wasn't fair. He crawled over Marvin's body and managed to raise up on his knees as the rain began to ease up. Desperately he looked around, having a difficult time seeing anything because of his tears and pain. He screamed Sadie's name. Paul's name. Over and over he called out to them.

"Oh, God, let them be alive," he sobbed. In spite of intense pain and dizziness, he grasped hold of a hoe lying near Marvin and used it like a cane to get to his feet so he could look around better. Again he screamed Sadie's name, and Paul's. He got no reply.

Leaning on the hoe, he slowly made his way to the soddy. Maybe, just maybe, Sadie and Paul were inside and had avoided being seen by the Indians. Yes, a man could always hope for miracles, couldn't he? God wouldn't let anything happen to his precious little son or his beautiful wife who'd put up with so much to come out here with him.

He kept screaming their names, kept looking around. He didn't see them. Thank God, he didn't see them. He made it to the soddy, the black pain in his head beginning to become even more unbearable. Balancing himself with one hand against the wall of the soddy, he made it to the door, noticing then that the cow, Jenny, lay slaughtered not far away. Dead chickens lay everywhere, and in the distance lay his draft horses and Jenny's grown calves. The wagons

131

that had brought them here from Ohio sat nearby, burned. A good deal of the prairie grass all around was also burned. Most likely everything would have burned a lot worse if not for the rain.

Still no sign of Sadie or Paul. He stumbled through the doorway. "Sadie? Paul?" The setting sun still shed enough light that he could see well enough to tell no one was inside. Dishes still sat in a bucket. Ham lay in a skillet on a now-cold grate. Yes, he remembered now. Sadie was going to make breakfast for all of them. It was her turn to do the cooking while the rest of them worked in the field. Her fresh-baked bread still sat on the table. He touched it lovingly. It was cold.

"Sadie," he wept. "Where are you? Where's Paul?" He collapsed in sobs. He'd failed her! He'd failed to protect his wife and child the way he'd promised to do! God only knew what kind of fate they'd suffered . . . if they were even still alive. "Oh, God, my son! My little boy!"

He fell to his side onto the wood plank floor he'd so proudly installed for her. Sadie loved that wood floor. He touched one of the rag rugs she'd made for it. "Sadie. My Sadie," he groaned, before a strange buzzing feeling moved through his body, from his neck downward. By the time it reached his feet the awful truth penetrated his thoughts. He couldn't move! When he tried to call for Sadie once more, he couldn't even open his mouth to speak! Then a blackness consumed him, mercifully taking away all thoughts, all agony, all pain.

21

March 30, 1811

Sadie clung to Paul, struggling with all her might to pretend calmness so as not to traumatize the boy any more than he'd already suffered. When the savages who'd taken her finally stopped for the night, they'd cut the ropes that held her. To her amazement she'd been led to a tree, and her captor, although his eyes showed a vicious darkness, spread out a blanket for her, then had someone bring Paul to her. One warrior stood by guarding her, and Paul clung to her as she watched a group of ten other natives sitting around a campfire talking among themselves.

Her captor sat eating and laughing as though this day had been just an ordinary day. Maybe for him it *was* ordinary! Maybe he went out murdering and terrifying whites *every* day! He turned, reaching out and handing her a leg from one of three rabbits they'd cooked over the fire. "Eat," he ordered her. The scar on his face looked even more grotesque in the firelight.

"Why?" she sneered. "Are you fattening me up so there is more of me to burn alive?"

He stared at her for several quiet seconds. "Is that what you think we want of you?"

She yanked the rabbit from his hand and turned Paul

sideways, handing him the rabbit leg. "Eat this, sweet-heart."

Paul had long ago stopped crying, but he'd not let go of her once since being brought to his mommy. He pouted as he gave a dark look of scorn to the man who'd offered the food. Then he took the rabbit leg and ate a small bite of it.

Sadie looked back at her captor. "If not to take your heathen pleasure in torturing me, why *am* I here? What did you mean when you said you'd finally found me? And where are my friends and my husband?"

The man scowled. "You ask many questions, white woman."

"Why *shouldn't* I? What is your name, and what do you *want?*"

"I took you because I saw you in a dream."

"What?" Was the man crazy?

"Dreams are very important to the Potawatomi . . . to men and women of *all* tribes. You whites should pay more attention to your *own* dreams."

"You make no sense! And you haven't answered me about my husband!"

He raised his chin proudly. "Your husband is dead. So are all those who were with him."

Naked reality stabbed Sadie in the stomach first, as keenly as if a knife had been put there. She wanted to scream, loud and long . . . and cry. She must cry. But here sat little Paul in her lap. More than anything else she wanted to keep him calm, shelter him from the ugly truths that pelted her emotions like the hail had

134

earlier pelted her back. It couldn't be true! It wasn't possible that a man as sure and strong and capable and kind and wonderful as Jonah Wilde could be dead! And if he was, who would come for her? No one! It would be days, maybe even weeks before anyone even knew they'd been attacked!

Never, ever in her life had she fought so hard to hide her emotions. She wanted to scratch out the eyes of the scarred man who looked at her now. If not for Paul, she would do just that, not caring what he did to her in return. How was she going to go on living without Jonah?

"Why?" she asked coldly. "Why have you done this horrible thing? None of us has ever done one thing to you!"

He snickered, then turned and said something to the others. They all joined him in the laughter, and her captor turned back to her. "You settled on land *stolen* from us!" he barked, making her jump when he shouted the word "stolen."

"*That* is what you did to me . . . to *all* of us!"

"That land is legally ours! Governor Harrison said—"

"*Harrison!*" the man interrupted. "Harrison is a *liar!* Harrison cares *nothing* about what is legal and what is not! And it is *his* fault that your husband is dead! *His* fault that you now belong to *us!*"

Jonah! Jonah! Oh, God, help me! "What do you mean, *belong* to you?" Sadie seethed. "What do you have planned for me?"

135

The man shook his head as he looked her over scathingly. He moved to face her more directly, crossing his legs and resting his elbows on his knees. "You whites think we take pleasure in torture, that we drink the white man's blood like demons, don't you?"

"What am I supposed to think, when you ride in and murder innocent people who've done you no harm?" Now the tears started coming. *No! No! Be brave! He'll respect bravery.*

"Please take me home," she asked, kissing Paul's hair.

"If I took you home, I would have to take you all the way across the big waters, past the land in the east, to the place your ancestors came from when they first set foot in country that belongs to *us!* We will not accept it, any more than *your* people would have if *we* had gone across the big waters to *your* country and tried to take it from you!"

Sadie quickly wiped at the tears she desperately did not want to shed. She was too weary to argue the point, and she hated the fact that his statement made sense in some respect. She closed her eyes and rocked Paul. "Just tell me what you want," she asked, feeling suddenly ready to pass out.

"I told you I saw you in a dream. I am taking you to my friend at Prophetstown. You will become his wife. I will explain more later. Know only that you are not in danger of death, unless you cause trouble! Nor is your son in danger. The Potawatomi and the Shawnee, *all* Indians honor the young. Over the years many young white children have been adopted into our tribe and have lived long and happy lives. It will be so for your son." He leaned closer, grasping a section of her hair. "But remember this, white woman. You can stay alive and always be near your son to love and protect him . . . or you can be foolish and try to run away or make trouble. If you do, your son will be raised by us *without* his real mother! I alone have the power to make sure no harm comes to you . . . I and my friend once we reach Prophetstown. There are those there who would enjoy torturing you to death. The light hair of a white woman is a great prize to them! Do you understand?"

Paul! She had to do whatever was necessary to be here for her baby. She met the man's dark gaze with fierce feelings of protectiveness and hatred. "I understand," she seethed. "But if you harm my child in any way, I'll sink a knife into *your* heart!"

The man actually grinned. "Windigo will be very happy with my choice," he told her. "You do not cringe and whimper and beg like other white women. You are brave and strong, like Potawatomi women." He breathed a deep sigh as someone greatly satisfied. "What do they call you?"

She smoothed Paul's hair, realizing that after a few bites of the rabbit, the boy had fallen asleep against her breast. "Sadie. Sadie Wilde. My son is called Paul."

He nodded, still sitting erect and proud. "I am called Wapmimi." He stood up. "I will bring you more food.

Then you must sleep. We have many days of riding yet."

He walked away, and Sadie leaned against the tree. "God, help me," she whispered. "Show me what to do. And please, please let Jonah be alive." Perhaps it was a foolish hope, a way of making herself want to live, but she just could not picture Jonah dead. Still, for now she had to think about survival, for herself and Paul. Apparently they were headed for Prophetstown, the place where the infamous Tecumseh lived.

22

March 29, 1811

The second day of travel brought more mercy from Sadie's abductors. She was allowed to ride upright and hold little Paul in front of her. She presumed this was due to the fact that they'd traveled so far that her captors considered it less likely she would try to escape.

A night of no sleep for fear of her baby being stolen away had left her time to think about her predicament. Survival was the key word now, for Paul's sake . . . and in case . . . just in case . . . Jonah had survived. If he was alive, her husband would come for her. His own grandfather had hunted down Jonah's grandmother when Delaware Indians murdered her whole family and stole her away. The whole family knew the

138

story of Noah Wilde. Trouble was, Noah was part Indian himself and had lived with them, knew their tongue, understood how to barter with them.

Jonah had fought Indians before, but he didn't have his grandfather's experience in dealing with them. Maybe he would go to Governor Harrison. Surely a man like Harrison would have the wherewithal to gather together an army of men to come for her! And Jonah would be right there in the lead with Harrison! . . . if he was alive.

Was it foolish to hope for something like that? She glanced around at the still-painted warriors who'd captured her. One of them still wore Louise's bloody scalp on his belt.

Of course Jonah was dead. Such men killed in the most brutal ways . . . ways that no man could survive. They enjoyed leaving behind horrid remains so that those who discovered the maimed, tortured bodies would tell others what they'd seen . . . stories the Indians hoped were so awful they would frighten away the surviving whites. That was, after all, their goal . . . to banish all whites from land they considered theirs. They did it by brutal raids, murder, and torture; by stealing the white man's means of survival, their food, supplies, and livestock; and by stealing their women and children.

Now Sadie had to face the sick reality that she would likely become some savage's wife, more likely a slave than a wife. Little Paul would be brought up as a Shawnee. One day he might even forget who his mother and father really were. She'd heard stories of how captured white children usually learn to like their life just fine and become just as Indian as those who stole them away.

She looked around the expanse of prairie through which her horse was led, and she realized there was absolutely nothing to use as a landmark in case she might escape, not a tree or a rock to go by. Just prairie, prairie and more prairie, grass and wildflowers that all tumbled and flowed into a monotonous pattern. Even the grass they smashed down as they traveled through would soon bounce right back up to the sun too soon for a person to follow a trail back.

What good would it do to escape? These heathens who knew this land so well would find her in no time, and only God knew what they might do to her for misbehaving. Or they might take it out on Paul, torture him to death before her eyes. She'd heard such stories. How any human beings could be so brutal was beyond the imagination.

No. If she was to try an escape, it would take a great deal of planning, and she would need all her strength for such a thing. The ordeal of yesterday's capture and a sleepless night left her too weak and confused to even consider escape, let alone how glad she was at the moment just to hold Paul in her arms and know they would both be fed and given water.

When would they stop? These men seemed to have no mercy for their horses, and an uncanny ability to stay on horseback for hours and hours at a time. Her inner thighs felt rubbed raw from riding bareback. Every fiber of her being ached and cried out for rest. The sun beat down on her exposed face. She longed for her slat bonnet. Little Paul was also getting burned. Right now his head lolled against her chest in sleep. His homespun pants were wet from an accident he'd had because they were not allowed off the horse often enough to relieve themselves when necessary. Right now Sadie's bladder felt ready to burst.

"God, help us," she said softly. "Save my baby from terror and harm. That's all I ask, except that if my Jonah is alive, bless him and take care of him, Lord. Take away his pain. Help him."

Wapmimi rode up beside her. "Keep still!" he ordered.

She faced him defiantly. "I am praying! You can't stop me from that!" So ugly! That scar was so white and ugly in the sun! What did his friend look like, the one called Windigo?

Wapmimi looked straight ahead then, holding his chin proudly. "Do you think the Shawnee do not pray?"

Sadie also turned away. "I don't care if you do or don't."

"You *should* care! And we *do* pray, to Wiske, the Master of Life. Wiske created all that you see, the land, the waters, the sky, the sun and moon and all the stars. He meant for us to care for all these things. You whites tear at the heart of the earth with your plows, making the prairie grass cry out in agony as you rip

141

her to pieces. You cut down trees and dump filth into the waters. You do not honor that which the Master of Life gave all of us so freely. You lie and cheat and burn and murder and steal!"

"You do the same."

"We do not destroy the land and the trees and the waters! We give back whatever we take from Mother Earth. And when we kill and burn and steal from the white man, it is only because he has done the same to us in greater numbers! We do what we *must* do to protect our own and our land!"

Sadie was too worn out and in too much pain to argue with him. "Can we please stop for a while?"

"Soon. There are more cabins ahead, more whites living where they do not belong. We will get fresh horses there . . . and food." Wapmimi looked at her with a wry grin. "Perhaps one of those strange hats you white women wear so that your skin does not burn."

Sadie's heart filled with dread. They were going to attack another settlement, kill more innocent people! "Please, can't you . . . can't you just leave them be? Can't you just sneak up and take their horses and let the people live?"

He smiled wickedly. "One day you will understand, Sadie Wilde." He tossed his long, dark hair behind his shoulders, and from the side, Sadie realized he might be quite handsome without his hideous scar. He looked young, perhaps only her age. "We have already tried being kind and leaving the white man alone," he continued. "It did not work. Every time we agreed to abide by white men's promises, they broke their side of the agreement. Our leader, Tecumseh, wishes to wait and try a bit longer for peace; but some of us are tired of waiting. The only action the white man pays attention to is when we kill and torture and steal, especially when we steal his women and children. Then he listens to us. And only when he stops building his houses on this land that is still ours, and stops making the roots of Mother Earth bleed, will *we* stop killing and torturing the white man in return. There seems to be no other way to deal with you people."

"Wapmimi—"

"No more talk!"

Sadie's heart nearly stopped when the man suddenly whipped out a huge, ugly knife and reached over to wave it in front of Paul. Instinctively, Sadie moved a hand over the boy's face.

"Do not forget that I took you because I felt you are the one I am to take to my friend. I could just as easily think that of some woman I find here at this new settlement. *Then* I would have no use for you *or* your son! I am already thinking what a prize your sun-colored scalp would be on my belt, as would your *son's* white-haired scalp! Do you understand?"

Sadie swallowed, fully realizing she was at the mercy of this temperamental, young, bloodthirsty man's whims. She remembered a tale she'd heard once about Iroquois Indians torturing a white woman's baby before her very eyes and smashing its head against a rock. "I understand," she seethed.

An arrogant smile passed over the young man's scarred lips as he put his knife back into its sheath. He barked an order to another warrior, who rode closer and dismounted, then took hold of the rope bridle of Sadie's lathered, panting horse. Without another word, Wapmimi and the rest of the young men with him gathered in a circle to talk, most likely planning their strategy for the next raid. The man holding Sadie's horse motioned for her to get down. He reached up and took Paul from her, and Sadie slid off the horse. Her guard pushed her down into the grass and handed Paul back to her, then sat down facing her, placing a musket across his lap.

Sadie surmised they were to wait here while the others conducted another raid. While she sat there in the grass, her now-soiled and partially tattered dress spread out around her, she relieved her bladder into the grass without her guard knowing the difference . . . and she prayed there were no women or children at the settlement about to be attacked.

23

Jonah's injured brain conjured up odd images. He saw Sadie riding away from him on a plow horse, screaming his name. He ran after her, stretched out his hand . . . but every time he nearly touched her fingers, her horse ran faster, while his own legs kept getting heavier and heavier. Then the grass through which he ran became so high he could see nothing. Suddenly a painted warrior jumped in front of him and raised a tomahawk. As it came down, Jonah ducked and deflected the blow. He fell into a sea of green and began to drown, voices becoming muffled. Under the water he saw Sadie again. Her eyes were wide and wild, and her mouth was open as though screaming for him, but he heard only an odd, water-laden sound that made no sense. Then she swam away from him, buckskin fringes on her toes.

He tried hard as he could to swim through the murky, green water to find her, crying out for her. The water became heavier and heavier, and he then swam toward a bright light. When he reached it he could breathe again, but warriors surrounded him and began beating on him so that his head ached with sickening severity. Someone knocked him to the ground, then rolled him over.

He reached up to fight, punching into the air, trying to scratch at a human face that suddenly loomed before him, but his arms would not move.

Someone leaned close, touching his arm. "Mister?" It was a man not much older than he but bearded and smelly. The man jostled him. "Mister?" he repeated.

Jonah wanted to cry out from the awful pain at the feel of the back of his head against something hard, but he could only manage a grunt. A second man lifted him slightly and put something soft under his neck and head, and Jonah felt the room spinning.

"Mister? Can you talk?" the bearded man asked.

Jonah could only stare in reply. He looked up and recognized the beige netting hanging there, remembering Sadie used that same netting in their soddy to catch dirt and bugs that might drop from above. He realized then that he was lying on the floor of his own house, the wood plank floor of which Sadie was so proud. He remembered waking up once and managing to get to his knees and pull down a water bucket from a table so he could drink. He'd been so thirsty! Then the awful pain and numbness had again engulfed him.

"Get him some water, Jake!" The bearded man told the other. He leaned over Jonah again and felt along his ribs. "You took an awful blow to the head, mister, probably from a tomahawk. You're one lucky man, I'll tell you that. Everybody else out there is dead, and they didn't go easy."

Everybody else out there is dead . . . Sadie? Was she among them? He struggled to clear his mind. He vaguely remembered stumbling, crawling, finding bodies . . . Louise . . . Marvin . . . Jack . . . but Sadie . . . he didn't remember seeing Sadie.

The man called Jake came over and held a ladle of water to his lips, raising Jonah's head enough that some of it trickled into his mouth. Jonah managed to choke some down, relieved that he could swallow, if nothing more. Moving his head again brought the ungodly pain, and he again grunted, thinking how he sounded more like a snorting hog than a man. He tried hard to speak, wanting to ask if they found more

146

than one woman, or a little boy.

"My name's Hank and my friend is Jake," his rescuer told him. "We're traders, mister, comin' through here to see if new settlers might need somethin'. We've got a couple wagons full of goods. We headed this way when we saw your soddy and the burned wagons. When we came closer, we saw the bodies out there . . . a couple of men, an older woman, all your chickens and horses. Sorry to say they're all dead, even the unborn calf. Indians cut it out of the cow's belly and cut it up—probably figured it would give them some real good, tender meat."

Jenny! Poor, faithful Jenny. Why did he feel sorry for the animals, even the chickens? Out here in this lonely place even a man's animals seemed like good friends.

Jake had mentioned only two men and one woman. Could Sadie and Paul still be alive?

"You're awful bad hurt, mister. Me and Hank will take you to Vincennes. We're headed that way anyway. Came through here out of Ohio."

Ohio. Home. Jonah could feel the cool shade of a hardwood tree. He could see Jeremiah working out in the fields, see his nephews out there helping. Visions of the family farm swam through his head. He'd left it all to come here, to fight the prairie roots and rip them up to build his own farm. He'd made Sadie come with him, made her live in a house hardly better than Indians lived in, and where she had to worry about dirt and bugs falling onto little Paul in the night. But she'd not complained, not even once. And now, because of him, only God knew what she might be suffering this very moment. And Paul! Little Paul! Sometimes Indians killed little children.

He had no control over the tears that slipped from his eyes. This was his fault. If he even managed to find Sadie, how could she ever forgive him for bringing her here? And how could *he* ever forgive Governor Harrison for assuring them that they would have no trouble with the Indians. He didn't even know what tribe they were or in which direction they'd gone. By the time he healed enough to start tracking them, there would be no signs left.

"I'll report to Harrison what we found here," Hank was telling him. "Maybe he can do something about this."

Jonah tried so hard to talk, but it was impossible. Sadie! Paul! He wanted to scream the names, but nothing would come, and he felt as though a large stone was lashed to the back of his head. He had no idea how long he lay there listening to the two men talk until he screamed at being jostled as they picked him up. He felt himself being carried, heard a lot of grunts and "be careful" and "try not to jostle him too much." He screamed more when someone laid him down on his back.

"We'll get you to help soon as we can," came Hank's voice.

Suddenly Jonah could tell both men were gone. He managed to open his eyes again to see pots and pans hanging from hooks inside the wagon, as well as towels and clocks and the like. The wagon began to move then, and every bump felt like getting smashed in the head all over again.

"Oh, God, let me live," he begged inwardly. "Take care of my son and my Sadie. Let me live to find them!"

24

Sadie closed her eyes and covered Paul's ears, hoping to keep him calm. If the screams they heard made him cry, their blood-thirsty captors just might decide to add his white hair to their scalp belts. Wapmimi had said Paul would not be harmed as long as she cooperated. He'd even told her the Shawnee did not kill children, but she knew better. What kind of fool did he take her for? She'd lived with the danger of Indians all her life, and she'd heard plenty of stories, even of babies being killed and scalped.

She hated being at the mercy of such an unpredictable people. If only she better understood their way of thinking, their customs and beliefs, maybe then she could feel more confident about how she should behave. She heard the gunfire as yet another settlement was attacked, heard the screams . . . screams of women, a young child crying. Then the crying suddenly stopped.

She thanked God she and Paul had been left behind

in the high grass so Paul could not witness whatever was happening. Wapmimi and his cohorts had no idea just how angry Harrison and his militia would be over this new raiding. They would come against the Shawnee and those who'd joined them with a vengeance. She was sure of it. If she could just wait out whatever was her fate and keep her precious Paul alive and unharmed, help would surely come.

She had to think positively. There was nothing else left if she wanted to go on living and bear whatever was to come. If Jonah were alive, he would tell her to do whatever she had to do to save their son, and she was trying to prepare herself for just that, steeling herself against panic and terror, trying to put Jonah's death and the deaths of Louise and Jack and Marvin to the back of her mind. Someday when this hell was over, there would be time for mourning. For now she dared not show fear or cowardice.

Now she smelled smoke. She could see black billows of it rising above the high grass. She glanced at the greased, painted warrior who watched her and saw nothing in his dark eyes. She wondered whether he was devoid of any human emotions.

"Mommy," Paul said, cringing against her breast. "Where Daddy?"

A lump rose in Sadie's throat. "Daddy is . . . he went for help, Paul. He'll send us help and we'll get to go home in a few days." She grasped his face in her hands. "And until then, you have to be very brave and not cry. As long as Mommy is here with you, you have no reason to cry, okay?"

The boy nodded, his big blue eyes showing his implicit trust in her. *Dear God, please let my words be true,* she prayed. *Don't ever let us be parted. Send us help! And let my Jonah be alive!*

The distant raid seemed to last forever. When would the shooting and war whooping and screaming stop? She waited for what seemed another hour, until finally she heard laughter and whooping and talking coming closer. Minutes later Wapmimi appeared in the small clearing where she waited with the unnamed warrior who'd just stared at her the whole time they waited. Sadie dreaded what he might be thinking, and she was actually relieved to see Wapmimi come back . . . until she saw two women's scalps hanging from his belt. His blood-spattered body looked even more hideous than when he was just painted for war. He led two new horses, and he grinned with pride at his bounty. He then handed her a slat bonnet with bloodstains on it.

"Put this on," he ordered. "White woman should keep her face from the sun."

Shuddering with horror, Sadie obeyed, feeling ill.

"Get on horse," Wapmimi then told Sadie. He stooped and cupped his hands for her to step in, and she mounted the horse he'd indicated. To her relief he then handed Paul up to her. She positioned him safely in front of her and grasped the unbridled horse's mane. It was then she had a chance to look around, and she shuddered. Several cabins and outbuildings were in flames, and she saw the bodies of three women sprawled on the ground, one with a spear through her back pinning her to the earth. All three were stripped and bloody, and all three showed ugly gashes on their heads where a good deal of their hair had been removed. One lay on her back, and it was obvious she was big with child. Her chest was split open.

"Oh, God, oh, God," she whispered. "Help me not to scream."

Was the baby in her belly still alive? She dared not give it a thought.

"Mommy, they hurt?" Paul asked.

"Yes, but they'll be fine, darling," she lied. "Let's go." She gently kicked the horse's sides to get it moving to follow Wapmimi and the others away from the scene of horror and destruction. She saw more bodies strewn about, and when she dared look back she realized only then that two of the raiders led three male captives, being led on foot with ropes around their necks. Their wrists were tied behind their backs, and they looked bloody and beaten. Surely they were the husbands or some other relatives of the horribly murdered women.

What about children? Surely with men and women, one of the women pregnant, there had been children at the settlement. She looked back again, but she saw none. Wapmimi had told her they did not kill children! He'd lied! He'd surely lied! Would he decide to do away with Paul once they reached their destination? Or would whoever he claimed she must marry decide

152

that Paul was an unnecessary burden?

She hugged Paul closer. Renewed terror engulfed her. She would do anything she had to do to keep her little boy alive and free of pain. This precious child depended on her to protect him. He believed her when she said they would be rescued and promised him he needn't be afraid. She made up her mind about one thing. If she thought for one second that these murderous savages had any ideas about harming her son, she would grab a knife if she could and sink it into the boy's heart herself, and then into her own.

25

April 4, 1811

Sadie's heart ached for the three captives who'd walked the last six days to reach the destination of their captors. One looked old enough to be her grandfather, the other two appeared to be about Jonah's age. They'd actually had to run part of the way to keep up with the horses to which they were tied so as not to fall and be dragged, and choked to death in the process. They'd been given just enough water to keep them alive, along with raw meat. They were bloody from beatings and sunburned from the long exposure to the sun without hats. Their clothes were filthy and their pants soiled from not even being allowed to properly relieve themselves.

Paul kept asking where his daddy was, and Sadie was actually glad to say he was not here. She'd rather he was dead than to suffer what these captives were suffering now. It would likely be much worse for them now that they were arriving at their destination.

Several of the Indians who'd brought them here had painted themselves before entering the village with their "prizes," proudly war whooping, laughing, talking rapidly with those who came out to meet them.

So, this was Tippecanoe, or Prophetstown, as some called it. Domed huts made of branches and bark stretched as far as the eye could see. Campfires burned in front of them, and from a few of them smoke wafted upward from a hole at the center of the domes.

Word of their arrival spread fast, and Sadie clung tightly to Paul when the first trickle of a welcoming party turned into hundreds of brown faces, men, women, and children, all smiling and laughing and cheering their brethren. Several men dragged the prisoners to an unknown fate. Sadie quickly lost sight of them, and she said a quick prayer that perhaps the old man would die quickly of a heart attack or something else before he would suffer whatever awaited him.

Suddenly Wapmimi was jerking her off her horse, and hard as she tried to cling to Paul, several women pulled the crying boy out of her arms.

"No!" she screamed, turning to Wapmimi. "You said my son would be all right if I did what you said to do! Give him back to me!"

He grasped her arm tightly. "You will see him soon enough. It is time for you to meet your new husband."

"Not until I get my son back!"

Wapmimi squeezed her arm. "Be still, or you will *never* see him! Come!"

"Let go of me! I'll walk on my own." Sadie jerked her arm away, and several Indian women began pawing her, fingering her light hair, lifting her skirts to laugh at her bloomers. Sadie whirled and shoved one of them away. They just laughed, and an older woman shoved her hard from behind, causing her to fall on her face. They all laughed more, but then Wapmimi jerked her to her feet and shouted something to the women, who all backed away and seemed to be jeering at Wapmimi and making fun of him. Another woman poked Sadie hard in the side with a stick before Wapmimi gave her a light shove. "Walk toward the river," he told her, pointing toward a stretch of trees a hundred yards or so in the distance.

The river! That would be the Wabash. She knew that much. If a person could slip away in a canoe, all he or she had to do was paddle south . . . to Vincennes! How far was it? A good two hundred miles she guessed. Wasn't that the distance Governor Harrison once told them lay between Vincennes and Prophetstown?

She searched frantically for any sign of Paul. She heard him crying. Were they hurting him? Her heart and stomach both pained her so intensely that she nearly doubled over. She could put up with whatever fate lay ahead of her if only Paul was all right and with his mommy.

She was surrounded by so many Indians that it was impossible to see past them to wherever Paul was and wherever they'd taken the prisoners. She fought tears, suspecting the women would enjoy seeing her cry and beg. Most of them were naked from the waist up, some carrying little babies in their arms or in contraptions strapped to their backs. Some of the young ones were quite pretty, with bright smiles and long, shining hair. All were cleaner than she'd imagined Indians would keep themselves, and the village, or town, or whatever they preferred to call their settlement, appeared very organized, set up much the same way whites set up their towns, the huts organized in rows. Wapmimi led her along what might be considered the main street of a white man's town, past a huge "building" of sorts, also made of branches and bark. It reminded her of what would be called a town hall in one of her own people's towns.

The thought brought a miserable longing to her chest. She missed Willow Creek worse than ever now, wondered if she would ever again see the loving relatives and beautiful farm left behind . . . or even see Vincennes again. Worst of all, she'd never see Jonah again. She had to face the fact that these heathens enjoyed blood and death. Jonah could not possibly have survived whatever happened to him back at their little farm.

He was gone from her life forever. The only way to

bear the pain of it was to concentrate on survival now, not for her own sake but for Paul's. Jonah would want her to do whatever was necessary to make sure their son was not harmed, or taken from his mother's care.

Jonah! Her sweet, strong, brave, skilled, handsome Jonah. She would never meet another like him, and it was very possible she'd never even have the chance. Little Paul just might end up being physically and psychologically trained up in the Indian way. She'd heard stories about "white" Indians, children captured and then adopted into tribes. Often they became the go-betweens in treaty conferences. She noticed that many of the children she spotted here looked perfectly healthy and happy. At least these people seemed to take good care of their own, and she'd heard they usually took good care of child captives. She prayed the stories she'd heard were true.

"Windigo!" Wapmimi suddenly shouted the name, startling Sadie from her thoughts. "I have found her!"

Sadie searched the sea of faces. Where was this Windigo? Was he as hideously ugly as Wapmimi? Again Wapmimi had to order some of the women to leave Sadie alone as they approached the last in a row of huts that led to the river.

"Windigo!" Wapmimi shouted. He turned to Sadie. "Stay!" He ducked inside the hut, its door covered with a large bear hide. He emerged momentarily with a scowl on his face. He barked something to one of the women, who just giggled and shook her head.

"Windigo!" Wapmimi shouted then, very loudly.

Sadie heard a man shout in reply, using his own tongue. Sadie tried to remember the tribe. Wapmimi had said they were not Shawnee. They were Potawatomi. The voice came from behind her to the right. She turned to look, and a young man rode up to Wapmimi on a fine red roan mare. He wore nothing but an apron over some kind of cloth tied underneath like underwear. He appeared perhaps her own age. If this was the one called Windigo, she could only be grateful he was clean and handsome, for an Indian. The lean, muscled young man dismounted and greeted Wapmimi by grasping wrists, then a quick embrace.

Sadie was amazed at the show of affection, much like two white men who were good friends or brothers might greet each other. She felt astounded at how these people seemed so normal and affectionate, the mothers cradling their babies, friends hugging each other, a literal town made up of neat, organized huts, people laughing and talking like white people at a town gathering . . . and yet they could be so cruel as to murder white women and little children, torture their husbands and fathers, steal wives from their husbands and babies from their mothers, burn and ransack their homes, murder their livestock, and in general do horrifying things to other human beings not of their own blood.

She watched the young man who'd dismounted the roan mare. His nearly waist-length, black hair looked shiny and clean, and was decorated with an abundance of tiny braids into which was wound beading and feathers and tiny pieces of tin. After speaking with Wapmimi a moment longer, the young man turned to study her, looking her over as though a prize cow.

Her stomach sank. This must surely be Windigo, the man she supposedly must wed because of Wapmimi's dreams. How crude and incredibly ridiculous! She felt sick at the thought that she just might have to bow to Wapmimi's prediction in order to keep little Paul safe.

The man's dark skin glistened in the sunlight. He was rather tall for an Indian, and in his dark eyes she saw a glint of kindness, albeit a man's hungry appreciation for what he might consider a pretty woman, or worse . . . his "bounty" from war. He grinned, a smile that would be handsome if not for his intentions. He turned back to Wapmimi and said something that included the name Tecumseh. Wapmimi frowned and seemed to argue with him for a moment. Windigo argued back, but not in an angry way. He used his hands to accent whatever he was saying, obviously trying to point out that whatever he was arguing was the right thing to do. Sadie waited, heart pounding.

Wapmimi turned to her then. "This is my friend Windigo, who will take you for a wife. He says we first must talk to our leader, Tecumseh, as Windigo is now one of Tecumseh's aides. Soon he will leave with Tecumseh to visit tribes in the south and the east, to bring more back to Prophetstown. If Windigo marries you, you will go with them."

Go with them! To the east and the south? How far? What about Paul? If they took her away from here, how would any rescuers find her? *If Windigo marries you,* Wapmimi had said. Did that mean he might *not* marry her? What would happen to her then? She had a feeling that having to take Windigo for a husband was the lesser of whatever other evils could happen to her here at the mercy of these savages. Wapmimi might decide to take her for his own wife, or perhaps trade her to some old toothless warrior who wanted a young woman in his bed. Or they could simply decide to burn her at the stake, as she'd heard some captives suffered, or skin her alive, or . . .

No! She had to stop thinking the worst. Perhaps someone had found the remains of the raid, and at this very moment Governor Harrison was gathering troops to come for her and Paul.

Wapmimi and Windigo exchanged more words, then Windigo took hold of her arm, but gently. "Come," he said in English. "We go to Tecumseh."

Sadie had no choice but to obey. They headed back toward the huge building she'd seen earlier, which she suspected was what the Shawnee called a longhouse, where they held important meetings. Her legs felt like they were filled with water and would collapse on her at any moment.

❦

26

April 4, 1811

The voices sounded mumbled and distant. Jonah
struggled to understand the words.

"Massacre . . ."

"Scalps . . ."

"Women . . ."

"Near half dead . . ."

"Head split open . . ."

"Miracle . . ."

"Dirty savages . . ."

"Bloodthirsty . . ."

"Buried what was left . . ."

"Left the livestock to the buzzards . . ."

Men's voices. Women's voices. Once in a while the
squeal of a child.

"Get away from there!"

"Mommy, is he dead?"

"No, and he doesn't need any noise right now. Let
him rest."

Who were they talking about? And who *were* they,
anyway? He tried to open his eyes, but they wouldn't
budge. He tried again, managing only a slither. Just
that little bit of movement brought ungodly pain to his
head. He wanted to scream from it, but he couldn't
make a sound.

He noticed people walking about in the room where he lay, a room that his impeded gaze did not recognize. All he could see was some flowered wallpaper and what looked like a rather fancy ceiling light, a chandelier, actually, its candles lit.

"If they took them captive, it's likely they're dead by now. And the mood the Shawnee are in lately, there's no sense going after them. They'd kill them for spite."

Where on earth was he? And why did everything seem so odd, as though this were all a dream? Perhaps it was, after all.

"Look, dear, his eyes are open!" A rather plain-looking woman leaned closer. "Mr. Wilde? Can you hear me?"

Of course he could hear her. Was she daft? Something about her looked familiar. Now a man leaned closer. "Jonah? Jonah Wilde?"

The man had dark, bushy eyebrows and a very narrow, prominent nose. Jonah struggled to think . . . Harrison! It was Governor Harrison! He tried to say his name, but his mouth would not move.

Why! What was wrong? It took every last ounce of strength he had to slowly blink his eyes.

"Good God I think he's indeed paralyzed," he heard the governor tell the woman. His wife, that's who she was. The governor's wife. Was he in their home? Was that the squeal of their children he heard?

Children . . . children . . . he had a child, didn't he? Yes, a son! A little boy with blue eyes like his own but light hair like his . . . mommy's.

Sadie! Oh, God, where was Sadie? And where was Paul? What had happened to his precious wife and son? He had to get up! He had to go find them! He tried to rise. Oh, he tried so hard!

God, no! Nothing would move! Nothing! And he couldn't even feel the bed upon which he lay! He felt nothing at all! This couldn't be happening!

"Mr. Wilde, do you recognize me?" The governor leaned closer. "I'm Governor Harrison. Some traders found you and brought you here. It's obvious you and your family suffered some kind of Indian raid. They're all dead—all but you. It's truly a miracle you're alive, Mr. Wilde. We'll do all we can for you. Blink if you understand me, will you?"

Jonah again struggled for that one little flutter, his heart crashing in on him as reality took precedence. He could not move anything more than an eyelid! He couldn't even tell if he was breathing, but he must be, or he wouldn't be hearing these voices and seeing these faces.

All dead? No! He would not believe that! He remembered now—remembered seeing Jack, and Marvin, and Louise, and Jenny the cow, the chickens, the horses. He remembered the smell of burning prairie. But he did not remember seeing Sadie or Paul. Indians took captives sometimes, didn't they? And if Sadie was a captive, he might be able to find her, barter for her. Paul, too.

Had the traders found their bodies, too? Had they reported burying *two* women? A little boy?

163

If they took them captive, it's likely they're dead by now. And the mood the Shawnee are in lately, there's no sense going after them. They'd kill them for spite.

He remembered someone saying that. That meant they *did* realize Sadie and Paul were missing! But it also sounded like they were going to give up on finding them. They couldn't! It wasn't fair!

He *had* to get up! Again he struggled to move. Nothing! Nothing! Tears began to fill his eyes at the realization of his helplessness. Never in his life had he known such utter terror. He'd rather face more attacking savages than this!

Sadie! He should have been ready for an attack! He shouldn't have left her alone at the soddy! Her and his precious son! Sadie! Sadie! He had to go find her!

"Oh, you poor man," Mrs. Harrison said, leaning over and pressing a cloth to his eyes.

"Oh, Bill, he's weeping."

Thank God he could feel the cool cloth on his face. That was a start. Surely this horrible helplessness was only temporary. All his life he'd been strong and able. He'd farmed and fought Indians and sometimes beat Jeremiah at arm wrestling. He'd raced horses at the Willow Creek picnics, and he could pitch hay higher and in larger quantities than any man around.

But this wasn't Willow Creek. Why had he left there? How he'd love to see Jeremiah's face right now, and the faces of his younger brother, and Regina, and his nephews. How he'd love to hear Marvin's sloppy English, and hear Louise admonishing him about something, hear young Jack's good-natured laughter.

He sensed others were in the room—citizens of Vincennes, no doubt, wanting to know what had happened. Again he heard a child's voice.

"Go on with you now," Mrs. Harrison said. "Let's leave the man alone. Let him rest. He just might come around. One never knows with a head wound as bad as his."

Head wound? No wonder he felt the pain again. But if he was paralyzed and couldn't feel anything from the neck down, why could he feel the pain in his head? In spite of its fierceness, he took it as another sign that eventually feeling would return to the rest of his body.

"Don't worry, Mr. Wilde," Harrison told him. "We'll take good care of you. Others will take turns helping. If you don't get to where you can move any time soon, we'll work something out so you'll always be cared for."

Mrs. Harrison again bathed his face. *We'll take good care of you.* Good God, what if he was paralyzed for the rest of his life! He'd rather be shot! If he could move his hands, he'd do it himself . . . if not for the thought that Sadie and Paul might still be alive. He wished he could talk, tell the governor he had to go look for them. But he'd heard someone say there was no sense in that. Why not? It always made sense to try to save a white woman from Indian captivity, didn't it?

Harrison! He'd like to kill the man right now for promising them that if they settled where they did they would not have to worry about Indian trouble! It was all a lie! And now here the man sat in his fancy mansion in a protected town, telling others it was useless to go after poor Sadie and Paul!

His emotions ran wild. He hated the man, yet he was grateful he'd opened his home to such a helpless patient.

"Bill, what if the woman and boy are still alive?" he heard Mrs. Harrison ask her husband.

"It's very unlikely," Harrison answered her. "Not with the mood of Tecumseh and the others right now. Riding into Prophetstown to find out is out of the question. Tecumseh is up to something and is still willing to talk peace, so let's just wait and see for a while. In the meantime I'll build up the Indiana militia and be ready for whatever comes. If they have Mrs. Wilde and the boy, they took them either as captives for torture, or they intend to adopt them into the tribe for some reason. We have to hope it's the latter so when the time is right we can get them back."

When the time is right? Jonah wanted to scream. He could do absolutely nothing now but lie here and pray inwardly that indeed, Sadie and Paul were safe and sound, albeit terrified and heartbroken. They probably thought he was dead and they had no hope of being rescued. Sadie was a smart, strong woman. She'd know what to do . . . and she'd do whatever might be necessary to protect little Paul.

The thought sickened him.

Harrison and his wife left the room, and Jonah lay

there alone, staring at the chandelier and the flowered wallpaper. More tears slipped down his cheeks, and he felt his body jerk when a sob engulfed his throat.

Sadie! My beautiful Sadie, I failed you, and Paul, too. Dear God, I failed you both! I'll never forgive myself. May God protect you until I can come for you. And I will come for you! I will!

27

April 5, 1811

For lack of something better to do, and to keep her sanity, Sadie began studying the structure of the longhouse where she'd been kept since arriving the day before at Prophetstown. The building was surprisingly huge, supported by thick tree limbs, those along the walls literal trunks. Everything was strapped together tightly and covered with bark and hides. Overnight she heard it rain hard, but everything inside stayed dry.

She struggled not to think about what her fate might be. Windigo had brought her here yesterday and tied her wrists together, then tied her to a tree around which the longhouse had been built. Twice three Indian women had come to untie her long enough to take her outside and let her relieve herself away from the village. One of the women was quite large and carried a sturdy stick that she posed threateningly over

Sadie as she took care of business, obviously telling her she'd beat her with it if she tried to fight or run away.

Sadie had no such plans, certainly not while she had no idea what had happened to Paul. She still had not seen him since he was torn from her arms the day before. She could only hope he was being well cared for, as Wapmimi had promised would be the case as long as she cooperated.

The organization and near civilization of the Shawnee surprised her, considering their ruthless treatment of their supposed enemies when out in the field. Here, although not living in wood or brick homes, the village layout was well planned. The place where they took her for personal duties was well away from the village, as it should be. So far everyone she'd seen appeared clean, albeit dressed far differently from any whites. Half the women didn't even cover their breasts, and the men were even more naked. Their skin was shiny, from some kind of animal fat, she guessed, probably to ward off mosquitoes; but they did not smell bad . . . just different . . . more like the earth and smoke and plants. Their hair appeared clean, often tied neatly or braided, and some wore cloth turbans. Most were in her eyes hideously pierced. Even the men wore earrings and necklaces.

Here in the longhouse it looked to her as though whole families lived in divided areas on either side of the building. The center was open, and last night there was a gathering here of Wapmimi and those who'd raided with him, as well as other men from the village. They had talked and laughed and smoked and drummed and danced, women later joining them, all obviously celebrating the victories and spoils of the Indian raids against the hated whites. Wapmimi had brought back many horses, blankets, rifles, clothing, flour, sugar, pots and pans, and assorted other booty.

He'd also brought scalps . . . one of them Louise's . . . one of them obviously a child's. It sickened her and also confused her that he and the others could be so violent and ruthless and unfeeling. She'd seen women nursing their babies, holding and hugging them. She'd even noticed men and women being affectionate with each other, real families, apparently. Yet they could decide at any moment to burn her and the other prisoners at the stake, or run them through with a spear and scalp them.

She'd not seen the three male prisoners since arriving, nor had she heard one word in English since being tied here not far from where all the celebrating and dancing took place. When this morning they all sat in a circle nearby and talked, sometimes raising their voices, sometimes pointing to her, sometimes seeming to be reasoning with each other about something, she knew the discussion was over what to do with her and the other prisoners.

Where was Windigo in all of this? He'd left her here yesterday and had not returned. She remembered he'd said that her fate needed to be discussed with the infamous leader Tecumseh himself, but from what she could tell, the man had not yet made an appearance. Perhaps Windigo was with him right now, arguing that she be spared the normal fate of a prisoner; and, she prayed, arguing that Paul should be allowed to be with her.

She wanted, needed, to mourn for Jonah; but this was not the time. Maybe the time would never come. As long as she was at the mercy of these people, she was determined to appear strong and unafraid. Oh, how she missed Jonah! How she would relish the sight of him right now, the feel of his strong arms around her, reassuring her that she was safe. Never again would she know that feeling of lying close to him, the taste of his mouth, the glory of being his woman. Never would she give him another child like they'd both wanted, or hear him whisper in her ear that he loved her, or feel the gentle touch of a man who could break her in half if he had the notion. Never again would she look into those blue, blue eyes or see his handsome smile or run her fingers through his thick, dark hair or hear him laugh or . . . .

Wapmimi came into the longhouse then, interrupting her thoughts with the way he strode proudly with his warriors behind him. This time Windigo was with him. The young man glanced her way with a rather arrogant look in his dark eyes. Had some decision been made? More men came inside now, led by someone she hadn't seen yet, but who stood a little taller than most of them. He was clean and good-looking, and he held himself almost regally. He wore a white man's calico shirt with fringed, deerskin leggings and a fancy, beaded apron. His hair hung straight and was topped with a red turban wrapped neatly around his head, accented with beading. A beaded knife sheath was strapped to his side, and he wore knee-high moccasins. He stopped to turn and look at her as he passed, staring at her intently for a moment and saying something in the Shawnee tongue. He walked on then, sitting down at a central fire around which the rest of those present sat in a circle. The man remained standing and began speaking in a rich voice resonant with authority.

Tecumseh! It had to be the infamous Shawnee leader. Something about the way he carried himself and the way he spoke told her so. Maybe, just maybe, if she mentioned Governor Harrison—that Harrison had said Tecumseh was usually a fair man and wanted peace—maybe she could talk to the Shawnee leader and convince him to let her and Paul go free. After all, how could there be peace if the Shawnee held white captives?

The obvious leader of the meeting carried on for quite some time. He seemed to be admonishing Wapmimi. Good! He was upset about the raids! She began to take hope in what appeared to be a chastisement. Wapmimi had his turn, and then Windigo. Her heart dropped when Tecumseh nodded his head and seemed to agree with something.

The meeting lasted for what Sadie guessed was at least an hour. Then to her horror, the three white male prisoners were led inside the longhouse, ropes still around their necks. Their shirts and shoes were gone, their trousers ripped and bloodstained. The old man could barely walk, and their backs and chests were so covered with ugly bruises, cuts, and welts that Sadie had to look away.

Now the group of warriors became excited, and Sadie changed her mind about their being civilized. To her their excitement was like that of a pack of wolves that smelled blood and wanted to attack their helpless, wounded prey. There came further discussions, and then Tecumseh, if indeed that was who the obvious leader was, seemed to make a final decision of some sort, waving his arms and appearing to be giving directions.

The gathering suddenly broke into whooping, cheering, laughing warriors, who dragged the prisoners back outside. Wapmimi followed, but Windigo approached Sadie. He untied her from the tree but left her wrists tied.

"You are mine now," he told her. "I will take you to the women who will dress you as a proper Potawatomi bride, and your ears will be pierced, your hair greased and braided. Then you will be brought to my *wigawa*."

"What?" Sadie tried to think. Everything happened with such finality. "I . . . can't I talk to Tecumseh first? Is that who led your meeting? Was that Tecumseh?"

"It was. And he is too important to talk to a mere captive white woman. Soon he will leave again to visit tribes in the south. I will go with him . . . and so will you . . . as my wife." He kept hold of the rope tied at her wrists and pulled her closer. "I will not be cruel, if you simply do as I say and behave like a wife should."

Sadie fought panic. Didn't this young man realize she mourned for her husband? And what about Paul? "Where's my son?" she demanded. "I was promised that he could be with me! If I can't be with my son you might as well put me to death! I'll be no wife to you unless my son can live with us, too!"

Windigo said nothing as he pulled her out of the longhouse and toward an area where the three other prisoners were being tied to the trunks of three dead trees that were scorched from previous fires. Several women were stacking wood around the trees, just far enough away that heat from a fire could scorch the skin without the flames touching it. The three men had been stripped naked.

"Oh, dear God!"

"Today they will slowly die," Windigo told her. "Their skin will first blister, and women will poke the blisters with sticks. After a while their lungs will burn inside of them whenever they take a breath, and their flesh will roast like that of a pig or a fresh-killed deer."

"Stop it!" Sadie screamed at him. She looked away when one of the men began sobbing. "How can you be so cruel"—she glared into his dark eyes—"and then expect me to have any kind of feelings for you as a husband! You're animals! *All* of you!"

He grasped her arms. "Hear me, Sadie Wilde! Today I saved your life! *And* your son's! When the women are through washing and dressing you, you will be brought to me, and I will make you my wife. Then your son will be brought to live with us. This I promise. But never forget that if you try to escape, or if you try to harm me when I sleep or do anything to disrespect me as a husband, I will have no control over what will be done with you! Do you understand?"

The fires were lit, and the old male prisoner began screaming for God to take him quickly. Sadie stared into Windigo's eyes. Her fate was sealed, if she had any hope of holding her son close again.

"I understand," she answered coldly.

Windigo nodded matter-of-factly. "If you are truly the woman in Wapmimi's vision, our children will be the ones to bring peace, for both white blood and Potawatomi blood will run in their veins, and it will be good. You will see. One day you will even come to me willingly, when you learn what a good husband and provider I will be. I am an honored warrior, a man you should be proud to call husband. I am even honored by Tecumseh and am considered one of his closest aides. That is why you are not burning at the stake with the other three prisoners." He turned and started walking, jerking her with him. "Come."

Shivering with dread, screaming inside with grief, Sadie had no choice but to follow. The horrifying screams of the prisoners made her want to cover her ears and scream herself, but she could do neither. Her hands were tied . . . and if she screamed, it might denote disrespect.

She had to think of Paul, her poor, small, chubby, angel-faced little boy who needed his mommy. That was all that mattered.

28

"I am Serena, Windigo's mother."

The words came from the stern woman who shoved a thin cord of leather through Sadie's sore and still-bleeding earlobe. Tied to the cord were several tiny pieces of tin that tinkled as Serena tied them in place. She then tied another dangling earring to Sadie's other ear.

Both ears still burned and stung from being pierced with a pointed piece of bone, and now she felt ashamed of the gaudy, heathen decorations. The holes in her ears would forever brand her as an Indian captive. Even if she was rescued, women would whisper about her, and if he was alive and found her, Jonah surely would never love or want her in the same way he once did.

That thought alone, and knowing this was the only way to keep Paul protected, helped her face the inevitable. Serena stepped back and looked her over, actually smiling with what looked like pride. "You are a beautiful white woman. My son will be well pleased."

I don't care if he is pleased or not, Sadie thought angrily. *He'll not see an ounce of desire or pleasure in my eyes! I hate him! I hate all of you!*

175

Aloud she said nothing, afraid to displease Serena, who seemed highly respected by the other Potawatomi women who'd taken part in bathing her, greasing her hair, weaving tiny braids into it that were decorated with beads. She wore a beaded, bleached buckskin dress that though she hated the reason for wearing it, she could not help but notice was exceedingly beautiful. She thought the beadwork must have taken weeks. Serena told her she'd made the dress over two years earlier, knowing that someday her son would marry.

"I'd hoped my son's wife would be a respected Potawatomi woman," she pointed out to Sadie now. "But to us dreams have great meaning. To ignore them is to bring bad luck and perhaps even death on the one who refuses to act. Wapmimi is Windigo's best friend, and a respected warrior. His dreams carry much meaning. And so Windigo will marry you because Wapmimi says he must."

Sadie tossed her head. "Wapmimi! Why should his dreams affect Windigo?"

Serena eyed her narrowly. "In our own lifetimes we might never know the reason for this. The answer might come only through the children you have with Windigo."

Sadie felt the fire of dread move through her blood, and she turned away. "I already have a child, and a *husband*. I neither love nor desire your son. Why would he want to marry me instead of a young virgin of his own blood?"

"I already told you. It simply must be so. And you do *not* have a husband. He is dead. Wapmimi made sure of it. And your son will now be adopted by Windigo and the Potawatomi. He will be raised our way, learn our language and customs. He will be given a new name, and at his young age he will soon forget his old life, and his white father. He—"

"Stop it! Surely you have a husband, too! How can you think I could so easily forget my own? I *loved* Jonah!" She whirled around. "And I'm *white!* My *son* is white! Nothing can change that!"

Serena sighed deeply. "Yes, I had a husband. I was right beside him when a white man with the Michigan militia shot him in the head as he came out of our hut unarmed! He then rode off with me and raped me, he and several others!" Her dark eyes flickered then with anger and hatred. "I assure you that lying with my son as his legal wife will be *nothing* like what I suffered! And no, I will never forget *my* husband either. I *do* understand what you are saying. But the circle of life goes on, and because of Wapmimi's dream your life must now be here, with the Potawatomi. And you must protect my son by submitting to him so that Wapmimi's dream will be fulfilled. You have no choice! You are a very lucky woman to be allowed to keep your son with you. There are many Potawatomi women who would gladly take him. If you refuse to do this, he will be given away, and you will be turned away and become a slave. Is that what you want?"

Sadie closed her eyes. "What I want is to go home

to my own people. If my husband is dead, then I will go back to Ohio, where his brothers live. Surely you know I don't belong here. I'm sorry for what happened to you, but your people do terrible things to *my* people, too! It has to *end* somewhere, Serena!"

The woman nodded. "Yes. But who will take the first step? We have signed treaty after treaty, tried to keep our word. But it was *your* people who continually broke their promises. Tecumseh will stand for us, for the Shawnee, the Potawatomi, the Delaware, the Miamis, the Kickapoo, even some of the Sioux to the west of us follow Tecumseh now. He will unite all of us into a force the Americans cannot defeat! They will *have* to listen to us! And *then* it will all end, Sadie Wilde, all the fighting and killing. Come. It is time to go to him."

Serena ducked out of the hut, and for a moment Sadie stood frozen in place. She could hardly believe this was real. Surely it was all a bad dream. Terror and dread engulfed her so that she could hardly feel her own feet when she finally forced them to move.

She made up her mind that the longer she lived, and the longer she was able to keep Paul with her, the more chance she would have to find a way to escape this living hell. To cooperate would mean no harm would come to her, and that was important. She couldn't escape if she was highly watched as a slave and if Paul was taken from her to a place where she couldn't find him. She couldn't escape if she was beaten and sick. Perhaps becoming the wife of an honored warrior was God's way of giving her a chance to live . . . and eventually to escape.

She followed Serena to Windigo's hut. Women lined both sides of the pathway, smiling, giggling, whispering. Some began to sing a rather lilting chant, swaying side to side with the rhythm of the song. Serena stepped aside and motioned for Sadie to enter the hut.

Feeling as though she was being led to her execution, Sadie ducked inside, surprised at the neat condition of Windigo's round home, and the pleasant smell from something burning inside.

Windigo stood tall and dark, his skin shining, his hair looking clean, and he, too, wore white buckskins. He smiled, walking closer and touching her hair. Sadie forced all emotions deep inside to that place where only she could find them again when she was ready. For now she would think only of Jonah. Jonah. It would be Jonah touching her . . . Jonah taking her. She would close her eyes and he would be there. In spite of any physical interaction, no man on earth could truly touch her the way Jonah had, deep into her heart, mind, and soul. There was a difference between taking a woman, and actually owning that woman to the very fiber of her being. That part of her belonged to Jonah and would never belong to another.

Windigo pulled her down to a soft, bearskin-covered bed of robes. She closed her eyes and took deep breaths to keep from screaming, reminding herself that as soon as this was over, she could be with Paul.

29

June 6, 1811

Betsy Jarvis moved about the room quietly, gently tucking the covers at the foot of Jonah's bed, picking up his water glass and going out, returning shortly with fresh water. Jonah followed her every movement, wondering how he could ever thank her and her family enough for what they'd been doing for him. He'd lain here in a bed in what was Betsy's room for two months now, cared for by Betsy and her mother, lifted and helped by the husband and father, Tom Jarvis, whenever he needed to relieve himself.

Betsy was only allowed to feed him and keep the room clean, and only after Tom and Betsy's mother, Fiona, got Jonah out of bed and into a chair was Betsy, eighteen and unmarried, allowed to then come in and change the bedding.

With a great deal of effort Jonah spoke Betsy's name, having finally gained his ability to speak just one week ago.

Betsy looked at him and smiled, her green eyes and light hair reminding him of Sadie. "Good morning, Mr. Wilde."

He managed a smile and was actually able to scoot himself up a little, although it tired him greatly. He thanked God every minute of every day that he was able to move again, although he still could not walk. "Surely you can call me Jonah by now," he told Betsy.

Betsy actually blushed a little, something he'd noticed she did a lot now that he could speak and move and was more aware of people around him. "If you say it's all right."

"Of course I do. And I've been thinking about something." His voice was still weak, and talking made him feel out of breath. How he hated being this way, especially hating the fact that he could not get on a horse and go look for Sadie. God only knew what she'd been through by now, if she was even still alive. And where was his precious son?

Betsy pulled a chair closer to his bed. "What have you been thinking about, Mr. Wilde?" She sat down and folded her hands in her lap.

Jonah was slightly taken aback for a moment when he could have sworn a look of love flashed into her eyes . . . well, maybe not love, but certainly concern and adoration. Good Lord, did the girl have feelings for him?

He rubbed at his eyes and pretended not to notice. "I'm considering sending a letter to my brothers in Ohio," he told her. "I never got the chance to write last year when we first arrived, and now after all that's happened . . . I guess my family should know."

"I think that's a good idea, Mr. . . . I mean, Jonah. They would want to know."

"Yes, but I'm worried my older brother, Jeremiah,

will think he needs to come here and help; but he's needed at the farm."

"I guess only you know what's best."

Jonah stared at the low log ceiling of the Jarvis cabin. "It was my idea to come out here. I hate to bring Jeremiah into this. He'll think he has to go riding off to find my wife, and he could get himself killed."

Betsy touched his arm. "You shouldn't blame yourself for all of this. A man has to do what's in his heart to do, and this country would never grow if there weren't men like my father, and you, who are brave enough to go into new lands and settle."

Jonah grunted a laugh of self-chastisement. "At least your father had sense enough to settle close to Vincennes where it was safer."

"Well, now, you never know. Pa says it wouldn't surprise him at all if that Tecumseh and especially his crazy, one-eyed brother, the Prophet, decided to gather together an army of Shawnee and attack this town. Being here doesn't always mean you're safer."

"Maybe not, but it's better than what I did." He closed his eyes. "Every time I think about what could have happened to my wife and son . . ." His voice choked, another thing he hated about being so weak and vulnerable. He broke down easier, and that angered him, especially in front of a woman.

"Can you even be sure they were taken alive?" Betsy asked cautiously.

"They must have been." Jonah wiped at his eyes.

"Those who found me said there was only one woman found killed, and they didn't find a little boy's body." He breathed deeply. "Poor Louise Stockton. And her son, Jack, what a nice young man he was. And Marvin . . ." He swallowed. "Such nice people. We couldn't have got through those first few months without them. It isn't fair that they had to die that way. And it sure isn't fair that my poor, loving wife, who I know didn't really want to come here, had to suffer for my dreams. And my little boy . . ." He sniffed. "I don't think I'll ever get over the guilt of it. I don't deserve to still be alive."

"Yes you do, Jonah Wilde!" She squeezed his arm. "You shouldn't feel like this. No man can predict what will happen in his life, and when a woman marries, she expects to have to do some things she doesn't agree with. That's just the way it is. A man has dreams and ambitions, and if a woman truly feels loved and protected by him, she doesn't mind following her man wherever he takes her."

Jonah felt the words were spoken with a little too much passion. He wiped at his eyes again and breathed another deep sigh to keep his composure, his curiosity over Betsy's grand words helping ease his pain by giving him something else to think about.

"Soon as I'm able to walk again, I'm going to look for my wife and son," he told her. He shifted in bed again, an excuse to get the girl to let go of his arm. "I'll find them or die trying."

"After all we've done to keep you alive?"

Jonah grinned a little, then saddened. "I wish I could think of the best way to repay you and your family, Betsy, taking me in like you did for such long-term care. If I don't get all feeling back in a few more weeks, I'll have to find someone to take me back to Ohio and let my own family care for me. I can't keep putting all of you out like this. And I'm sure you'd like your room back."

"I don't mind, really. Helping someone in need is the Christian thing to do. Ma fixed up a nice bed for me in the loft with my little brother. We've got plenty of room, and Pa, he does good with his tanning business out back, which leaves him close to home all the time, so he doesn't mind coming in to help you when you need it. Ma does laundry and mending for others, so we've always got plenty of food and all that. Having one extra person isn't all that bad. I hope you'll stay here till you're completely well. Ma hopes that her working with your legs, even though you can't really use them yet, will help keep the muscles strong so it won't take long for you to walk again once you get all your feeling back."

He studied her slender build for a moment, appreciating her nice shape. "You sound awfully sure I *will* walk again."

"Of course you will. I pray for it every night before I go to bed." Her full lips parted in a literally loving smile.

Good Lord, Jonah thought again. Maybe he needed to get out of this house quicker than he thought. "Well,

I thank you for that, Betsy. God surely listens to someone as giving and sweet as you."

She blushed again. "Thank you, Jonah." Their eyes held for a moment, then she pushed back her chair as though suddenly alarmed. "I'd better go help Ma with the butter churn. She's waiting for me." She stood there rather awkwardly for a moment. "If you decide to write your family, you let me know, Jonah. I can write real good. I'll write the letter for you and Pa will make sure it gets back to Ohio. What town would it go to?"

"Willow Creek." Jonah suddenly felt melancholy with memories, remembering the first time he'd kissed Sadie . . . at a harvest dance. Even before that he knew he was in love with her.

30

June 30, 1811

Sadie presented Windigo with a pair of beaded moccasins. "How do you like my work?"

Windigo looked them over. "It is good. My mother has taught you well."

Her feelings mixed, Sadie sat down across from the man with whom she'd shared a *wigiwa* for two months now. She would never truly think of Windigo as her husband, but so far he'd at least kept his promise, and other than when he decided to exercise

185

his husbandly rights, she slept with Paul close to her. Windigo did not often impose upon her for conjugal visits, for the young man knew she still did not care for him as a wife should. In return, Sadie did her best to be a wife to him in every other way, partly out of a secret gratefulness that he'd kept his promises not to harm her or Paul, and partly because she could not get over the worry that if she displeased the man, it could change everything for the worse.

There was one other reason: feelings she had for Windigo. Not feelings of love, but rather grateful obligation . . . and a growing dependency. Windigo represented warmth, food, supplies, and protection in this frightening new world into which she'd been thrown. He was handsome, strong, and brave, and her only safe refuge. The longer she lived here in Prophetstown, the easier it became to dress like the other women, learn their work, how they cooked and made their clothes, learn to help Windigo make weapons . . . *weapons that will likely be used against whites* . . . learn some of both the Potawatomi and Shawnee tongues, and learn to admire their leader, Tecumseh.

Just two weeks ago more prisoners had been brought to the village after raiding, and Tecumseh ordered that they not be tortured. For now they were being held in the longhouse, for what purpose, Sadie did not know, nor would Windigo say.

She glanced over to see Paul napping, then addressed Windigo as she picked up a blue calico shirt he liked to wear. It needed mending. "Your mother told me something today that disturbs me, Windigo," she said, taking to the shirt with needle and thread sold to Serena by English traders.

Windigo leaned against a backrest made of woven reeds. "What is that?"

"She said the pretty young Potawatomi woman named Tima has always dreamed to catch your eye, and that her heart is broken over you taking me for a wife." She watched him closely, saw his smile fade.

"Tima is just that—a dreamer. There can be nothing between us. She is seventeen summers now, old enough to allow some other warrior to court her."

Sadie had been with this man long enough now to at least feel easier about talking with him. She'd learned he was twenty-two summers, knew what he liked to eat, understood the right ways to approach him with requests. She'd gratefully learned that women had considerable say in what went on inside a couple's private hut, which gave her the privilege of often turning Windigo away in the night, often enough to bear what she must put up with.

She breathed deeply for courage to ask the next question. "Do you wish there *could* be something between you and Tima?"

Windigo took a white man's pipe out of his mouth and studied it as he spoke. "Sometimes."

The admission surprised Sadie. "Then take me to Vincennes, Windigo, and take Tima for your wife."

His dark eyes shot her a look of literal disappointment. "You know that I cannot. I have explained that to you." He sat up straighter. "Will you never have feelings for me?"

Literal sorrow shone in his eyes, and Sadie thought how proud she would be as his wife if she were of his own kind. "I do have feelings for you, Windigo, of gratefulness, and dependency; but not of love. How can I love a man whose people murdered the man I *truly* loved, and took me away from the only life I've ever known?"

Now he snickered and leaned back again. "Surely the longer you are with us, the more you see this is a good life. We are human beings, just like you and your kind. We love the same, have children, eat and drink and sleep the same. It is no different here than where you came from. And we only fight the white man because of what he tries to take from us. If he would stay off our land and keep his promises, there would be none of this trouble. The redcoats tell us that war is coming, war against the Americans. When it does, we will join them in the fighting. Perhaps by then you will be Potawatomi here"—he put a fist to his chest—"in your heart. I wish it could be so."

Sadie would not tell him that she had not given up hope of being rescued. How she missed her old friends, her husband and family, Willow Creek, even the dirt house Jonah had built for her with so much sweat and hard labor. And yet, she wondered if she truly should try harder to adapt. After all, she'd given up hope that Jonah could have survived the slaughter at their farm . . . and for all she knew it could be months before she was found, maybe years. By then . . .

Please don't let it be so! she prayed. She'd not had her time of month since that first night she gave herself to Windigo. It had sickened her to betray Jonah that way. That's what it had felt like. The only way she managed to lie still for Windigo since that night was to always, always think of Jonah touching her, entering her, filling her with his life . . . and love.

Yet now, if she carried Windigo's child, could she ever be accepted into her old life again if she *was* rescued? Was it best to accept this life and never go back? Living like other Potawatomi women was not so different from the hard work she'd put forth as a new settler on the prairie. She just went about performing her chores much differently than a white woman would; and in fact, the way the Potawatomi dressed was much more comfortable than the restrictive clothing of white women.

She had to face the real possibility that if she was rescued, Jonah's family might disown her and her Indian baby and keep Paul from his shamed mother. She could end up being shunned and cast out, never able to rejoin white society.

"Sometimes I also wish I could give my heart to your people," she told Windigo, "because . . ." She decided to tell him. After all, her key instinct was still survival for her and for Paul. Knowing she might be carrying his child would only help seal Windigo's promise that she would never be harmed. Ever since seeing prisoners tortured by fire, hearing their screams until finally God, in His mercy, took them out of their misery, had forever instilled in her a fear of the same demise.

"Because I am carrying your child," she finished.

Windigo's dark eyes brightened as he bolted upright again. "You are sure?"

"One more month will make me sure." It was evident by the look in his dark eyes that he was very pleased.

"I am glad! My mother will also be glad! And so will Wapmimi."

Sadie's slice of peace vanished at the mention of Windigo's scarred friend. She didn't care what Wapmimi thought of anything. He was the man who'd led the raid that ended in Jonah's death and her captivity. And just because of his dreams, Windigo listened to everything Wapmimi said to do. For all she knew the ugly warrior could turn around and tell Windigo that Sadie and/or the baby must die, or that Paul should be given away!

Before she could reply there came a commotion from outside the *wigawa*.

"We will talk more about this tonight!" Windigo told her as he rose and set his pipe aside. "I will go and see why the dogs are barking so wildly and men are shouting. You stay here."

He ducked outside, and Sadie waited. Minutes later two older warriors came inside. Sadie frowned. "What do you want?"

"We watch you. You stay here. Keep boy here," one

who spoke a little English answered.

"Why? What's happening?"

The man frowned, showing with his threatening eyes that he meant what he said about her not leaving. "White soldier come, from Vincennes. Bring letter from Harrison. Windigo not want him see you."

A *white* man! If he knew she was here, he could get help for her and Paul! And maybe he knew something about Jonah, if he was dead or alive! How tempting it was to duck and run, to scream to the soldier her name and beg him to help her!

She glanced at Paul, then looked up at the older warriors. She would never get past them, and to try to do so could be considered an unforgivable betrayal that might bring dire consequences. She didn't worry for herself anymore, but she would put up with anything to protect Paul.

She sat quietly mending, screaming silently to the soldier to please come and help her.

31

A council was quickly called, Windigo being asked to join Tecumseh inside his large *wigawa* to act as the official representative of the Potawatomi. The Indian leader thanked the hundreds of Indians who'd gathered around to greet the soldier minutes earlier, then invited the uniformed man inside for a talk. The white soldier, who introduced himself as Captain Walter

Wilson of the Fourth Regiment of the United States Army, appeared pale and apprehensive, as did most whites who dared come to Tippecanoe. He was accompanied by three Frenchmen, something that certainly did not meet with the favor of the Shawnee, but the fact that he'd announced he was sent here with yet another message from Governor Harrison kept him safe from harm, for now.

Wilson was shoved into Tecumseh's *wigawa,* where the man gawked at his surroundings. Windigo could tell he was impressed with the room and furnishings inside the tidy dwelling. Tecumseh even had a white man's desk, where he kept journals in the white man's writing.

As was custom, Tecumseh first offered food to his visitor. Windigo smiled at the way Tecumseh had of charming the enemy into making them feel easy and perhaps give away a little more information than necessary. The compelling Indian leader engaged in a friendly conversation while the soldier ate and began to look more relaxed and confident. Finally Tecumseh got to the point, asking the soldier's business at Prophetstown.

"I have brought you a letter from Governor Harrison," the captain answered. He reached into his shirt and pulled out an oilskin-wrapped parchment, opening it and offering to read it to Tecumseh.

Raising his chin proudly, Tecumseh replied, "I will read it myself."

Windigo smiled, thinking how Tecumseh's knowledge of English reading and writing gave him even more power against the enemy. As the leader read the letter, Windigo studied the fancily dressed captain, wondering what Sadie's husband had looked like. Would he be considered handsome by white man's standards? Sometimes he could tell by Sadie's eyes that she thought that he, Windigo, was also handsome. Much as he hated to admit it, he'd come to have feelings for his white wife, deeper feelings than he thought possible. He actually wished she would show some kind of emotion and affection toward him, wished she would take him in the night as though she truly wanted him.

Wapmimi had made the right choice, for Windigo was beginning to cherish Sadie. That could only mean the woman was indeed meant to be a part of his life, and the presence of the white soldier here today worried him. It was important that he not see Sadie or her son, or the man might go back with stories of an imprisoned white woman who needed rescuing.

Never! Never would he allow white men to come and take Sadie from him. She belonged to him now, and one day soon, she would be *glad* she belonged to him!

Tecumseh folded the letter, glancing at Windigo before speaking. "You ask about white prisoners," he said.

Windigo's heart beat faster.

"We have none," Tecumseh continued.

Windigo glanced at his leader. Tecumseh was protecting him from losing Sadie!

"There is no one here who is not Indian at heart," Tecumseh added. He turned to Windigo. "Is that not so, Windigo?"

Windigo gave the man a grateful glance. Yes, Sadie seemed more Indian than white now, and little Paul played with little Indian boys, behaving just as they did. "Yes, that's so," he answered, turning to nod toward the captain.

Captain Wilson sighed. "It's just that there is a white man in Vincennes who survived an Indian attack. Those who found him say that not everyone from his party was found at the place where they were attacked. This white man believes his wife and son might still live. His name is Jonah Wilde, and his wife's name was Sadie."

Windigo struggled with his emotions. Sadie's husband was *alive!* Sadie must not know this! It would destroy any chance he had of winning her love! He looked at Tecumseh again, begging with his eyes not to disclose Sadie's presence. Tecumseh's deep gaze showed a wise understanding. He looked again at the soldier.

"As I said, there is no one here whose heart is not Indian. You can tell Governor Harrison that we have no white prisoners here—none who are alive, that is."

The soldier stiffened. "Then did you or any of those here kill a white woman with light hair, and a small boy who also had white hair and eyes the color of the sky?"

Tecumseh shook his head. "We did not kill any such prisoners. And I should tell you that I do not condone torture and death for prisoners. I have often pleaded with my people to stop such practices. Now, let us get on with the real reason for your visit. In the governor's letter, he warns that I should not stir my people against him and the Americans, that to do so would be futile. He tells me he wants a sign that we do not intend to make war and urges me to visit the President of the United States. I have told the governor many times that all he has to do is stop whites from moving into our land, and that he must nullify the treaty he claims gives him permission to open up most of southern Indiana to Americans. He claims that he cannot nullify the treaty, that there is no stopping the whites from coming. He says there is nothing he can do about it, that I must speak with the president about it."

The soldier nodded, and Windigo had trouble following the conversation now, his heart still rushing with the news that Sadie's husband was alive. Somehow he had to get her away from here for a while, and he most certainly needed to make sure she never knew the truth!

Tecumseh and the soldier continued their conversation, and finally Tecumseh told his visitor that he would write a reply letter to the governor and consider yet another council in Vincennes.

Vincennes! If he went with Tecumseh to another meeting with Harrison, he might even meet Sadie's husband and see for himself what the man looked like. It gave him great satisfaction to think that he could look the man in the eyes, knowing secretly that Jonah

Wilde's wife belonged to Windigo now, as it should be! If white men wanted to keep coming here to steal Indian land, they should expect to suffer for it, to lose their women and children!

He watched Tecumseh leave them to sit at his desk. Windigo eyed the now-calmer soldier while Tecumseh took pen and paper and carefully wrote his reply to Governor Harrison. The thought of going to Vincennes excited Windigo . . . but he would most certainly leave Sadie behind.

The *wigawa* seemed tense with quiet while Windigo and the captain waited. Finally Tecumseh blew on the wet ink of his note, then folded it and returned to where the captain sat, handing it to him.

"I have told Governor Harrison that I will come to Vincennes in thirty days. I hope we can at last settle our differences; however, tell your governor that I will not come alone or even with just a few men. It is important to our people that for a council of this importance, many of our people and chiefs come with me to hear what is said. I will also bring women, to show you and the other Americans that we indeed come in peace. They need not fear a surprise attack."

The captain nodded and tucked the note into his shirt. "I'll tell him." He put out his hand. "Thank you, Tecumseh, for assuring my safety."

Tecumseh nodded, shaking his hand. The captain left, looking very relieved. Tecumseh, Sauganash, and Windigo walked out behind him, and Windigo noticed the captain made quite a hasty retreat to the river with the three Frenchmen who'd accompanied him.

Windigo turned to Tecumseh. "May I go with you to Vincennes, Tecumseh?"

Tecumseh grinned. "You wish to see your woman's white husband."

Windigo nodded. "I will leave her behind. She now carries my child, Tecumseh. It is best she never knows her white husband still lives. It is even better for him, now that she carries the life of a Potawatomi in her belly."

Tecumseh nodded. "I understand." He looked after the captain again. "Yes, you may go. But the woman must stay here. It is too risky to take her."

"I hoped you would say so. Thank you, Tecumseh." His heart racing with what he'd learned, Windigo hurried back to his own hut. He took a deep breath before entering, ordering the two older warriors guarding Sadie to leave. He sat down and again took up his bow.

"What happened?" Sadie asked anxiously.

He kept his eyes averted. "Governor Harrison wants another council with Tecumseh. In thirty days Tecumseh will go to Vincennes with many others."

Finally he found the courage to face her. "I will also go, but you will stay here. Now that you are carrying, I want you to rest more. My mother told me that if a woman is going to lose a child, it usually happens in the early months."

He felt her eyes searching deeply. "You are *afraid* to take me to Vincennes, afraid someone will see me."

He kept a stern look on his face. "You are mine now. The child in your *belly* is mine. There is nothing more to be said about it. I have made life good here for you and your son. One day you will be happy with this life . . . and with *me*."

His conscience bothering him, he looked away again and set his bow aside. "I am going to see Wapmimi," he told her, needing to get away for a while. Besides, Wapmimi needed to hear this news! He would not be pleased to learn he'd not killed Sadie's husband after all! Jonah Wilde must be a very strong, resilient man, which could mean he might come looking for his wife once he was well. Windigo could only hope that Captain Wilson believed Tecumseh's story that Sadie and Paul were not here, and that Sadie's husband would in turn also believe it.

32

July 29, 1811

At the sound of voices outside the door and heavy footsteps on the front porch, Jonah started pulling himself up with crutches Tom Jarvis had made for him. Before he could fully steady himself, the door opened, and a man his own size practically filled the doorway.

"Jeremiah!" The first moment of true joy he'd known since losing Sadie and Paul filled his heart as his older brother closed the door and walked over to greet him. Jonah let his crutches fall as Jeremiah embraced him. "My God, it's good to see you!" Jonah told him, his eyes tearing.

"I'm just glad to see you alive and standing on your own after what I read in that letter," Jeremiah answered. "I came soon as I could. I saw Mrs. Jarvis outside and she told me to come on in." He stood back and looked Jonah over. "My God, Jonah, look at you. You're thin and pale and . . ." He frowned. "The letter said you couldn't walk at all."

"I'm improving every day." Jonah held on to Jeremiah's arms for support. "Tom Jarvis made these crutches for me, but I have every hope that I'll walk on my own within a month or two. In that respect God's been good to me, but—" Pain tore through Jonah's heart again, so often and so severe that he wondered how much longer he could take it. "I still don't know anything about Sadie or Paul," he finished. "All my stupid dreams and plans . . ." He turned away, grabbing the arms of the rocker and sitting down again.

"I'm not here to say I told you so, Jonah. Down inside I never thought your plans were stupid. I just knew I'd miss you so much, I tried to talk you out of leaving." Jeremiah took a chair from the kitchen table and sat down across from him. "Don't forget that you're just one of thousands of people who've had the courage to branch out and settle new country and who've ended up the victims of Indian attacks, so don't blame yourself. Just tell me what I can do to help."

Jonah's eyes teared from being so overwhelmed at seeing his brother after so long. Why did he ever leave their farm in Ohio? "That doesn't make me feel a whole lot better," he answered. He quickly wiped at his tears. "Tell me about the farm first—Regina and Matthew and the kids—"

"They're all doing great, and they said to tell you they're praying for you and Sadie and Paul. Matthew wanted to come with me, of course, but I ordered him to stay and help out at the farm. Not all the harvesting is done, but he and Mark and Regina can get it done. They all said they'd pitch in so I could come for you. I want you to come home with me to finish mending, Jonah. You'll get stronger a lot faster if you're with family."

Jonah sighed and leaned back. "Going home sounds good, but until this happened I'd really come to think of our miserable little spread in the middle of the prairie as home. And until I know about Sadie—"

"First things first, Jonah. You can't do anything about Sadie if you aren't strong and well. I've given it a lot of thought. You know the endurance it can take going into Indian country. You're in no shape for it. I want you to come home with me and get completely well. I promise that when you do, I'll go with you to search for Sadie and Paul, unless . . ." Jeremiah leaned forward, his elbows on his knees. "Unless we somehow learn there is nothing to look for."

Jonah groaned at the thought of it, putting his face in his hands. "I can't even think about it." He sighed. "One of Harrison's men went to Tippecanoe to see about another meeting with Tecumseh." He faced Jeremiah again. "While he was there he asked about Sadie and Paul—described them and the attack. Tecumseh swore they weren't there and that he knew nothing about them even being prisoners. I believe he was lying, but Harrison said that wouldn't be like him. Still, even Harrison admits that the mood Tecumseh is in, he might not cooperate in any way about anything."

Jeremiah thought a moment. "Well, the reality is that it's very possible they are no longer alive, Jonah, especially not Sadie. She could have died after being captured but before she even made it to Tippecanoe. That would explain why Tecumseh wouldn't know anything about her. I'm sorry, but I think the best thing you can hope for is that Paul could be alive and well. The Shawnee have a soft spot for children, which could explain their reluctance to give him up. They adopt them into the tribe and by the time they're grown they hardly know they're white. You've heard of Blue Jacket."

Jonah nodded. "Him and a lot of others." He rubbed his forehead, staring at the floor. "It makes me sick to think of it . . . and to think of what Sadie might be going through if she *is* still alive." He swallowed. "I'm such a goddamn fool, Jeremiah."

"No more the fool than our grandpa Noah was, or

our father or Uncle Jeremiah. They all took the same chances, and God knows Grandma Jess suffered for it, and our mother, too. But they knew they were loved, and that Grandpa and Pa both would do everything they could to find them, just like you and I will do everything we can to find Sadie. We both have to know one way or another what really happened to her and Paul."

Jonah sniffed and met his brother's dark eyes. "I can't ask you to take the chance, Jeremiah. You've got a wife and children and a farm to run and—"

"There's no arguing and you know it. We'll find a good guide to help us."

Jonah leaned back again, running a hand through his hair. "It's awfully dangerous now. There has been more raiding. The Shawnee are enraged about people like me settling in that land Governor Harrison claims they sold to the United States. Tecumseh swears it's not a legal sale and that we have no right on the land. Word is he's gotten quite a force of Indians together up at Prophetstown. He's uniting several different tribes, which can mean real trouble, maybe even for you back in Ohio. This isn't going to go away anytime soon, and walking into the lion's den will be a big risk, us being Americans. Now the British are befriending the Shawnee because they know we'll most likely end up at war with England, so that will make matters even worse."

"We'll just have to find someone who speaks their tongue and knows how to deal with them; and we'll have to take things with us for presents, maybe even horses and guns."

Jonah let out a soft whistle. "It'll be difficult and expensive, but we have to try."

"It will be worth every dime we have to spend if we find Paul and Sadie."

Jonah nodded. He searched Jeremiah's eyes quietly. "What would you do, Jeremiah, if they took Regina and . . . you know . . . what if Sadie is some buck's wife now? I know she wouldn't want it that way, but if it meant survival—"

"She'd do whatever she had to do to survive, especially if it meant Paul's safety and happiness. You know that. It's something you have to deal with, Jonah, emotionally. If that's what she's done, then be proud of her for not cowering and whimpering and doing something foolish that could cost her and Paul their lives. Indians respect bravery. You know that. So does Sadie."

Jonah felt the pain shoot through his innards again. "Yeah." He looked away, and Jeremiah reached out and touched his arm.

"I know it hurts, Jonah. You asked what I would do. I'd go to the ends of the earth to find Regina and any one of my children. And if some damn buck decided to claim her, it would take a while to get our lives back the way they were, but I'd sure as hell try. I'd just be glad to have her back."

Jonah cleared his throat. "Yeah, well, we have one starting point. If you can stay a couple of days before heading out, we can sit in on a big council the governor is having with none other than Tecumseh himself, right here in Vincennes, day after tomorrow. Harrison promised me he'd ask again about Sadie. He sent a captain to visit Tecumseh about a month ago to take a letter to him to again plead for peace, and the captain asked at that time if they had a white woman and boy with them. They claimed they didn't, but I want to ask that Shawnee tyrant myself. I want to watch his eyes when he tells me they aren't holding any prisoners that match Sadie's and Paul's descriptions. If I see any flicker of a lie, we're going to Prophetstown and find out for ourselves!"

Jeremiah nodded. "I'll stay for the council. I wouldn't mind seeing this Tecumseh myself. He's got quite a reputation, and it's not all bad. He's quite a leader and a statesman, and he really does seem to want peace."

"Well, that won't happen until he gets his land back, and neither Harrison nor even the President of the United States is about to let that happen, so I don't see a good outcome. It just irks me that when we first got here Harrison talked like there were no problems with that land sale."

Jeremiah leaned back and sprawled his long legs out in front of him. "So, what's it like trying to plow prairie land?"

Jonah finally had to chuckle. "You saw plenty of it coming here, I'm sure. Did you try jabbing a knife or a spade into it?"

Jeremiah grinned, shaking his head. "Unbelievable root system."

"To say the least. But what's underneath is the best damn soil a man could ask for. It'll all get plowed up someday, you just watch. We had a pretty good section broken in before all this happened. Another year or two and we would have had a nice little farm started." He took hold of a crutch and toyed with it as he spoke. "Came here with another couple, older folks, and their grown son—real nice people they were. We helped each other, built our little soddies . . ." He stared at the crutch. "I'll miss them." He met Jeremiah's eyes again. "I'm damn lucky to be alive. Those warriors bashed my head in so bad I couldn't even remember anything for a long time, let alone move anything. The Harrisons helped me at first, then the Jarvises took me in. Real good people. Trouble is, they have a daughter who has taken a shine to me, but she's too young and besides that, there is room in my heart for only one woman."

Jeremiah smiled softly. "Out here you sure wouldn't be the first man who's had more than one wife. Life has to go on, Jonah."

Jonah closed his eyes. He could see Sadie so clearly sometimes. "I suppose so, but going on without Sadie is not a pleasant thought. I survived, Jeremiah, and it makes me feel so guilty. I can only hope my wife and son are also still alive. I'll never rest easy until I know for sure."

Just then Fiona Jarvis came inside with a bucket of

wood. "Don't mean to interrupt you two, but it's time to start supper. Jeremiah, you're sure welcome to stay and eat with us! Me and Tom was so happy to realize who you were when you came riding in. Fact is, there wasn't much doubt, you two lookin' so much alike and all, except for them dark eyes of yours. I've never seen bluer eyes than Jonah's." She set down the bucket. "I know you have a lot to talk about, and I don't mean to butt in."

"You're not butting in, Fiona. Heaven knows that's what *I've* been doing here for months now," Jonah told her.

The woman waved him off. "Nonsense! We're glad to be of help, and thrilled to see you making so much progress."

"I want to thank you for taking such good care of my brother and for getting that letter to me," Jeremiah told Fiona. "I'll be taking him off your hands soon as the council with Tecumseh is over in a couple of days. I'm taking him home to mend."

Fiona nodded. "I figured that's what you'd do." Her smile faded. "We'll miss you sorely, Jonah, but I know what your real plans are once you're well. All I can say is God be with you, and I'll pray your wife and son are still alive."

Jonah struggled to his feet again. "Right now that's about all anybody *can* do."

Jeremiah rose to face him, and the two brothers embraced again. "Thank you for coming, Jeremiah," Jonah told him. "God help us both."

"He already is, Brother. I've found you, and you're starting to walk. With the whole family back home praying for both of us, I see nothing but that light at the end of the tunnel."

Jonah clung to him a moment longer. "It's been a long, black tunnel, Jeremiah. A long, black tunnel."

33

July 31, 1811

The air felt heavy with tension. Jonah and Jeremiah were among those seated behind Governor Harrison, who sat at a table flanked by interpreters and government representatives, about fifty armed soldiers and several dragoons who carried only swords but no firearms.

Jonah eyed the imperious Tecumseh, who'd arrived two days earlier with upward of three hundred warriors, all fancied up with paint and feathers and looking quite impressive . . . and intimidating. As Tecumseh had agreed with Harrison, most of the warriors did not carry firearms, but they carried knives and war clubs, enough of a weapon for men who were better at using such instruments than many white men were at using guns. Jonah would forever bear an ugly scar on the back of his head to attest to that.

To show they came in peace, Tecumseh had brought about thirty women with him. Jonah felt like going to their camp and inspecting every female to make sure one of them wasn't Sadie. They could have painted her to look darker, covered her beautiful, golden hair with a dye or made her wear a blanket over her head. Still, as Jeremiah had assured him, if they did have Sadie, why would they bring her here with them? It would only cause trouble, and Tecumseh was here to talk about peace.

Peace! There was no peace in Jonah's heart, and there never would be! He'd like to sink a knife into the heart of every red man at this council! Many citizens also sat in on the council, and talk was rampant about worry over the strength Tecumseh had built in numbers. Citizens were taking alarm, for from what scouts told them, Tecumseh indeed had managed to form an amalgamation of numerous Indian tribes. Even now, he'd brought to this council Kickapoos, Potawatomies, Wyandots, Winnebagos, Ottawas, and Chippewas. This was not just a Shawnee threat, but a threat from every tribe from Michigan and Wisconsin down through Illinois, Indiana, Ohio, Tennessee, and Kentucky. Jonah's hopes of being able to go and find Sadie were already dwindling.

The council was to have started the day before, but a thunderstorm prevented it, and Jonah felt as though the thunder came from his own heart. To face these painted warriors after what he'd suffered and lost brought renewed pain and hatred.

Once everyone was in place, introductions began, Harrison giving the names of the commissioners present and explaining the reason for their presence. His secretary wrote hastily, frantically dipping and redipping his pen into an inkwell. Jonah kept a steady gaze on Tecumseh and his closest advisers as Harrison continued the introductions to include him.

"This citizen here on crutches, Tecumseh, is Jonah Wilde, a man who has lost his family to a raid by your people, the very kind of thing we don't want to happen again."

There! Jonah nudged Jeremiah. "Look at that young warrior second from Tecumseh's right," he said quietly. "Look at his eyes."

Indeed, the young man stared at Jonah oddly, seeming to take a greater than normal interest in him. He glanced at Tecumseh, then back to Jonah. Jonah glared right back at him, his heart pounding.

"He knows something," he told Jeremiah quietly.

"Don't get your hopes up. Maybe he's just heard about Sadie, or it could be they are just interested in seeing the white man who survived getting his head bashed in with a war club." Jeremiah faced Jonah, half grinning. "That doesn't happen often, you know, unless you're a Wilde."

Jonah couldn't help returning the smile, it felt so damn good being with his brother again. "Didn't Ma used to say that Wilde men were hardheaded?"

Jeremiah chuckled. "Maybe she meant that in more ways than one."

The joking helped ease Jonah's own tension, but he couldn't help watching the young man who seemed to be paying him uncommon attention as Tecumseh returned the introductions—his personal aide, Sauganash; Seekaboo, a Wapakoneta prophet who spoke many tongues; Jim Blue Jacket, son of the white man raised as a Shawnee, Blue Jacket, who'd died the past winter. When he reached the young man upon whom Jonah centered his attention, he was introduced as Windigo, a respected Potawatomi warrior learning from Tecumseh how to speak, read, and write in English. Again Windigo raised his chin proudly and literally glared at Jonah. "See?" Jonah said to Jeremiah.

"I'm watching."

Harrison opened the meeting with a literal scolding for the deaths of two whites in Illinois, as well as more in Indiana; then he chastised Tecumseh for coming to Vincennes with so many warriors, as though to threaten the Americans. Jonah watched Tecumseh stiffen, his pride obviously hurt. He could see the now-famous Tecumseh did not abide being talked down to, which was just what Harrison was doing. If Harrison intended to soft-talk Tecumseh into finally accepting the terms of the Indiana land sale, Jonah suspected he was not getting off to a very good start. When he finally got to the subject of the land sale, he reminded Tecumseh that he could not himself enter into any negotiations regarding the subject. It was something only the President of the United States could do anything about.

Tecumseh rose then, with an air about him that commanded attention and respect, even from the whites. Jonah could see this was not a man with whom others should deal lightly. Looking angry, he sarcastically asked Harrison why he wanted to meet with him if he could not handle the matter of the land sale himself.

Irritated, Harrison abruptly adjourned the meeting to the next day.

"Damn it!" Jonah swore. "He didn't accomplish a thing!"

Jeremiah sighed deeply. "I'm going to see if I can talk to that Windigo." He hurried off, and Jonah slowly followed using his crutches. Both Indians and whites were grumbling among themselves over what seemed a wasted morning, and Tecumseh was talking intently with Sauganash and Windigo when Jeremiah approached them.

Jonah's ego was strengthened when he saw that Jeremiah stood taller than Tecumseh, who was himself of unusual stature for a Shawnee. Jonah was just as tall as Jeremiah. "And before long I'll by-God be just as strong as ever!" he mumbled to himself. "If any of you has Sadie or my son, I'll come for them!"

By the time Jonah reached the others, Tecumseh said something to Windigo in the Shawnee tongue and left with his closest aide, Sauganash. Windigo remained, folding his arms in an obvious attempt to show Jonah and Jeremiah his hard muscle, but he had to look up at them.

You should look up to us, you bastard! He reached Jeremiah's side, and Windigo looked him over as though he were a ghost. "So, you are Jonah Wilde," he said.

"Why does that matter to you?" Jonah asked.

Windigo shrugged. "Only because it was my good friend, Wapmimi, who attacked you. He thought he had killed you." Windigo grinned. "Now I can tease him that he is not the great warrior he *thought* he was."

"Is that the only reason we noticed you took such interest in Jonah?" Jeremiah asked.

Windigo put his hands on his hips. "I have no other reason. Why have the two of you come after me like this? I must go rejoin Tecumseh." He nodded toward the other side of the meeting site. "Your Governor Harrison does not seem to have much to offer. And I can see from their eyes that many of those here at Vincennes fear Tecumseh's strength."

"Quit changing the subject!" Jonah told him, hating the young man's smugness. "What do you know about my wife and son? If Wapmimi is your best friend, you must know something, because they weren't found at our homestead along with the other innocent people he murdered!"

Windigo's dark eyes flashed with heated indignation. "And what about all the Shawnee and the Potawatomi and Wyandot and Kickapoo and all the Iroquois who have been murdered by the *white* man, including my own father! What about my mother, who was raped by six of you filthy Americans!"

"Tell me what you know!" Jonah growled.

"Calm down, Jonah," Jeremiah advised, putting a

hand on his shoulder. "You'll get nowhere this way."

Windigo faced Jonah squarely. "I will tell you this, Jonah Wilde. Your son died of a sickness, and your wife died more bravely than any white woman I have ever seen tortured to death."

The warrior's dark eyes gleamed with obvious joy at giving Jonah pain.

"You *bastard!*" Jonah roared, dropping his crutches and plowing a hard right fist into Windigo's face. Both men went sprawling in spite of Jeremiah's attempt at catching Jonah. Unable to use his legs properly, Jonah was unable to keep Windigo from wrestling him onto his back, and in the next moment Windigo sat on top of him, knife drawn.

"How does it feel, *white* man, to know your loved ones suffered!"

In the next moment Jeremiah grabbed Windigo off Jonah, yanking at his right wrist and twisting so that he let go of the knife. By then soldiers and Indians alike had gathered. Two soldiers pulled Jeremiah away, and another hurriedly helped Jonah to his feet. Opposite them, several warriors stood hunched for battle if necessary.

"What is going on here!" Governor Harrison himself stepped in then, as men held both Jonah and Windigo at bay.

"This son of a bitch told me to my face that my wife was *tortured* to death and that my kid is dead!" Jonah growled. "With a *smile!*"

"Windigo, my apologies. Go on with the others. I'll

take care of this," Harrison told Windigo.

"Don't apologize to him!" Jonah yelled.

Harrison shot him a warning look. "It's going to be hard enough to deal with Tecumseh and those like Windigo without something like this happening," he said calmly. He glanced at Jeremiah. "Take your brother up the hill there where the rest of the soldiers are. I'll talk with both of you there."

Windigo shook his long, partly braided hair behind his shoulders defiantly, then grinned again as he bent down to pick up his knife. "You are a lucky man, Jonah Wilde," he told Jonah. "If you were not crippled, I would have killed you. But Windigo is a proud warrior who fights only men who can truly give him a challenge." He shoved the knife into its sheath and walked away, motioning for the rest of the restless warriors to follow. Harrison walked partway with them, still talking to Windigo.

"Goddamn bastard!" Jonah seethed as Jeremiah handed him his crutches. He couldn't help the tears that came to his eyes. "When I get my strength back I'm going after him, Jeremiah. I'll *kill* him, *and* that friend of his, for what they've done to me and my family! If he wants a man who can match his strength, he's damn well *found* one! I'll slice his *guts* out and feed them to the buzzards! How can any man watch a woman be tortured to death! Sadie!" His voice choked with the horror of what Windigo had told him.

"He could have been lying." Jeremiah spoke the words calmly.

Jonah swallowed and faced him. "What?"

"What if he was lying?"

"Why would he do that?" Jonah frowned at his brother's suggestion.

"Maybe he's afraid for you to know the truth. Maybe he took a liking to Sadie and doesn't *want* her found. Or maybe he sold her off to some other warrior for a few horses and feels it's not his place to betray the man."

Harrison was approaching them now, shaking his head. He pulled a pocket watch from his vest and glanced at it, then slipped it back into place. "I could see by Tecumseh's attitude this morning that it would be best to stall our talk until at least tomorrow," he told Jonah and Jeremiah. He faced Jonah. "That little tirade you just went into won't help."

"What would *you* have done!"

Harrison put up his hand. "Now, now, calm down, Jonah Wilde. You're in no condition to be duking it out with a wild Indian. You could have had a major setback getting into a fracas like that. Now just listen to me for a moment, will you?" He nodded toward the top of the hill. "Follow me."

Jonah glanced at Jeremiah, who helped him up the hill after Harrison. Once well away from others, Harrison turned to Jonah. "I understand how you feel, Jonah, and I'm sorry. But getting into a scuffle like that doesn't help the greater cause here, which is to find a way to convince Tecumseh to accept the land sale."

"The *greater* cause? Greater than my wife's death?"

"I'm not saying that. Let me get to the point. I'm not obligated to make any special deals with Tecumseh. I can tell we aren't going to get much settled at this council, because Tecumseh is not about to back down on this land sale thing. It's going to come down to breaking up Tecumseh's amalgamation and destroying his power if we're ever going to be able to allow men like you and their families to continue settling that land. Otherwise, Tecumseh's numbers will grow to the point where we truly *can't* stop him." He drew in his breath, eyeing both men. "Prophetstown has to be destroyed."

Jonah frowned, glancing at Jeremiah before speaking to Harrison. "You mean—you already have plans in that direction?"

Harrison put a finger to his lips. "I've heard you intend to go home to Ohio with Jeremiah to finish mending. Why don't you do just that? If you're well enough by, let's say, October, come back to Vincennes and talk to me about what's been decided. If you want to join the Indiana militia, you're welcome to come with us. Maybe it would help you with the revenge I know must be boiling in your guts over your wife . . . and just maybe . . . just maybe you'll find out that Windigo was lying."

Jonah's eyebrows shot up in surprise. "That's exactly what Jeremiah told me."

Harrison grinned. "There, you see? It's two against one."

"Why do *you* think he might be lying?" Jonah asked.

Harrison shook his head. "It's just a hunch. I've dealt with the Shawnee and Potawatomi for years, and one outstanding attribute I do give them is that they are a truthful people. I saw something in Windigo's eyes when I asked him how your wife died. He didn't quite know what to say at first. Then he just turned away and said she died bravely. He walked away too quickly."

"I *told* you!" Jeremiah said, giving Jonah a look of support.

"Don't get your hopes up," Harrison warned. "I just know that you and a lot of other Indiana volunteers are eager to vent some rage over atrocities committed against them. They'll be joining us when we've finalized our plans against Prophetstown, but that won't be until the fall. If you decide to go with us and things go well, you'll have a chance to see for yourself if your wife and child might be there."

"They could be killed in an attack," Jonah mused.

"Yes, they could. But is that any worse than living out their lives with the Shawnee? Either way, you never get to see them again." Harrison put out his hand. "You need answers, Jonah. I might be able to help you. But it has to be done my way. Lighting into one warrior won't get you what you want. I hope you'll come back and join the Indiana militia."

For the first time since the attack Jonah felt a glint of hope and saw at least a chance for retribution. He grasped Harrison's hand. "I'll by-God be back, Governor Harrison! Sign me on!"

Jeremiah grasped both their hands in his. "Add me to the list. Harvesting will be over by then and I'll come back with Jonah." The three men squeezed hands, and already Jonah felt stronger.

34

August 10, 1811

"You've said nothing about Vincennes," Sadie told Windigo cautiously. "Or how you got that bruise on your jaw." She handed him a bowl of berries she'd picked near the river this morning. Every time she went to the Wabash she thought how easy it would be to jump into one of the canoes banked there and start paddling south to Vincennes. It couldn't be all that far, could it? But there was no doubt in her mind that Windigo would come after her. Knowing the river and the woods so well, it would not take him long to overcome her. If that happened, others here at Prophetstown might decide she was not worth Windigo's time and frustration. Her fate might fall out of Windigo's hands. She could lose her precious Paul. "You've hardly spoken to me since you returned, Windigo. As soon as you got back you rode off to hunt. And since you returned from hunting last night, you've slept away from me and haven't said two words—"

"Enough!"

Sadie stopped sorting through the berries, instantly trying to determine what might have gone wrong at Vincennes. Why was Windigo so changed? Those women who'd gone along with him and Tecumseh told her they were not present at the actual meetings, but that their men said things did not go well, that it was likely Tecumseh would join the English and make war on the Americans. None of them knew how Windigo got his bruise, and their men would not tell them.

"My husband said it is Windigo's choice to tell or not to tell," one young Potawatomi woman had told her. "He is a respected warrior. To show a bruise like his hurts his pride."

Sadie waited quietly. She could swear Windigo had been literally sulking ever since he returned from Vincennes. She'd tried to get something out of a few of the other young braves herself, but they looked at her strangely and told her it was not their place to speak to her about such things and that she should be careful not to offend her husband.

Windigo downed a few berries before finally speaking again. "Women do not ask a warrior, even if he is her husband, about his injuries. If they are from making war, from killing the enemy and taking his weapons and his scalp, then a warrior proudly shows his injuries. They were won honorably. The bruise on my face is not from such a cause. I was thrown from my horse and hit a stump."

Sadie almost burst out laughing at the thought of

such a sight. "*You?* You ride a horse as though it were a part of you."

He cast her a dark look that convinced her he was telling the truth. Such a fall would truly be an embarrassment to a man like Windigo. No wonder he didn't want to tell his own wife how he'd got the bruise.

"If you laugh, I will beat you."

In all the months Sadie had been captive, this was the first time she truly did want to laugh. She couldn't stifle a snicker. Almost instantly Windigo darted to where she sat and laid her back. "What did I tell you?"

She kept smiling. "You won't beat me, Windigo. It's not in you to beat a woman you care about."

He softened, leaning closer and smiling. "Is that what you think?"

She sobered. "Yes."

He leaned closer and rubbed his cheek against hers. "Did you miss me?"

Sadie tried to think quickly. Joking with him probably made him think she cared about him . . . and a tiny part of her *did* care. Why? Was it just because this man was her only hope now for life and love and to be with her son? "Yes," she answered, always wanting to keep him pleased with her. The fact remained that he was Potawatomi, which meant certain beliefs could sway him and his people against her no matter how much he cared about her, or she for him. She reminded herself she could never truly trust this man.

"*I* am your man now," he told her.

Something about the way he said the words made it

seem almost as though he was worried someone else might take his place.

"It is *my* child you carry in your belly—no one else's." He ran a hand over her now-swelling stomach.

"Of course, Windigo. Why do you seem angry?"

He studied her deeply for several long seconds. "Because I wish you could *care* for me. For *me*— Windigo.*"

The look in his eyes almost made her feel sorry for him. She touched his hair. "*I do* care for you. I've told you that before. But I don't know how you can expect me to care the way I would for a man who properly courted me and won my heart."

"Your heart should belong to me, now that my life grows inside of you. Your white husband is . . . dead . . . and I am aware of how some white women captives are sometimes treated once they are returned to their own people. Your only happiness is here now, with me."

He pressed against her, pushing up her tunic. The strange mood he was in, she was afraid to push him away, even though she'd learned from other Potawatomi women that they sometimes did just that if they did not feel like mating. They would laugh about how frustrated it would make their husbands, who sometimes stomped outside in a grouchy fit.

Still, she was *not* Potawatomi. She was white, and her fate would forever depend on this man's mood.

As always she shut away all feelings as Windigo took her. He was never mean about it, which was the only reason she could bear his intrusion upon her most private self . . . that part of her that had once belonged only to Jonah.

Your husband is dead, Windigo had reminded her. Dead. Jonah was dead. Would his family even accept her if she ever got the chance to go home, especially if she toted along a little half-breed baby? She'd been with these people so long she was beginning to lose her sense of right and wrong, of where she belonged now. Should she truly accept the fact that Jonah was dead and stop wishing it was not true? Should she give up hope of anyone coming for her?

She hated living in this constant middle world, belonging nowhere and to no one. She wasn't sure how much longer she could go on fighting for her own identity, hers and Paul's. It was like being partly dead, but not completely.

Windigo finished with her and rolled away. "I am taking you south with me," he said then, "when Tecumseh leaves to speak to the southern tribes again."

Leave Prophetstown? That would mean even less chance of her ever being found. "Will we come back here?"

"Yes, of course. But when we go, we will leave Paul here with my mother."

Alarm stormed her heart. "Why?"

"Because I want some time alone with just you. I want you to care for me not because I protect your son but because of who I am, and because you are carrying

222

my child. Paul will be fine here. He has such fun playing with the Potawatomi and Shawnee boys that he will not even miss us. You have seen how he is."

"Yes." Paul was becoming as wild as the Indian boys, dressed like them, ran naked when it was extra hot, played with make-believe bows and arrows, was learning all the Indian games little boys played. He was fast losing connections with his white world. He was actually happy, never showing fear anymore. He'd been accepted by the elder Indians as one of their own, and he even called Windigo's mother "grandmother."

So, it was happening. She and Paul were being melded into the lives of these brown-skinned people as surely as cream could be churned into butter. Was there no stopping it?

"When will we leave?" she asked.

"Soon. We will return before the deepest winter comes."

Winter. She remembered last winter, huddled in the little soddy with Jonah and Paul, reading together, baking bread, visits from Marvin and Louise and Jack, playing checkers and other games to keep busy. Another life. Another world. Something she might never enjoy again.

35

October 12, 1811

It was three miles from Jeremiah's farm into Willow Creek, and every day for the past two weeks Jonah had walked to town and back. In spite of pain through his right hip and the right side of his back, he kept walking, determined to get stronger and stronger.

Too much time had gone by. It had been six months now since the attack, six long months since his wife and child disappeared from his life. How could a man's life change so dramatically and so quickly? What would Sadie be like if she truly was still alive and he found her? Would she even still want to be his wife? Would all this change everything between them? Would little Paul remember his daddy?

Fool! You stupid fool! He chastised himself over and over again for ever leaving Ohio . . . and yet part of his heart still lay in the Indiana prairie and that little piece of land that was to be a future settlement, maybe even named after himself or little Paul. This past summer he was supposed to have started building a real house for Sadie.

All those dreams—gone. He tried to think positive, to be grateful he was even alive, as Regina often reminded him he *should* be thankful for. But what was the sense of survival if it meant living the rest of his life with broken dreams and without the wife and son he loved so much?

A tiny part of him had been tempted to give up hope and just consider starting over, maybe with Betsy Jarvis, whose affection for him had burst into words of love the day before he left Vincennes. The sweet young woman had cried and told him if he found out Sadie was dead to please come back to Vincennes, for she loved him and would help heal his heart.

He'd hated telling her that could never be. It would take months, maybe years to get over Sadie. Betsy was too young to understand the kind of love and loss he was talking about. She'd run off crying and part of him ached to go after her and hold her close, just to feel a woman's softness against him again; but it would be cruel to use Betsy that way. That's all it would be, just a woman's comfort, not true love like a man had for his wife. The Jarvises had been too good to him for him to hurt their daughter.

He increased his pace to a run to work off his frustrations. He would find Sadie and Paul. He had to believe that. His heart pounded, but the pain in his hip actually eased, although his head began to throb as he ran ever faster. God only knew what kind of damage he'd suffered inside his skull. An ugly long white scar remained, where his hair would not grow.

Run! Run! He began panting. He couldn't stop himself. It seemed the running helped vent his anger and frustration. He visualized attacking Prophetstown and killing as many Indians as he could shoot down or strike down with sword and hatchet. He envisioned seeing Sadie and Paul, both running to him with open, grateful arms. He could see the three of them hugging and crying and laughing and thanking God they'd found one another again.

He reached the fields of Jeremiah's farm and finally began to slow down, his vision blurring, his lungs feeling ready to burst. He sprawled into a stack of hay where a few cows were feeding. A couple of them scuttled back at the sudden intrusion, then ambled closer again and continued feeding in spite of Jonah lying in the middle of the mound.

Jonah kept breathing deeply, waiting for his vision to clear, reminding himself to be careful not to overdo anything just because he had his strength back. He shouldn't risk doing something that might aggravate whatever brain injury he might have suffered. He had to stay well now. Soon he and Jeremiah would leave for Vincennes.

One of the cows nibbled close to Jonah's ear, snorting warm breath through its nostrils. Jonah couldn't help a chuckle as he rolled to his side to pat the cow's jaw. "Do you plan to include me with your meal, girl?" he asked.

The cow licked the side of his face and Jonah laughed again, scooting farther away and thinking about how nice it used to feel to roll over and pull Sadie close in the mornings, when they were both still warm in bed—how soft she was, how sweet she smelled, her full lips, the feel of her breast cupped in his hand. What was it about a woman's breasts that brought a man such comfort?

"Jonah!" Matthew yelled his name.

Jonah's vision finally cleared and he sat up, then rose to brush straw from his clothes. The weather was beautiful today, crisp and cool, perfect for running. He walked around the cows to see Matthew walking through the field calling his name. "Over here!" he shouted. He couldn't believe how much Matthew had grown in the year and a half he'd been gone. The young man was as tall and broad as he and Jeremiah now, even though he was only sixteen. "Going on seventeen," he always reminded them.

"Jeremiah sent me to look for you," Matthew told him as he ran closer. "Said you should have been back a long time ago."

"I did some visiting in town before coming back this time," he told his brother. "You guys don't need to worry about me."

"Can't help it, big brother. Jeremiah's afraid you're doing too much too soon."

"It just feels good to be able to walk and feel strong again," Jonah answered. "I need to be ready to leave soon for Vincennes."

"I sure wish I could go, too."

"You're helping just as much by staying here with the rest of the family. We couldn't feel right about doing this if all three of us went and left Regina and the kids here alone. I know there hasn't been Indian trouble around here in a long time, but you just never know. You see one sign of trouble, you take everybody into town, understand?"

"Sure. I know what to do. It's gonna be hard on Regina, though, knowing you two are for sure going to ride into that big Indian settlement and attack it. You be sure to let us know as soon as you can how it went and that you're both okay."

"We will." Jonah drew in a deep breath. "I feel good about this, Matthew. I think I'm going to find Sadie and Paul."

Matthew stopped walking. "What if you don't, Jonah? What will you do?"

Jonah sobered. "I can't think about that now. I have to stay positive or go crazy."

Matthew frowned and shook his head. "I just can't believe Paul and Sadie are out there somewhere living with the Shawnee. It just seems so unreal, you know?"

Jonah started walking again. "Well, it's all *too* real, I'm afraid. And we have to hope they *are* out there somewhere and not dead."

They continued walking silently, making their way through chunks of turned-up dirt from plowing after the corn harvest. Jonah wondered if he could ever get his prairie land into good working soil like this. It would take one hell of a lot of plowing, over and over, and now he'd missed a whole summer of working the farm.

It struck him then that he'd thought about the place again as though it were home. He stopped to take in the sight of the old homestead. "If I find her, Matthew,

I guess I'd have to go back to Indiana, if she'd go."

"After what happened?"

Jonah felt a catch in his throat. "To not go back would be to let them win, Matthew. There are settlers right here in Willow Creek who've gone through some pretty horrible things, too, but they stayed. My mother and father came back here, in spite of the original house being burned and the awful things that happened to both of them because of the Indians and the Revolution. They came back, and look what a grand farm this is now. It's ours—yours, I should say, because of them. I want to do the same thing for my son. If all men gave up right away, this country would never get settled."

"Regina says men like Grandpa and you are either brave or crazy."

Jonah smiled sadly. "Probably a little bit of both."

Matthew sighed deeply. "We'll be praying real hard for you, Jonah. Regina says if you find Sadie and Paul, you bring them back here first for a while, on account of it will be winter anyway, and most likely they'll be needing some time to get over whatever they've been through."

Again the thought of Sadie possibly being claimed by some Indian buck, maybe even that one called Windigo, stabbed at Jonah's guts. "I expect they will, Matthew. I expect they will." He put an arm around Matthew's shoulders. "Let's get to the house. It's time for me and Jeremiah to start planning our trip."

36

November 2, 1811

Sadie wrapped herself against the freezing cold, using a bearskin blanket. In spite of having traveled untold miles east and then far enough south that it should be much warmer, the day was wet and chilly, the kind of cold dampness that seemed to go right to the bone.

She walked with other women behind the warriors, her feet sheltered by fur-lined, knee-high moccasins, a fur, hooded cape wrapped around her shoulders and covering her head. She was glad now that Windigo had insisted Paul stay behind. He was surely warm and cozy inside a *wigawa* with his "grandmother" Serena, who most likely was telling him stories about the Potawatomi and their beginnings . . . doing all she could to turn Paul from his white ways and white memories.

Now seven months' pregnant, she was close to giving up on ever escaping her plight, ever returning to any kind of normal life again. No one in white society could possibly accept her and a half-breed child . . . not even Jonah . . . *especially* not Jonah.

The sun peeked from behind puffy, gray clouds, but it did little to warm her. Tecumseh and all those with him made their way along a narrow pathway somewhere on a hillside. Windigo claimed that today they were traveling through Mississippi . . . so very far from Indiana, even from Ohio. Jeremiah, Regina— none of them had any idea that miles to the south Sadie Wilde was walking with the infamous Tecumseh and some of his followers, traveling south to recruit even more Indians for Tecumseh's grand plan to bring all tribes together against the Americans.

In her wildest imagination, she could not have predicted her fate last spring when she and Jonah were looking forward to working up more prairie land and starting to build a house. What strange turns life could take, and what strange things people could do to survive.

They came through a clearing where she could see a few log cabins in a valley below, smoke wafting from their chimneys.

A white settlement! She couldn't help staring, a lump rising in her throat. Down there surely lived white families, men, women, and children, sharing chores, living in real houses, cooking over hearths, baking bread, making clothes, sharing quilting time . . . perhaps making plans for Christmas. She wasn't sure what the date was, but from the chilly wind and the fact that most trees had lost their leaves, she knew it was probably late October or early November.

The sight below brought back memories of last Christmas, baking cookies, the scrawny tree Jonah had brought from the riverbank . . . scrawny, yet so beautiful. She remembered playing games with the Stocktons, drinking coffee, listening to the endless winter winds outside but feeling surprisingly cozy inside their little soddy.

She longed to run down this hill and try to find shelter with those below. But the way she looked now, they would probably not even believe she was a white woman. And if she ran off, Windigo would come after her, and she could end up causing a lot of trouble for the innocents below who didn't even know a good-sized band of Indians was moving past them.

"Sadie!"

Sadie turned, realizing then that she'd been staring at the settlement below so long that the others had kept going without her. Windigo came toward her on his horse, looking grand in paint and feathers and a wolfskin coat. As always, the tiny pieces of tin in the many skinny braids through his long hair made a tinkling sound as he tossed that hair behind him. He rode closer, glancing down to where she'd been looking.

"You are thinking of going to them for help?"

She met his eyes. He'd been good to her this whole time. Her refusal to care for him was beginning to soften. "The thought crossed my mind, just for a moment. But I wouldn't want to cause them trouble, and I wouldn't want to leave you while I'm carrying your baby," she answered.

"And *after* the baby?"

She gave him a smile. *Always keep him happy and satisfied,* she reminded herself. "After the baby, we'll just be one big, happy family, won't we? We'll just have *more* babies."

Windigo grinned and dismounted. "I was worried when I could not see you behind me. Come." He picked her up like a feather, in spite of the weight she'd gained, and put her on his horse, then leapt onto the horse in front of her. "Can you hold on with your belly in the way?"

She put her arms around him. "I think so."

"I was afraid for you to ride because of the baby, but too much walking might also be hard for you. You can ride with me for a while."

"Thank you, Windigo. My feet need the rest."

The pathway ahead widened, and Windigo rode his horse at a faster trot to catch up with the men, then slowed down for her sake. "We will go home soon," he assured her. "Tecumseh has won over many more southern tribes to his side, but there are many others who refuse. They think like white men now, bow to the white men. They are afraid to make war against them, but they will learn that soon the white man will drive them even farther away and take everything they have. The white man always breaks his promises to the Indian. It is only a matter of time, which is why we must band together and stop the Americans from coming any farther into our lands! Those tribes who will not join us are fools and cowards!"

Sadie wished she could make him understand just how many "whites" there were farther east, and just how many thousands more there were like Jonah, men who would be determined to keep plodding westward to make a place and a name for themselves. Surely

Tecumseh knew the odds, but even he seemed to believe this amalgamation would work in the end.

If it didn't, what was to happen to her? If the Shawnee and Potawatomi were chased farther west, would she have to go with them, living like an Indian forever? She felt as though someone was slicing her heart in half, for part of her had grown so used to this life and was so worried about being accepted by whites that she felt she could, indeed, stay with Windigo and his people, wherever they went.

What was happening to her? She glanced back at the disappearing settlement below and thought about Jeremiah and Regina, Matthew, the children, Willow Creek, the Stocktons. Then silly things came to mind, things from her past life . . . a doll she'd kept since she was a little girl, her good china, a warm quilt her grandmother made for her years ago, churning butter . . . all the small but important things she would never again experience.

37

November 3, 1811

Tenskwatawa raised his one good eye to greet the two scouts he'd sent south. Tecumseh believed there was no chance of Governor Harrison taking any more action before spring; but the Prophet believed otherwise. Perhaps his brother might be wrong for once.

He both envied and hated Tecumseh. He, the Prophet, was the driving force behind Tecumseh's power and popularity. Yet *Tecumseh* got all the glory.

"What do you come to tell the Prophet?" he asked his scouts.

"A great army comes, Tenskwatawa, out of Vincennes! They are camped perhaps thirty miles south of Tippecanoe, and they are well armed, some in uniform, others just citizens who have chosen to join them. You were right, Tenskwatawa! Governor Harrison plans to destroy us! He even stopped and built a fort halfway here before coming even closer."

Tenskwatawa nodded. "I see." He drew a deep sigh. "My brother professes to be the savior of the Shawnee, a leader who will bring all tribes together to destroy the Americans. Yet where is he now, in our time of greatest need? He is *gone!* And many of the tribes he brought together here at Tippecanoe have gone home to visit relatives while Tecumseh is away in the south, preaching to tribes who once were our enemy, and many of whom will *never* follow Tecumseh! He wastes his time, and now there are few of us here to defend ourselves."

"What will you do, Tenskwatawa?"

The Prophet pulled the bandana wrapped around his head away from his bad eye. He sat hunched into the corner of his *hut,* where he'd stayed practically the whole time since Tecumseh left six weeks ago . . . thinking . . . thinking.

"I must contact the spirits," he answered. "My

brother told me that when he is gone I am to be in charge. We will greet Harrison and his army when he comes and see why he brings an army. Perhaps it is just to talk again, but it is too late for talking. I, Tenskwatawa, *say* it is too late! I will warn Harrison to be afraid." He wrapped his blanket closer around himself against the damp November day. "Go and tell the others to make ready. And tell them not to fear. Already I have been speaking with the spirits, and I am told that if the white men attack us, his bullets cannot harm us. They will pass through our warriors like magic."

"Tenskwatawa, did not Tecumseh tell you to make no major decisions until his return?" one of the scouts asked carefully.

Tenskwatawa threw a pinch of gunpowder into a central fire, causing a sudden poof of fire and smoke and causing the scout to jump back. "What my brother and I talk about is no one's business! I said that Tecumseh put me in charge, and therefore you will do what I say! Go now!"

The two scouts looked at each other and left. Tenskwatawa watched the fire, his hard-pressed lips in a downturn of grumbling determination.

"It is my spiritual powers that foretold the greatness of the Shawnee," he nearly growled. "Through me alone we burned all the witches and demons that lived among the Shawnee, making them weak. I alone truly recognize the enemy, and often the enemy is within one's own ranks."

Yes, Tecumseh had tarnished the strength of the Shawnee by bringing in all these other tribes . . . and by putting up with white intruders . . . like that white woman who lived with the Potawatomi man, Windigo. Such soiled trash among them would bring down the Shawnee in the end. It might even be that Harrison was coming here because of *her.* Her and that little boy of hers. It would be better to burn *both* of them at the stake!

Tenskwatawa sniffed in scorn. The boy might be the answer to staving off whatever Governor Harrison had planned. Perhaps if he took the boy out to Harrison, the governor would turn back to Vincennes. Then he, Tenskwatawa, could claim victory! He would be praised for his cleverness and quick thinking. He would be the savior of Prophetstown and the Shawnee!

He rubbed at his chin, thinking how he could paint himself gloriously, don his finest feathers and most colorful clothing. He could wrap his head in red and wear his finest earrings, then take the white boy out to Harrison to show his generosity and truthfulness. He might even tell Harrison that the boy's mother lived and that when she came back with Tecumseh, he would promise she would also be returned. By doing so he might save Tippecanoe! By using the boy and his mother for ransom, he could demand many things from Harrison. After all, wasn't that what prisoners were for . . . to ransom?

Of course they were. This silliness about Windigo

being required to take the white woman for a wife was just that—silliness! What did a young warrior like Wapmimi know about spiritual callings and demands? In his mind the white woman and even those of other tribes tainted the Shawnee and only made them weaker, not stronger.

The time had come for clear thinking and for pleasing the One Who Rules All. Not enough enemy blood had been spilled these past many months. That made the Shawnee look weak. Tecumseh's orders for no more torture of prisoners only worsened their situation. Shawnee warriors took their power through torture, as well as destroying the souls of their enemies!

Windigo's mother catered to the white boy now and truly seemed to care for him. She would be against giving him back, but she was not Shawnee! She was Potawatomi, living in a Shawnee town, and now that he was in charge of Tippecanoe, she would have to obey whatever he told her, especially knowing that Harrison commanded an army only thirty miles to the south.

It was time for action. Things would be done Tenskwatawa's way, and Tecumseh must accept that. He should not have left them yet again on this last, futile trip. He should be here, leading and helping his own people during this time of danger!

Tenskwatawa closed his one good eye and held his hands over the small fire, praying for guidance and power. Tecumseh couldn't possibly be angry with him for making these decisions in his absence. It was what he'd been instructed to do. How *dare* his brother tell him he could not make any major decisions? He was Tenskwatawa, the *Prophet!*

38

"What time is it?" Jonah pulled a wool hat closer around his ears as a freezing drizzle began pelting Harrison's camp.

Jeremiah glanced at a pocket watch by dim firelight. "About three A.M."

"I wish Harrison would quit sending messengers just to talk," he complained to Jeremiah. "Why can't we just get this over with? I'd like to tear into Tippecanoe and rip open every hut there to see if Sadie or Paul are with them. This is driving me crazy."

Jeremiah sat next to him on a log, puffing quietly on a pipe. "I think you'll get what you want pretty quick, Brother," he answered. "With one sentry shot and more Indians lurking about out there, this is going to come to a head by morning. That's my guess. Harrison is just waiting for full daylight."

They were camped within a half mile of Tippecanoe. In spite of a constant drumming sound in the distance and a sentry being shot, so far Harrison had done no more than call out to prowling Indians for the Shawnee to send out a delegation to talk. The invita-

239

tions were answered with hoots and catcalls and name-calling.

It was obvious the Indians were not ready to cooperate, and that for some reason they were also very confident, almost inviting Harrison to attack them. They'd already learned that Tecumseh was not even here, that he'd gone south, and that a lot of the other tribes who'd been living here had left for home to visit, unaware that Harrison was marching for Tippecanoe. That was a fact in their favor. Of the thousands of warriors that could be camped here, Harrison guessed there were only four or five hundred available to fight, if that many. Harrison's army consisted of over a thousand armed men, including a lot of white citizens who were tired of constant harassing attacks on their homes and small towns throughout Illinois and Indiana. It was time to put down Tecumseh and his threat for once and for all.

Suddenly a sentry ran up to Jonah and Jeremiah. "Harrison says to come quick!" he told them. "Three Shawnee men are coming in to talk, and they've got a white boy with them!"

Jonah's heart swelled immediately with joy and hope. "God, let it be Paul!" he prayed aloud as he and Jeremiah jumped up to follow the sentry about a quarter mile upriver to Harrison's headquarters. Harrison stood waiting with several guards, and he put his hand out as Jonah hurried closer.

"Don't get too excited," he warned, "and let me do the talking. It might not be your son at all. The whole thing might be a trick. You can't trust an Indian once he smells battle blood."

Jonah felt he could barely breathe as he waited, breathing deeply both from running and from hoping beyond hope he'd found at least part of his family. Paul, his precious little Paul!

Three warriors approached on horseback, and it was obvious a child sat in front of one of them. Jonah started away, but Jeremiah grabbed his arm. "Do what Harrison said," he told his brother. "Wait and see what they say. They could disappear into the darkness on a moment's notice."

Harrison stepped forward. "What is it you want?" he asked.

One of them, who looked quite old, nudged his horse closer. "I am called Hunter. Tenskwatawa would have come, but the drumming you hear is from the Prophet, who now sits on a hill praying to the spirits. He sent me instead to speak with you, as right now his prayers are more important. He asks why the white governor brings an army here. We have done nothing wrong."

"One of your warriors has already shot one of my sentries for no good reason, and there has been too much raiding against white Americans. We have come to show you our strength and to tell you for once and for all that the raiding must stop and the sale of Shawnee hunting grounds was good and fair and will not change."

The old man frowned. "We listen only to Tecumseh.

He is the one who will decide about the land. And until he returns, the Prophet is our leader. He says to tell you that it would be useless to make war on us, as your bullets will pass through us."

Jonah struggled against an urge to snicker, afraid of offending the man.

"Tenskwatawa tells you wrong, Hunter," Harrison warned. "You *should* be afraid of our bullets. And you should know that we are here to put an end to Tecumseh's efforts to bring all the tribes together. Most are already at peace with the white man. Why should they rise up against us again? They are wise to stay where they are so their women and children can live in peace. You tell Tenskwatawa that we are here to end Tecumseh's campaign, and that I don't care to listen to anything Tenskwatawa has to say."

The air hung silent for a moment, and Jonah feared Harrison had just ruined his chances for seeing if the white boy with the Shawnee was Paul. He worried it just might not be, for the boy shrouded under the blanket did not even seem to recognize his father.

"Then maybe you will listen to this," Hunter said. "Tenskwatawa has told us to bring this boy and give him to you, to show you our good intentions."

Jonah handed his long gun to Jeremiah, ready to run and grab his son.

"Bring the boy closer," Harrison said.

One of the other warriors dismounted, lifting the child down. He brought him forward and pulled away the blanket.

Jonah's eyes immediately teared. "Paul! It's Paul!" He ran forward and whisked the boy into his arms, unable to control his actions then. "My God, it's Paul!" He kissed the scowling child over and over, running a hand through his thick, blond hair that now hung long. "My son! My son!"

Paul pushed away. "I want Gwandmothew Sawena," he said.

Jonah hung on tight. "Grandmother?"

Paul pointed toward the Indians. "I go back to Gwandmothew."

The words shattered Jonah's heart. "Paul, it's me, your daddy. It's Jonah. You remember Daddy, don't you?"

The still-scowling youth studied Jonah for several long seconds. "I want Mommy."

"Mommy?" Jonah's heart pounded even harder. He glanced at Jeremiah, then to Harrison. "Ask them if his mommy is alive."

Harrison started to ask, but Hunter interrupted. "I know what he said." He, too, dismounted, stepping closer, a gleam of all-out victory in his eyes. He looked straight at Jonah. "His mother lives. She belongs to Windigo now, a Potawatomi man. She carries his child."

The words were like a club blow to Jonah's stomach. "My God," he muttered, still clinging tightly to Paul. Windigo! So, he'd been right that the bastard had lied about Sadie's death!

"She's *alive!*" Jeremiah reminded him. "Keep your senses, Jonah!"

"Where is she?" Jonah shouted at Hunter, stepping even closer to the old man, wanting to kill him. "Where is Sadie?"

"Mommy," Paul said, beginning to sniffle at Jonah's shouted words.

Hunter stiffened, and Harrison shot a dark look at Jonah. "Stay calm!" he ordered. "You're frightening your own son." He turned back to Hunter. "You bring only the boy," he said in a commanding tone. "But not his mother. This is not a sign of good faith!"

Hunter raised his chin proudly. "The mother is not with us. She is with Tecumseh and Windigo, in the south. If you want the mother, you will have to ask Tecumseh when he returns, but I would advise you in the meantime not to attack Tippecanoe, or the woman might be killed out of revenge when Tecumseh returns."

"Then I need a promise of no more raiding, especially into Indiana in the land that has been sold to us!"

Hunter sniffed. "I cannot speak for all. I have brought the boy for goodwill. That is all I can do. Tenskwatawa said to make no bargain with the liar, Harrison."

The old man turned and walked back to his horse, as did the warrior who'd brought Paul.

"If you make war against us," Hunter told Harrison before parting, "it will be a grave mistake, as we have shown our goodwill."

The three warriors turned and rode off into the darkness. Jonah broke into tears, hugging Paul closer again, groaning with agony over the news that Sadie was alive but had been taken by a Potawatomi man and now carried his child. He felt like vomiting at the revelation, even though he'd known such a thing could happen. "Sadie, my God!" he groaned. He remained on his knees, still holding Paul.

Jeremiah knelt beside him, putting a hand on his shoulder, and in the background Jonah could hear Harrison ordering his men to be alert.

"I don't trust Tenskwatawa any farther than I could throw him," Harrison was saying. "I wish I were dealing with Tecumseh, but it's got so I can't trust him either; and if the Prophet has told his warriors that our bullets can't harm them, there's no telling what they will do."

It didn't matter to Jonah. He had Paul, and Sadie was still alive. Alive!

"We'll find her," Jeremiah was telling him.

"How can I expect her to ever forgive me?" Jonah answered. "How can anything be the same again?"

"Because you *love* each other!" Jeremiah reminded him. "Because our grandparents got through something similar, and so did our parents."

"Neither Grandmother nor our mother ended up white squaws!" Jonah lamented.

"Hell is hell, Jonah Wilde! It doesn't matter what form it comes in. They still suffered terrible losses. They saw loved ones slaughtered before their eyes and spent months apart from their men. Sadie is just as

245

strong as they were, and whatever she's done it's been to survive and keep *Paul* alive! I'd bet my life on it! And she knows there is nothing to forgive you for. There is nothing you could have done, and for all she knows you were killed the day of the attack."

Jonah sat down on the ground, finally releasing his grip on Paul and studying the boy in the firelight. He appeared clean, and was warmly dressed in leggings and a fur jacket. The boy stared at him as though trying to remember him. "I want Gwandmothew," he repeated.

"You don't have a grandmother," Jonah answered.

Paul nodded. "Uh-huh. She's Sewena, Windigo's mama."

How he wished Windigo was in front of him now! He'd light into him and rip a knife from his balls to his throat!

"Jonah." Jeremiah grabbed his arm, as though he'd been reading his brother's thoughts. "Look at the boy. He's been well fed and is dressed well. And be careful how you talk about Windigo and the woman the boy calls grandmother. He obviously feels attachments now. They have apparently taken good care of him. Be thankful for that."

Jonah shot a dark look to his brother. "And what did *Sadie* have to pay for his good care?"

Jeremiah sighed. "One thing we know is that the Shawnee, and apparently the Potawatomi, care for their white prisoners once they are accepted. Paul even calls Windigo's mother grandmother. He's obviously been given care and even love."

"Love! What do *any* of them know about *love!*"

"Enough that we're both aware of white prisoners who ended up growing up happy with them, marrying into the tribes. You have to face reality, Jonah, and for now you have to thank God you have your son back!"

Jonah closed his eyes, pulling Paul close again. "If only I could find Sadie as easily."

"Well, for now be glad she *isn't* here. I have a feeling come morning, Harrison isn't going to hold back any longer. He and every man here are ready to sack Tippecanoe and leave a hard reminder for Tecumseh that all talk is done with. He'd better forget his plan for one Indian nation against America. It will never happen!"

Jeremiah had no more spoken the words than shots rang out and war cries could be heard from the darkness.

"I knew I couldn't trust that Tenskwatawa!" Harrison shouted. Immediately he began assembling his troops.

Jeremiah grabbed Jonah. "Let's get Paul to cover! You've been wanting to kill some Shawnee. Now's your chance!"

39

December 9, 1811

Sadie sat in the shadows, alert to the visit from two of Tecumseh's principal lieutenants from Tippecanoe, the Wyandot war chief Stiahta and the Potawatomi subchief named Metea. It was obvious by their countenance when they arrived here at Tecumseh's camp not far from New Madrid that something terrible weighed heavily upon them. They had traveled for over a month to find Tecumseh, who'd welcomed them to the central fire of the camp he'd made on his way to Apple Creek.

After failing to win over as many southern tribes as he'd hoped, Tecumseh was gradually making his way back home. He'd come farther south first to find his sister, Tecumapese, who'd run away from her husband and Tippecanoe with a white trader. Upon finding her, Tecumseh convinced her to come back to Prophetstown with him. She, too, sat nearby now. Sadie could tell that the woman did not really want to go back with her brother, but few people argued with the great Tecumseh, and Tecumapese had meekly agreed to his command.

After serving hot broth to the newly arrived messengers, Sadie and Tecumapese stayed in the background while Tecumseh, Windigo, Sauganash, Stiahta, and

Metea smoked a pipe together, passing it around as a sign of unity.

"Now, tell me what burdens you so that you have searched so long to find me," Tecumseh asked.

Stiahta sighed, glancing at Metea before turning his gaze back to Tecumseh. Sadie was surprised to see a trace of tears in the proud man's eyes.

"Tippecanoe has been destroyed by Harrison," the man told Tecumseh unwillingly.

Tecumseh and all his party gasped, as did Sadie and Tecumapese. Immediately Sadie's heart filled with terror. What about Paul? "My son!" she cried out. "Is he all right?"

A strange look came into Stiahta's eyes. "Your son is well," he answered.

"How did this happen?" Tecumseh demanded before Stiahta could say more about Paul. "Harrison promised to wait and talk more when I returned from the south!"

Metea rubbed wearily at his eyes. "I am sorry to say that your brother is partly responsible."

"Tenskwatawa!" Tecumseh exclaimed. "I told him to make no trouble, and no major decisions until I returned!"

Stiahta shifted his position where he sat on a blanket. "Harrison came claiming he wanted to talk. He had many soldiers with him and—" He hesitated, glancing at Sadie. "And many white men. We told him you were still away. He said that the morning of the next day he would talk with the Prophet, but before morning came, Tenskwatawa ordered us to attack first, sure that Harrison intended to do the same. He told us the white man's bullets could not harm us, but that proved untrue. Many of our people were killed, nearly the whole town burned. We believe all of this is because we attacked first."

Tecumseh's hands went into fists, and he rose. He paced a moment, his rage permeating the temporary lodge. Windigo and the others there were also obviously enraged, some of them cursing in the Shawnee and Potawatomi tongue. Sadie could not understand it all, but the meaning of their exclamations was obvious.

"I will have my brother *killed* for this!" Tecumseh roared. He went to his knees then, facing Stiahta again. "Did my brother make no effort to stem any attack?"

Again Stiahta got that strange look in his eyes, as though he did not want to say what he had to say. He looked at Sadie again, then at Windigo, before replying, directing his words to Tecumseh.

"We tried one thing. Tenskwatawa hoped to turn Harrison away by giving over the white woman's son as a sign of good faith. We did so, but after that Tenskwatawa still ordered the attack."

Sadie's heart pounded harder. "What happened to my son?" she again demanded to know. "Did they take him away before the attack? Is he all right?"

"Be quiet, woman!" Tecumseh demanded. "Stiahta already told you your son is well."

"I want to know more than that! Who took him?"

"Remember your place!" Windigo insisted. "Sit down!" Gritting her teeth, Sadie obeyed, but she sat close behind Windigo.

"Tell us what happened to the boy," Windigo told Stiahta.

The old Indian sighed, swallowing before replying. "One of the white men there, he was tall and big, with dark hair and blue eyes, he shouted out when we produced the boy that the child was . . . his son."

Sadie sucked in her breath. "*Jonah?* Was his name Jonah?"

"I believe that is what he was called. He had a man with him who claimed to be his brother. Somehow they knew Harrison was marching on Tippecanoe, and they came along."

Sadie turned away, grasping her swollen belly. "Oh, my God! Oh, my God! It's my *husband!* He's *alive!*" A myriad of emotions raced through her heart and mind, and she literally felt faint.

"It was wrong to lie to her about this!" Tecumseh shouted. "This woman and her son have brought us bad luck!"

Lie about it? Sadie turned, watching Windigo, who had a devastated look on his face.

"Did they demand the mother?" Tecumseh asked.

"Yes," Stiahta answered. "When we could not produce her, the white man was very angry. We told him she now belongs to Windigo and that she carries his child and that she was not at Tippecanoe."

"No!" Sadie exclaimed. He *knew!* Jonah knew she carried another man's child! An *Indian* man's child! What must he think? Where was he now? Part of her wanted to shout with joy and thankfulness that Jonah lived, that her Paul was with his father again; and part of her wanted to scream with devastation at the position in which this had left her, wondering at the horrors that must be going through Jonah's mind. And Windigo! She eyed him again.

"You *knew!* You knew Jonah was alive, didn't you! You've been *lying* to me!" she screamed.

Windigo rose. "You will still your voice! A greater matter must be discussed here! Tippecanoe has been *destroyed!* Tecumseh must learn more and decide what to do!"

"A greater matter?" she shouted in reply. "Greater than my husband being alive, while I lie with another man and now carry his *child?*"

Windigo grabbed her. "Come away!"

"Don't touch me!" Sadie managed to jerk herself away.

"This is all the *white* woman's fault!" Stiahta suddenly proclaimed. "She is a witch! She brings us tragedy and death! Wapmimi should be punished for bringing her into our midst!"

Sadie's eyes widened in shock and fear. Everything she'd dreaded could happen was beginning to take place. These people were turning on her! Terrified by Stiahta's accusations, she ran out of the hut and into the darkness. Windigo shouted after her, but she paid no attention. All she could think to do was run. Run! Run away from it all! Maybe if she ran hard enough and far enough, she would find Jonah, but once he saw her, he would surely turn his eyes from her in shame.

40

Run! Run! Sadie stumbled through undergrowth, having no idea in which direction she ran or how much longer she could keep this up. Then she tripped on fallen timber and fell, landing on her side.

She rolled to her back, grasping her belly, now eight months swollen with child. A heavyset Creek woman had loaned her three deerskin dresses large enough to give her pregnant midriff plenty of room, although the shoulders had to be taken up and sewn so the dress wouldn't fall off Sadie's much smaller frame.

Afraid of the pain that enveloped her, she lay still, trying to gather her wits, while in the distance she heard Windigo calling to her. How she hated him now, mostly because he'd made her actually begin to have feelings for him, thinking Jonah was dead and she could never go back to the white world and live a decent life. She'd actually been preparing herself to live this way forever, as long as Paul could be with her, and since now there would be another child, a Potawatomi child!

Now Paul was with his father. For that much she thanked the Lord. It would take time for the boy to reestablish his connections with the white world from which he'd been torn, but at least he would grow up loved by his real family. But what was *she* to do now?

"Sadie! Sadie, come back!"

Windigo's voice was closer now. What choice did she really have but to answer and let him help her? If she kept running and lost Tecumseh's camp, she would probably never survive in these wilds; and yet, did it really matter? The motherly instinct in her said she *must* survive, for the baby. The child inside of her was innocent of all that had taken place to create its existence, yet part of her almost hoped she was losing it.

Pain ripped through her again. She managed to sit up, then knew she had no choice but to call out to Windigo. "Here! Follow my voice!"

While she waited, calling to him twice more, the pain subsided. She suspected it had come more from a strained muscle from the fall than from the baby itself. She scooted herself against a fallen log and waited, the bright moonlight making it easier for Windigo to finally find her.

"Sadie!" He knelt closer.

"Don't touch me!" she ordered. "I hate you! I hate you for what you've done to me! In the white man's eyes and religion I've committed a terrible sin! I'll burn in hell for it! If I'd known my husband was still alive I would never have given myself to you!"

"Sadie, I, too, thought he was dead. I did not discover he lived until long after I made you my wife.

But what would it matter? You were *destined* to belong to me, and taking you as a wife saved your life and your son's life. Surely you are grateful for that. How can you hate me, the father of the life in your belly?"

The moonlight lit up his face by a shaft of light through the trees, and for that brief moment something tore at Sadie's heart. It was the forlorn look in Windigo's dark eyes. The young man had truly fallen in love with her! Until this moment she'd never really allowed herself to believe he could have such deep feelings.

"Surely you know by now how much I care for you, Sadie Wilde," he told her, his voice nearly to a breaking point. "It is sad enough hearing what has happened at Tippecanoe, our homes burned, all our winter supplies gone. For all I know my mother has been killed. Perhaps Wapmimi also, my best friend since I was very young. And now that your white son has been taken, I know that deep inside you feel no reason to stay with me any longer. Yet my heart would shatter if you left."

The handsome, proud warrior was pouring out his heart to her, feelings she never even considered an Indian could experience. In spite of what she'd seen of love and family life among the Shawnee and Potawatomi, it had not struck her until now how truly real their feelings could be, no different from her love for Jonah. And the child she carried—Windigo would love it just as much as Jonah loved Paul.

Sadie felt ripped in half. The part of her that had actually dared to consider loving this man when she thought Jonah was dead came alive to torture her heart and soul. Yet that same heart first belonged to Jonah Wilde. The very mention by Windigo of her last name brought all that to her in painful reality. *Was* it a sin to care for Windigo and to have lain with him when she honestly believed Jonah was dead and she had nothing to go back to? Even after he knew Jonah lived, she did not. How did God look upon her situation? What did He expect of her? What would *Jonah* expect of her? Her eyes filled with tears of agony and indecision. Windigo looked almost like a wounded, heartbroken little boy.

"I don't know what to tell you, Windigo." Her throat ached with a need to scream, to cry until there were no tears left. "I'm torn, and I'm afraid. Stiahta said what happened at Tippecanoe was partly my fault. If the others feel the same way, especially Tecumseh, what will happen to me if I *do* stay with you and go back? Will your people hate me? Will your *mother* hate me? Will I be put to death after the baby is born? And even if not, will I be forced to leave my baby behind and be cast out, sent back to my own people, where I might not even be accepted any longer?"

Windigo sighed and sat down beside her. "Are you all right? You should not be running when you are so big with child."

His concern softened her fear and hatred. "I fell, but I think I'm all right."

They both sat there quietly for a moment, and Sadie

remembered how terrified she'd once been of Windigo. Now she could talk with him almost as easily as she'd once talked with Jonah. She felt strangely removed from the real world, wished all of this could be just a bad dream.

"Come back with me," Windigo told her. "I promise nothing will happen to you. I will not let it. Stay with me until my child is born and we have a chance to talk with my mother, if she still lives. After the baby is born, then we will decide what to do."

Sadie covered her face with her hands. "Whether I stay with you or go back to my people, I will be an outcast."

After another few quiet seconds, Windigo responded in a strained voice. "Perhaps even *I* will be an outcast. I only know that I . . . feel love for you."

Love! Never before had he used the word! What a strange turn life had suddenly taken. She thought about Jonah, how often he'd told her he loved her. Could he still love her, knowing what he knew now? And where was he? In Vincennes? Back home in Ohio? Stiahta said another man was with him who called him brother. It must have been Jeremiah. That meant Jeremiah knew about her and Windigo, and so did Regina—and everyone else.

What were they thinking? What were they saying about her? What kind of pain was poor Jonah going through? Would he ever hold her again? Love her again? Could anything ever again be the way it used to be, when they laughed together . . . made love? She could see him so clearly, feel his damp skin against her own, taste his kisses. She could see the gentle, genuine love in those blue eyes.

Yet here sat Windigo, with the same look, but in such dark, dark eyes.

"I don't know what to tell you, Windigo. I wish I could fully return your love, but right now I am so horribly torn." She fought more tears. "For now I will do as you ask and go back with you, trusting that you will protect me from those like Stiahta who say this is my fault. The wiser side of me tells me to wait until the baby is born, because this child is yours. You have a right to see him or her. Maybe then the answer to what happens next will come to both of us." She faced him. "But until then I want you to respect my wishes that you not lie with me. And I want you to realize that a big part of me wants to go home, to see for myself that my husband truly is still alive and that my little boy is all right. My husband needs answers just as much as you do. It wouldn't be fair to leave him always wondering where I am and what has happened to me. He needs to know. I need to see him."

She felt him tense, and she knew that Windigo would like nothing better than for Jonah to be dead after all. He would likely never agree to let her go, but the fact remained that Paul was now back home. How could she live out the rest of her life without seeing her son again?

She sat forward again with her head in her hands. "God help me," she moaned.

41

December 11, 1812

Jonah sat on the porch of the Jarvis home watching Paul play with the family dog. "He's getting back to the little boy we all knew before he was taken," he told Jeremiah, who sat nearby on the porch steps. "Thank God kids are pretty resilient that way."

Jeremiah nodded. "He's barely three years old. He'll forget soon enough, probably already has. He hardly ever mentions his grandmother or Windigo anymore."

Windigo. The name grated at Jonah's guts. "I can hardly stand to hear that name."

Jeremiah sighed, turning to him. "I notice you've refused to broach the subject for over a month now, but the time has come, Jonah. Tecumseh will be returning to Tippecanoe any day, and Sadie and Windigo will be with him. We have to go and get her as soon as scouts tell us they're back, and you have to be careful how you behave. If we have to grovel in the dirt to get Windigo to give her up, then that's what we'll do. The important thing is to get Sadie out of there and bring her home. And somehow we'll all find a way to get back to a normal life."

Jonah put his head in his hands. "Easy for you to say. It's not your wife who was taken away and raped and God knows what else. It's not your wife who's carrying another man's child, an *Indian* child."

Jeremiah leaned against the railing. "Would you rather have found out she was dead?"

Jonah closed his eyes and rested his elbows on his knees. "Of course not." He shook his head. "I just don't know what to think about anything anymore. I'm grateful every second of every day that I have Paul back and he's finally calling me Daddy again, but I have to wonder if life can ever be the same again for all of us. I feel like I'm hanging in some kind of purgatory between happiness and rage and terrible grief. Nothing feels real."

Jeremiah paused before answering. "Jonah, before this happened, how did you feel about Sadie?"

Jonah met his gaze. "I *loved* her, of course, more than ever because of what she'd put up with because of my own stupid dreams."

"And why should those feelings change just because she's a smart, strong woman who figured out how to stay alive and protect your son?"

Jonah thought a moment and shrugged. "I didn't say they *had* changed. It's not that I feel any different about her, Jeremiah. I'll always love Sadie. I'm just worried over how *she* might have changed, let alone what her feelings will be for me. How can she not blame me for all of this? And what do we do about her Indian baby? I don't want folks looking down on her and insulting her like some scorned woman. It's not fair. None of them know what she's suffered. The guilt inside me is eating at my guts like a cancer."

Jeremiah puffed on a pipe before replying. "Well, my advice is to stop blaming yourself and wait until we find her before you go making any judgments about Sadie *or* yourself. If we find Sadie and get her back, just think what a miracle that alone will be. How many Indian captives survive to return to their old life? God has been watching out for both of you and for Paul. As far as I'm concerned we should all just thank God for that and let Him guide all our emotions through lots of prayer, all of us together. And don't forget that time is a great healer of wounds, both physical and emotional. Remember, too, that Regina and Matthew and the kids and I are all here for you and Sadie both."

Jonah nodded, feeling tired and beaten. "I can't thank you enough for coming to Vincennes and helping with all of this. For now I guess we just have to pray that—"

Jonah's words were cut off by an incredible roaring sound unlike anything he'd ever heard. Alarmed, he rose from his chair to look around, astounded when he noticed a whole forest in the distance literally rise up.

Jeremiah also stood up, setting his pipe on the porch railing. "What the hell?" he muttered.

In the next moment the railing began shaking violently, and the pipe fell off. The ground under Paul began rolling like waves on water, and the boy fell down.

"Paul!" Jonah yelled. He ran off the porch to grab up the child, and the earth shook so that it knocked him to the ground also.

The Jarvis family came running out of the cabin when it suddenly heaved, some of the logs popping out of place. The top part of the chimney fell onto the roof, the rocks tumbling off.

"Get off the porch!" Jeremiah yelled at them, pulling Mrs. Jarvis to the ground.

Up and down the streets of Vincennes could now be heard screams, barking dogs, whinnying horses, shouting men, cracking buildings. The roaring sound was nearly deafening, and the earth shook so that no one could stand up. Everyone lay on the ground, and Jonah could hear grinding, popping sounds in the nearby woods along the river. He lay over Paul to protect him, and when he glanced toward the river he saw trees pushed up by the roots and toppled, some splitting as they fell. Horses tied nearby fell to the ground whinnying and kicking. Jonah could swear that in the direction of the river he saw the earth cracking. Dust rose in choking roils then, and Jonah pulled a terrified Paul closer under him.

What was happening! Where was Sadie in all of this? It truly seemed the world must be coming to an end. Somewhere in the back of his mind he seemed to remember Governor Harrison joking once that he'd heard Tecumseh had predicted a great swelling of the earth as a sign of his power.

It was certainly no joking matter now! The earth quaked and bucked wildly, as though God Himself had decided to knead and pound it into a different shape. The astounding event made Jonah feel suddenly small and insignificant, and in that quick, terri-fying moment he realized that nothing mattered except love and having Sadie back in his arms where he could protect her forever, never again allowing her to suffer the hell she must have suffered these past many months.

"God save us," he prayed, holding Paul close. "And save my Sadie. Please let me have her back."

Surely God had decided to put an end to all life as it currently existed, perhaps destroy the entire earth and just start over. That was all Sadie could think as a deafening roar made her drop the reins and cover her ears. The horse she rode reared and threw her as the ground beneath its feet buckled. Amazingly she landed on a cushion of thick grass that rose as she hit it, breaking her fall somewhat and causing her to roll rather than land hard and flat.

She could see the wild look of terror in her horse's eyes, saw its mouth open in what she knew had to be a literal scream of a whinny, yet she could not hear it. It kept trying to get back up but could not. Sadie clung to bunches of grass as the earth continued shaking so violently it would be impossible to get to her feet.

She managed to look around at Tecumseh and the others, all of whom fell from their mounts and tum-bled in all different directions. It was obvious that they, too, were screaming, yet again, she could not hear them because of the ungodly roaring sound that made it feel as though her eardrums would break.

She screamed for Windigo, who'd been riding about fifty yards to her right, looking for deer tracks, as their food supply was nearly gone. They were only perhaps a hundred miles northwest of New Madrid, still a long way from Tippecanoe.

Her screams most certainly could not be heard amid the roaring that was mixed with the snapping, ripping sound of trees being uprooted and thrown to the ground all around them. Luckily they'd been in a small clearing when the awful eruption of earth started. No trees landed on them.

Then she saw Windigo running, obviously trying to get to her, but it was impossible for him to stand. He rolled and crawled, stood up and fell, over and over. Even at a distance she could see the desperation in his eyes to get to her.

Then, to her horror, the earth between them literally opened up, and in the next moment Windigo disappeared into the chasm.

"Windigo!" she screamed. "Oh, my God! Windigo!" The opening widened, then slowly moved together again, closing Windigo into its pit of hell, forever lost to her and to the rest of the world.

"Noooooo!" Sadie screamed. "Windigo! Windigo!" Not only was her last bastion of safety gone, but also the man who'd planted his life in her, the man she knew only in that moment that she'd truly loved, if only for a little while.

A scream rose from within her that seemed to match the roaring of the mighty quake that shook and rolled and buckled the earth around her. She suddenly remembered Tecumseh's prediction of a great shaking of the earth, followed by words of Christ that bolted into her mind like a sharp-edged sword.

My God, my God, why hast Thou forsaken me?

42

January 4, 1812

The baby was coming, and Sadie wished she could stop the precious life from leaving her, only because as soon as it was born her baby would be torn from her arms forever. Deep in the throes of pain Sadie saw the events since Windigo disappeared before her very eyes tumble through her mind, the aftershocks terrorizing her as she and Tecumseh and the others journeyed home to Tippecanoe, only to find nothing there but ruin. Sadie finished the journey in a daze, feeling more removed from reality than ever, the vision of her proud Windigo falling into the bowels of the earth haunting her.

Throughout their journey they saw devastation everywhere, whole forests laid flat, dead animals scattered in all directions. They were forced to constantly watch for deep chasms and holes that sometimes could not be seen until right in front of them. The air hung strangely still, as though all life had vanished. Even Tecumseh had trouble finding his way because some creeks and tributaries they normally followed had vanished or changed course. Constant tremors kept them all on edge, Sadie's terror made worse by not knowing what her fate might be when she reached Tippecanoe.

Now she knew. Upon reaching the devastated Shawnee town, a furious Tecumseh had led her and the others here to Wildcat Creek, where the survivors had come to wait for Tecumseh. There Sadie discovered Serena had survived Harrison's attack, but her hopes of protection from Windigo's mother were dashed when she saw the way Serena looked at her upon learning of Windigo's horrible death. She obviously blamed Sadie for her son's terrible fate, as did an angry and mournful Wapmimi, who'd agreed with Stiahta that Sadie must surely be a witch. Wapmimi promptly announced that once the baby was born, Sadie must leave and never return, or face death by fire.

Serena allowed Sadie to live with her, but the grieving woman refused to speak to her, and the hatred in the woman's eyes was unnerving, especially since Sadie had come to feel close to Serena before she and Windigo first left for the south. Now, as Sadie lay in labor with Serena's first grandchild, Serena gave her no consolation, nor did she show any compassion for her wrenching pain. Two other women acted as midwives, but they, too, showed no concern for Sadie's agony.

In spite of how her baby had been conceived, Sadie

could not fight the natural motherly instincts that formed the normal deep attachment any mother felt for her child. No matter what anyone else did about the situation, this was *her* baby—hers and Windigo's. How sad that Windigo would never see his son or daughter.

Finally, after nearly twenty hours of labor, Sadie gave birth to a son. Tired and weak, she asked to hold her baby just for a moment, but Serena immediately picked him up and took him away before Sadie even got a look at him.

"He will one day be as great and honored a warrior as Windigo!" she heard Serena tell the midwives proudly. While the midwives helped with the after-birth Sadie could hear shouting and celebrating outside the *wigawa*—a son for Windigo—something for Serena to treasure forever and help heal her broken heart.

Tears welled in Sadie's eyes, her only consolation knowing that indeed her son would be well cared for and loved. She'd lived with these people long enough to realize that mothers and grandmothers, no matter what race or background, all shared the same undying devotion and feelings of fierce protection for their children and grandchildren. Her son would not lack for physical or emotional support.

Still, Sadie longed to keep some kind of connection, something to make sure her son always knew who his real mother was and that she loved him. During her lonely wait to give birth after reaching Wildcat Creek, she'd prepared a letter for her baby, leaving out only the name until she knew the sex of the child. Thank God Tecumseh's aide, Sauganash, had allowed her the use of pen and paper.

It was over. Soon she'd be sent away to an unknown fate, her arms and heart empty. The midwives left, and quickly Sadie dug the prepared letter from her personal deer-hide satchel. She'd even thought of a name for either boy or girl. Keeping to the Wilde family tradition of giving their sons biblical names, she'd chosen Jacob for a boy, Ruth for a girl.

She opened the letter, forcing back tears that made it difficult to reread what she'd already written. Then, taking ink and pen, she again scanned the letter and filled in the baby's name at the end.

My dear child. I write this letter because I have been forced by the Potawatomi and the Shawnee to leave you with them. If it were my choice, I would never let you go, no matter what the consequences. No matter what your relatives tell you about me, your father loved me, and he would have loved you dearly and been so proud to present you to the world. As for me, you are part of my flesh and blood, and so I cannot help but love you with all the passion of any mother for her child. Though it tears my heart out to leave you, I know it is the best thing for you. You will be happier living in the world of your native people. But always remember that you are half white, and that is nothing of which to be ashamed. You should be as proud of your white blood as your Indian blood. Never forget that. And never forget your mother's name, Sadie Wilde. If you ever wish to find me, look through the white settlements of the Indiana prairie, or at an Ohio River settlement called Willow Creek.

She paused, wondering indeed if she'd live in either place. It all depended on whether Jonah and his family even wanted anything to do with her.

If you ever choose to use a white name, she continued, *I beg you to use the name I give you.* She dipped the pen and wrote, *Jacob Jonah Wilde.*

She had to set the letter aside then as deep sobs overwhelmed her. Her womb was empty. Her arms were empty. Her breasts were painfully full of milk that no child would drink. Soon she would return to her white world, leaving her precious son behind, having no idea how she would be accepted by friends and relatives. She wondered sometimes just how much emotional pain one woman could withstand.

She curled to her side then, folding the letter into her hand and waiting. "God help me through this," she wept.

After a good half hour Serena finally returned with her new grandson. Her eyes unreadable, she came closer, and to Sadie's surprise, she laid the boy beside Sadie.

"Only a few minutes," the woman said coldly. "And only because my son would want it so. We will watch all around so that you do not try to sneak away with him."

Sadie sat up and faced her squarely. "I would not try

such a thing, but only because it could bring harm to my baby," she answered, her angry glare boring into Serena's dark eyes. She picked up her son and pulled him close, the letter still in her hand. She looked down at a beautiful baby, her precious, precious son. "Know this, Serena," she said quietly then. "Remember the feelings of a mother for her child. You mourn for Windigo." She looked up at Serena. "*I* will mourn for this son that you have chosen to rip from my arms! I beg only one thing of you, and I ask you to consider this as you think of what it might have felt like if someone had torn Windigo from your arms as an infant. I plead with you to think only as a mother now, not as a woman who hates the mother of your grandson. I have something for this baby, and I want you to put it in his medicine bag and promise me, *promise* me, that you will never touch it or take it away from him!"

She handed the letter to Serena. "I have a right, as a mother, to leave behind some kind of connection to my son. This is a letter I have written to him, expressing my love. I say nothing against his father or you or the Potawatomi. Instead I have told him that living with you is the best thing for him and is the only reason I am able to leave him behind. I simply want to know for the rest of my life that my little boy has something of his real mother with him. Surely somewhere deep inside your hatred for me you can bring forth the mother's love that will help you understand how I am feeling right now."

Serena looked down at the letter, her eyes softening

slightly. She looked back at Sadie. "I promise to put it in his medicine bag. I am not a woman who lies."

Sadie swallowed back tears. "Thank you. And know that only minutes before Windigo died he told me he loved me. I hope that because of that you will not continue your hatred of me after time heals your own grief. I hope you will at least tell this child that his mother was a good wife and would have been a good mother. Make him understand why I had no choice in giving him up, because, Serena, with Windigo gone, I would have given him to you anyway. You didn't need to threaten me with death. I know in my heart this is what is best for this little boy, because in my world he likely would not have been happy or accepted, and that would have torn at my heart worse than giving him up."

Serena took a deep breath, her eyes also tearing now. "You are wiser than I thought." She stood up. "I respect you for that." She sniffed, then took on an uncaring look again. "I will give you ten minutes." She turned and left.

Sadie looked down at the babe in her arms. He was perfect, his red skin clear and unblotched, his little face pretty and detailed. She opened his blanket and counted fingers and toes.

"What a handsome man you will be one day, Jacob Wilde," she told him. "Just like your father. Forever you will be in my heart and in my prayers."

He looked at her with dark eyes that she knew probably didn't see her all that clearly yet. She wondered if their color would change in time . . . perhaps to green. He made a little gurgling sound, his mouth opening for a moment, then moving into a little "O."

Sadie leaned down and kissed the puckered little lips, then brushed her lips over his soft, soft cheek. "I will love you forever," she said softly into his ear. Then she untied her tunic at the shoulder and dropped it, allowing the baby to try feeding at her breast. He was so new that he didn't quite know what to do with the nipple, and she stroked a finger around his mouth to urge him to take his nourishment.

"Just once, Jacob Jonah Wilde," she said softly. "I want to remember that at least once you took your milk from your true mother."

The baby sucked weakly and slowly, but at least a little milk trickled into his mouth. It gave Sadie a feeling of connection that she knew nothing and no one could ever take from her. Her blood was in his veins, and her milk would be the first to nourish him. Her kiss was on his lips, and one day he would read her letter, and he would know his mother loved him.

43

January 12, 1812

For over a week Sadie was held in a hut alone while she recovered. Severe winter temperatures kept her hovered near a central fire, waiting for the time when, as she'd been told, two warriors would come for her and accompany her to the outskirts of Vincennes. From there she would be on her own to find help.

"Be glad you still live, witch!" Wapmimi had sneered at her scathingly, his hideously scarred face accenting the fact that he could be viciously cruel if he chose. "It is only because my friend cared for you that you have not been burned alive!"

A snowstorm put off Sadie's leaving, and the dreary weather seemed to match her own countenance. The ache for her baby would not go away, in spite of the fact that she'd not seen him since those few minutes spent with him the day of his birth. Since then she'd not seen Serena or the child, and no one would tell her where he'd been taken or who was nursing him.

Her loneliness had no comparison to any she'd known, for not only would she never see her precious baby again, but Windigo was gone, and she was not so sure she'd enjoy any kind of acceptance or love even if she found Jonah and Paul. She would not blame Jonah if he turned her away and kept Paul, deeming her an unfit mother now that she'd lived like a squaw for nearly a year.

Why would he want her now? Why would he want to take her in his arms again, make love to her the way he used to do? Maybe she shouldn't even try to find him. Maybe she should drown herself in the river, or shoot herself, rather than see the look in Jonah's eyes when and if she did see him again.

She lay down near the fire again, watching the flickering flames and feeling hopeless. When a commotion arose outside her hut, she paid no attention until she heard someone shout her name outside her *wigawa.* Feeling weak, she sat up reluctantly and called out, "Enter," thinking perhaps men had finally come to take her to Vincennes in spite of the frigid weather and deep snows.

A warrior entered and ordered her to put on her fur cape and her winter moccasins. "Come with me," he ordered, his cold, dark eyes unreadable.

Sadie felt alarm, wondering at first if they'd decided to burn her at the stake rather than let her go. "Where?" she asked cautiously. "Are we leaving now? Isn't it a little late in the day for—"

"Come!" he repeated impatiently. "Your husband waits."

It seemed a great hand suddenly reached inside Sadie's chest to squeeze her heart. "My *husband?*"

"A white man who calls himself Jonah is here. He takes a great risk coming into this place where some of us would enjoy torturing him. Come quickly, or we will not allow him *or* you to leave!"

Near panic rushed through Sadie's blood, making her feel light-headed. With shaking hands she quickly pulled on her fur-lined, knee-high moccasins and took up a hooded bearskin cape. Jonah! She found it amazing he was here. He'd surely had to fight his way through deep snows to make it, let alone the risk he was taking, walking into a Shawnee camp where so many were still reeling from the destruction of Tippecanoe! Tecumseh himself would know Jonah must have been a part of that destruction, because he'd been there with Harrison's troops when Paul was brought to him. Why had he done such a foolish thing, and how did he even know she was here? Not all the Shawnee were camped here at Wildcat Creek. Some had scattered to other places.

She followed the heavily clothed warrior outside, keeping to the path he made with his long strides through the snow to a longhouse the Shawnee had constructed since resettling here.

Oh, God, please help me! She prayed. *What should I do? What should I say? Will Jonah still want me? What is to become of me? Does Jonah know that Windigo is dead?*

Once inside the longhouse, her legs felt like lead as she hesitantly approached the central fire, where Tecumseh himself, as well as Wapmimi, Stiahta, Sauganash, and a few others waited. Tecumseh sat behind a desk. Across from him sat one man in a chair, his long legs sprawled in front of him. He wore leather boots and woolen pants, a flannel shirt under a fur vest. A pistol was tucked into the waist of his pants, and a long gun was perched against the chair. A fur coat hung over the back of the chair. His dark hair hung to his shoulders, and he sported several days of beard growth on his face.

He turned to look at her, and Sadie froze in place. There were those eyes, those blue, blue eyes! The reality of the fact that Jonah truly lived hit her then, and she literally gasped, keeping her fur hood pulled close around her face so he could not see her well. She could not imagine how she must look, after months of greasing her hair back and using no creams on her skin, her ears pierced. She did not want him to see earrings hanging from her earlobes, or see that her belly was still bigger than normal because of her recent pregnancy.

Her eyes filling with tears, her throat aching, she came closer at Tecumseh's command, part of her wanting to run to Jonah, yet also wanting to wilt right where she stood and weep until she dissolved into a puddle that would soak into the ground and disappear forever.

Jonah looked different, more rugged, older. What had he suffered the day of the attack? And what must he have suffered emotionally when first realizing his wife and son had been taken? She could not quite read his eyes yet, but when he spoke, the familiar voice awakened all the memories of the life they'd shared before she was taken so physically and emotionally by the Potawatomi.

"Have her take off that hood. I want to make sure it's really her."

Tecumseh turned to Sadie. "This man says he is your white husband. If so, you may leave with him. We have watched after his arrival to be sure he did not bring soldiers with him. The fact that he is alone is the only reason we allow him to live. His bravery is to be commended. We have no quarrel with one man, and so I will allow him to take you away so that we can be done with you. I have told him about Windigo's death, and about the child. I have told him that it is only because Windigo is dead that he will be allowed to take you. He came here willing to fight Windigo for you, but now that will not be necessary. Remove your hood so that he can see neither the Potawatomi nor the Shawnee have brought you harm."

Sadie met Jonah's eyes again. Now she saw the anxious anticipation, the worry over how she might look. Slowly she pulled back the hood of her cape to reveal blond hair that she knew looked dark from being greased and braided. She remembered Jonah loving to watch her brush her hair, loved running his hands through it.

She saw pain in his eyes at the sight of her. With her hair pulled back, her earrings were obvious. She heard him gasp, watched him close his eyes for a moment. His hands went into fists and he drew a deep breath before turning to Tecumseh. "You said she was well cared for. Look at her! She's thin enough to blow away with the wind!"

"If she is thin, it is her own fault. We have fed her well, but she has refused to eat."

"And do you wonder why?" Jonah asked, his face darkening with anger. "You ripped her baby from her arms and left her completely alone! You told me she'd been deemed a witch!"

"Be careful what you say," Tecumseh answered, his dark eyes drilling into Jonah's. "I would advise you to take your woman and leave! *Quickly!* If you value your life, you will do as I say! Right now I am in no mood to be kind to *any* white man, or *woman!* You have come for her. You have seen for yourself it is she whom you've searched for! Go! And tell Governor Harrison he has not heard the last of Tecumseh!"

Some of the warriors present raised their fists and cried out war whoops. Jonah rose, taking up his fur coat and pulling it on. He put a wool hat on his head and picked up his long gun. Saying nothing more, he walked over to Sadie, a look of apology visible in his eyes, eyes that teared as he pulled Sadie's hood back over her head.

He put an arm around her and led her out of the longhouse and to a place where three horses were tied, two of them saddled, one heavily packed.

"I have a camp south of here," he told her. "We'll talk there. Let's just get out of here before we both lose our scalps." He started to help her onto her horse, but Sadie collapsed against him.

"Jonah! Jonah!" she wept, clinging to him.

He held her close. "I know," he groaned, rocking her slightly. "I know."

44

"Can you ride?" Jonah asked.

Sadie spotted a hollow tree trunk not far away and wished she could crawl into it, away from the world, away from reality. "Yes."

Jonah pulled away from her hold and grasped her

arm, leading her to the second horse. Sadie wished she could determine the meaning of his overly firm grip. Was it from anger? If so, was it his anger at the Shawnee and Potawatomi . . . or at her? Was it simply a grip of possessiveness? Maybe it was his way of making sure no one ever took her from him again.

"You nearly bled to death when you had Paul. I just don't want you doing something that could endanger your health. How long since you had the baby?" he asked as he lifted her into the saddle.

"Eight days," she answered quietly, feeling both embarrassment and deep sadness.

Because of the cold Sadie wore fur-lined leggings, which she gratefully realized would make riding astride a saddle horse easier.

Jonah mounted his own horse, and Sadie thought how at least he cared enough to ask about her health. Still, he seemed strangely authoritative. When he first held her she felt the old Jonah for those few moments. Then he seemed to stiffen and grow quiet. She didn't doubt he was still very apprehensive about his safety as long as they were anywhere close to Wildcat Creek and the Shawnee, and she couldn't get over thinking what courage it took for him to come here alone like this.

He took up the reins to his packhorse, and Sadie thought how he looked more like an Indian scout and trapper than her farmer husband. Circumstances had surely changed him . . . as they had indeed changed her.

"Why did you risk coming here alone?" she asked as he moved past her with the packhorse. "After what happened at Tippecanoe, the Shawnee could easily have decided to torture you to death just for being white."

He halted his horse for a moment, looking around as he spoke, most likely still not trusting the many warriors not far away. "Harrison offered some men but not for another couple of weeks," he told her as he kept watch. "But I didn't want to wait any longer." He finally met her gaze, and self-consciously she looked down, pulling her hood farther around her face.

"Don't hang your head, Sadie," Jonah ordered. "You're too fine a woman for that."

She took hope in the words, but they also brought tears to her eyes when she looked at him again.

"Scouts told us Tecumseh was back and I knew that meant you had to be back, too," he continued. "I wasn't going to wait one minute longer to come and get you." He kicked his horse into motion then, moving ahead of her with the packhorse. "Follow me."

Angry. Yes, he was angry, but she sensed he was most angry with himself. He was blaming himself for this. Poor Jonah! There was no one to blame.

"Where is Paul?" she called out, desperate to see her little boy again, especially now.

"He's fine," he shouted back. "After the earthquake Jeremiah decided he should go back to Ohio and check on the family and make sure the house was still standing. He took Paul with him because I didn't know how much longer I'd have to wait in Vincennes. We figured Paul needed to be with the family for a while—get himself reoriented."

Reoriented. They *all* needed to get themselves reoriented, if it was even possible to get back to their old life. For nearly an hour Sadie followed Jonah along a pathway near the Wabash, well worn by Indians and whites alike who traveled north and south between Vincennes and the Great Lakes. It made Sadie realize how inevitable it was that one day all this area would be inhabited by whites.

Where would the Shawnee and the Potawatomi and the Delaware and all the others go? One day they would have no choice but to leave their beloved lakes and prairies or die. She wondered if Jonah would understand why she cared. Mostly she wondered what kind of future her little Jacob would have. The thought provoked more tears, a sudden need to let it all out, for it hit her harder now that she would never see her baby boy again. Her sorrow erupted into a sudden surge of sobs that she could not control, and she had to stop her horse.

Moments later she was in Jonah's arms, so lost in her sorrow that she didn't even realize he'd stopped and come to get her. He sat down in the snow and pulled her against him. She could do nothing but cling to him as she wept.

"I'll never see my baby again," she cried. "I'm so sorry, Jonah! So sorry! I've found you at last, but I can only weep over a baby that wasn't even yours."

He only held her tighter, both of them oblivious to the cold and snow. "I'm the one who's sorry," Jonah said gruffly. "You're a survivor, Sadie girl. You did what you had to do to survive."

Now she felt him shaking. He, too, was crying. He couldn't hold her tight enough, and she felt the same way.

"Your baby is where he belongs," he told her. "You know that. You have to let God take care of him now."

The words were all the comfort she needed. He understood. When finally she regained control of her senses, she pulled away slightly but remained sitting between his legs in the snow. She had no choice but to rub her eyes and nose with the fur of her jacket. "Oh, Jonah, how did you survive? And how did you find out where I was?"

"It's a long story, and it doesn't matter." He grasped her face, wiping at more tears with his thumbs and blinking back his own tears. He pushed the hood off her head, looking her over. "We'll unbraid this hair and wash the grease out of it," he told her. He touched her ears. "And we'll cut the rawhide looped through your ears. Maybe in time the holes will heal, but it doesn't matter, Sadie. Do you understand? It doesn't matter. When I think of what your fate could have been, yours and Paul's, I don't give a damn what you had to do to save the both of you."

She studied those blue, blue eyes. "I thought you were dead, Jonah. Wapmimi said you were, and I couldn't imagine how it couldn't be true. I knew I had to adjust to that life or die. They made me watch prisoners being burned at the stake. It was so horrible! I was terrified they'd do the same to Paul!"

"I know." He leaned forward and kissed her tears. "It's all right now, Sadie."

"How, Jonah? How did you manage to survive?"

He pulled her close again. "When you see the scar on the back of my head you'll be even more amazed that I lived," he told her. "I lay completely paralyzed for months. Finally someone got word to Jeremiah, and he came and helped me, then took me home to Ohio to recover." He told her about coming back to Vincennes and joining Harrison on his march to Tippecanoe. "When they brought Paul out to us—" He literally shivered. "My God, I never truly believed in miracles until then. And when I learned you were with Windigo and carrying his baby—" He kissed her hair. "It was Windigo and the Shawnee I hated, Sadie. Part of me wanted to blame you, but I knew better. I knew you couldn't be blamed for anything." He grasped her shoulders and studied her eyes. "You were never truly with him, Sadie. Not like you've been with me. Do you know what I'm saying? You're mine, and no damn Indian or anything else can change that."

She closed her eyes. "I know." She would not say anything now about how she'd learned to care for Windigo. The day would come when she would explain and he would understand. It was enough to be here together, in each other's arms, with the bright hope that they would find each other again emotionally and physically, return to the life they'd shared before the awful attack.

"I'd have started searching for you right away, Sadie," he told her. "I hope you know that. But I lay in a coma for a long time, then couldn't move. I thought I'd go crazy not being able to help you, protect you! I'll never forgive myself for bringing you out here—"

"Don't say that!" she interrupted, touching his lips with a gloved hand. "Fate is fate, Jonah. You followed your dream, and I would never ask anything less of you. I'm not even going to ask you to go back to Ohio now, other than for us to go there and see the family again and get Paul."

"Get Paul?"

"Yes. We're coming back here, Jonah. We're going to rebuild, right where we first settled."

He frowned and shook his head. "We can't. I won't take that risk ever again. I thought at first I could, but—"

"Jonah, this is what you wanted. And I've lived with the Shawnee long enough to know that we'll be safe now. After what happened at Tippecanoe, Tecumseh will concentrate farther north now, most likely try to hook up with the English up around the Great Lakes. He didn't have the success he'd hoped for in the south." She pushed his woolen cap away and ran her fingers through his hair. "I'm not afraid anymore, Jonah. I'm not even afraid of how others might treat me, as long as I have you and Paul, and as long as I know you still love me."

He grasped her hand and kissed her palm. "I never stopped loving you. How could I possibly blame you for any of this or ever stop loving you? We pledged ourselves to each other when we married, and nothing can change that. But both of us still have a lot of healing to do. Harrison has a guest cabin that he told me we could use for the rest of the winter if I found you. Come spring we'll go get Paul." His voice choked. "We'll be a family again, Sadie." He kissed her lips lightly. "And this time I'll build you a real house, before I do anything else. I'll not touch a plow until you're living in a decent house. Jeremiah said he's doing so well that he's willing to give up one summer to come here with Matthew and help build a house—that is, if you and I decided to stay in Indiana."

Sadie threw herself against him again, clinging tightly. "We *are* staying, Jonah. We are!"

Oh, the feel of his strong arms around her again! The joy of knowing he still loved her! How many men would still want a woman after she'd been "tainted" by another man, especially by an Indian? But the Wilde men understood. Their own mother and grand-mother had suffered in settling this land, and their men stood by them.

"I left a letter with my baby," she told Jonah then. She pulled away again and relished the love in his eyes. "His grandmother promised to put it in his medicine bag and never touch it. It tells him who his mother was and where he can find me if he ever wants to. That's another reason we have to stay here in Indiana. This is where he will look for us . . . if he ever decides that's what he should do." She swallowed with apprehension. "I . . . gave him a white name, Jonah. I hope you'll understand. He's got my blood in him . . . white blood."

He touched her cheek with the back of his fingers. "What did you name him?"

"Jacob Jonah Wilde. I wanted him to have a name that belonged to a proud, strong white blood line. Please don't be upset by my giving him your last name."

He shook his head, actually giving a hint of a smile. "I'm not upset. Maybe someday men like Jacob Jonah Wilde will help bring some kind of peace to this land. Somehow Indian and white will have to find a way to get along, and God knows there are plenty of half-bloods already roaming this land, and more to come. And maybe someday Jacob Jonah Wilde will even come knocking on our door, wanting to find his mother, and his half brother."

Her lips quivered from the deep agony of leaving her baby behind. "Maybe he will," she said in a near whisper. "And maybe by then he'll have lots of half brothers and sisters."

Jonah kissed her forehead. "Not maybe," he answered. "There is no doubt about it." He pulled her into his arms again, rocking her gently as fresh, fat snowflakes gently drifted over them on the cold, windless prairie winter day.

The peace Sadie felt in that moment belied the terror and hell she'd suffered over these last many months. Peace. Such a precious word, and such a fleeting joy it could sometimes be. But always, always she felt it here in Jonah Wilde's arms.

The great Shawnee Chief Tecumseh continued his dream of uniting all tribes against the Long Knives. He joined forces with the British in the War of 1812 and was a key figure in several decisive victories against the Americans. He was killed in October, 1813, during a battle in Canada at an Indian settlement called Moraviantown. He wore a British medal around his neck.

To this day Tecumseh remains a symbol of unity and courage, a man of intelligence and even generosity, one who strived to end the torture of enemy captives. The Americans who won the fight at Moraviantown that brought Tecumseh's death were led by none other than William Henry Harrison.

Center Point Publishing
600 Brooks Road ● PO Box 1
Thorndike ME 04986-0001 USA

(207) 568-3717

US & Canada:
1 800 929-9108